PAUL HOWARD

ALDRIN ADAMS
AND THE LEGEND OF
NEMESWISS

Illustrated by Lee Cosgrove

PUFFIN

PUFFIN BOOKS
UK | USA | Canada | Ireland | Australia
India | New Zealand | South Africa

Puffin Books is part of the Penguin Random House group of
companies
whose addresses can be found at global.penguinrandomhouse.com.

www.penguin.co.uk
www.puffin.co.uk
www.ladybird.co.uk

Penguin
Random House
UK

First published 2023
001
Text copyright © Paul Howard, 2023
Illustrations copyright © Lee Cosgrove, 2023
The moral right of the author/illustrator has been asserted

Text design by Ken de Silva
Printed and bound in Great Britain by Clays Ltd, Elcograf S.p.A.

A CIP catalogue record for this book is available from the British
Library

The authorized representative in the EEA is Penguin Random
House Ireland, Morrison Chambers, 32 Nassau Street, Dublin D02
YH68

ISBN: 978–0–241–44170–1

All correspondence to:
Puffin Books
Penguin Random House Children's
One Embassy Gardens, 8 Viaduct Gardens
London SW11 7BW

PUFFIN BOOKS

ALDRiN ADAMS
AND THE **LEGEND** OF
NEMESWISS

To Cuisle and Lux

NIGHT OF TERROR

The sky above her head was fiery red and it roared with the sound of approaching thunder. Little Esther Okobi from Duxbury Drive wiped the sweat from her forehead and stared at her feet. She had to focus now.

Slowly, and with great caution, she placed her foot on the wooden plank in front of her. It gave way and fell from the rope bridge into the bubbling-hot lava below. For one awful moment, she thought that *she too* might fall, down into the belly of the volcano, but she grabbed the rope handrail and held on for all she was worth.

And that was when she heard it. The terrifying beating of wings. Valdor the Remorseless had released his Giant Raptor Birds . . . to bring her back to the **Castle of Dread**!

There was no time for caution now. She had to reach the other side of the volcano. She started to run along the wooden planks. But, in her haste, she **tripped**. Behind her, she heard a sudden gust of wind, like the crack of a whip.

She looked over her shoulder as one of Valdor's **ENORMOUS** eagle-like birds swooped down and tried to pick her up with its blade-like talons.

Esther screamed:

'AAARRRGGGHHH!!!'

The bird narrowly missed her, snagging one of its talons on the rope bridge, which s_wa_yed violently from side to side.

Esther stood up again. She looked up. She counted SIX Giant Raptor Birds circling overhead. She took three more hurried steps, then she stopped.

One of the birds was now hovering just above her. It was ENORMOUS – as big as a TWO-STOREY HOUSE and its wings were so wide that the very act of flapping them blew back Esther's hair.

The bird stared hard at her with its dark, unblinking eyes. Then it let loose a loud and blood-curdling squawk:

'**WAAAAAAHHHHHHKKKKKK!!!!!!**'

Esther screamed again:

'**NOOOOOO!!!!!!**'

The bird opened its hooked beak, filled its lungs with air, then breathed a jet of fire directly at Esther. She jumped to the side, narrowly missing the flames, which now torched the bridge behind her. And suddenly, in that moment, the entire thing . . .

SNAPPED!

Again, Esther screamed . . .

'AAARRRGGGHHH!!!'

. . . as she held on to what remained of the bridge and found herself swinging through the air on the rope. A second later, she was slammed against the inside wall of the volcano.

SPLAT!

When she got over the initial shock, she discovered that she was still holding on to the rope – and dangling just sixty feet above the seething red lava below!

She took a deep breath. With all the strength she could summon, she began to slowly pull herself up the rope towards the lip of the volcano. It took a **HUGE** effort, but she had just enough strength left to reach the top.

She scrambled down the rocky slope of the volcano and took refuge behind a giant boulder to consider her next move.

She sat there for a moment, hugging her knees and listening to the terrifying wingbeats of the giant birds circling overhead. And that was when something VERY unexpected happened.

She started to get the feeling that she wasn't alone! Slowly, she turned her head. And there, sitting next to her, behind the boulder . . . was a boy!

He was about twelve years old, short and slightly chubby, with a friendly face, two front teeth that stuck out prominently and a head of wavy russet hair. Like Esther, he was dressed in pyjamas, except where hers had rainbows and unicorns, his were covered in yellow wedges of cheese.

'All right, Esther?' the boy said in a calm voice.

'*All right?*' she repeated confusedly. 'No, I'm NOT all right! I'm having a nightmare in case you haven't noticed!'

'I was only making conversation,' the boy said.

'Who *are* you anyway?' Esther snapped. 'And what are you doing here?'

'You're dreaming that you're trapped in a computer game,' he explained, 'called *Night of Terror*.'

'Yes, I *know* that!' she said in an exasperated voice. 'I have this nightmare EVERY night!'

'A lot of kids do,' the boy told her. 'It's a VERY scary game.'

'*You've* never been in it before,' Esther said. 'Why are you here now?'

'I'm here to help you!'

'Help me *how*?'

'By showing you . . . a way out.'

Esther's face took on a look of sad resignation.

'There is no way out!' she said sadly. 'Any second now, one of Valdor's Giant Raptor Birds is going to land in front of us, and he's going to breathe fire at me, and I'm going to wake up screaming. Then I'm going to run crying into my mummy and daddy's room and tell them I've had another nightmare and ask them if I can sleep in their bed tonight.'

'That *could* happen,' the boy said.

'It's what ALWAYS happens,' Esther insisted.

'Or,' the boy said, raising one eyebrow, 'you *could* fight back.'

'Fight back? How?'

'Have you ever played *Night of Terror*?'

'No, I've only seen my brother play it. He doesn't let me touch his games console.'

'Well, *I've* played it,' the boy said, 'with my friends Frankie and Harry. You have weapons at your disposal, Esther.'

'What weapons?' she asked.

'You can shoot **BOLTS OF LIGHTNING** from your hands!'

Esther looked at him like he was out of his mind.

'Bolts of lightning?' she repeated. 'From my hands?'

'Here,' he said. 'Make a fist like this.'

Esther closed her right hand as he showed her.

'Now,' the boy said, 'you have to sort of throw your hand forward and open your fingers at the same time. Can you do that?'

Esther tried. Nothing happened.

'OK, pretend you're throwing a tennis ball,' the boy suggested. 'Like this, Esther.'

He demonstrated the action for her again.

'Do you think you can do that?' he asked.

She tried it a second time – again, with no result.

'I think you're possibly opening your fingers too early,' the boy suggested. 'Try it in one smooth movement –'

The boy suddenly stopped talking. Because standing in front of them, eyeing them from a distance of twenty feet away, was a Giant Raptor Bird!

Esther looked at it with a sense of weary dread. As usual, this one was different from the other birds – it had golden plumage and curly ram's horns on the side of its head. It let out its horribly familiar squawk:

'WAAAAAAHHHHHHKKKKK!!!!!!'

'Er, NOW would *probably* be a good time to get the hang of the whole bolts-of-lightning trick!' the boy suggested.

'I've already *tried* it,' Esther said, 'It doesn't work!'

The bird moved closer to them.

'Yeah,' the boy said, 'I think he's about to turn us into toast, Esther.'

He watched as the bird drew in a deep breath. And then . . .

PADOOOOOOMFFF!!!

. . . suddenly exploded in a shower of golden dust!

Somewhere above him, the boy heard a computerized voice say:

'FIVE HUNDRED POINTS!'

Esther was staring at the palm of her right hand in astonishment.

'Did you SEE that?' She laughed. 'Did you SEE what I did?'

'You got one of the golden ones,' the boy said. 'They're worth five times as much as the ordinary ones. And, by the way, you can shoot lightning from your left hand as well.'

'That is SO cool!' Esther said, standing up and examining her two palms. She clearly wasn't frightened any more. As a matter of fact, she seemed very much ready for a fight!

She looked up, squinting into the flame-coloured sky, then, with a flick of her left wrist, sent a bolt of lightning fizzing through the air to take out another Giant Raptor Bird.

'ONE HUNDRED POINTS!'

the computerized voice said.

'If you can get three golden ones,' the boy told her, 'you'll be able to BREATHE FIRE for the next thirty seconds!'

'Oh my God,' Esther squealed excitedly, 'this is SO much fun!' Then she ran off, her hands a blur of movement as she launched lightning bolt after lightning bolt into the sky overhead.

A few seconds later, she returned, out of breath.

'I don't even know your name,' she smiled.

'My name is Aldrin,' the boy told her. 'Aldrin Adams.'

'Thank you,' Esther said, 'for showing me how to do this.'

'Selles-sur-Cher,' the boy replied.

'What?' Esther asked.

'Oh, it's a type of goat's cheese that's made in France. It's covered in ash and mould and it tastes like grass.'

'Er, what does *that* have to do with my nightmare?'

'Absolutely nothing. It's on a poster on the wall at the end of my bed. *Fromages de France*. I suppose it means I'm waking up. Hey, don't you have Giant Raptor Birds to terrorize?'

'It was nice to meet you, Aldrin Adams,' Esther said.

Then, all at once, Aldrin found himself lying in his bed, with his pyjama top soaked through with sweat, a throat so dry that he could barely swallow and a thumping pain in his head.

'It was nice to meet you too,' he groaned, 'Esther Okobi.'

2

'I WANT THAT BOY DESTROYED!!'

In his secret lair, deep inside the fake frontage of the Codfather Packing Company, a fish-packaging factory on the outskirts of the West Yorkshire town of Todmorden, Habeas Grusselvart was working late into the night.

Beddy Byes, his loyal Personal Assistant and Vice President of Global Operations, was bringing him up to speed on how splendidly business was going. And business, in this case, meant the spreading of fear, anxiety and misery throughout the world through the medium of terrifying dreams.

'Nightmare production is up by thirty-three per cent,' Beddy Byes announced, pointing at a graph on a flipchart. 'We are now creating nightmares for five thousand new people per week! And scarier ones too! We have increased our production of Monsters-in-the-Wardrobe nightmares, Drowning-in-the-Sea nightmares, Falling-from-a-Height nightmares, Buried-Alive-by-Snow nightmares,Bitten-by-Dog nightmares . . .'

But none of it was giving his boss any pleasure at all.

Habeas stared past Beddy Byes to the thousands of TV screens that made up his **WaLL of Torment**, each one broadcasting live footage from some of the MILLIONS of nightmares being experienced at that exact moment by people all over the world. But all he could focus on were the handful of screens that had nothing on them except static.

'These are all *his* work, I presume,' Habeas said.

'*His* work?' asked Beddy Byes.

'The Adams boy,' Habeas growled. 'Each one of those empty screens represents a nightmare that he's managed to bring to a happy resolution.'

'My apologies,' Beddy Byes simpered. 'I should have filled those screens with something else.'

Habeas put his elbows on the desk and made a steeple of his fingers.

'He's getting stronger,' he said.

'Sir, we are in the midst of a period of record growth,' Beddy Byes insisted. 'The boy has helped only five people in the past twelve weeks.'

'He is gaining complete mastery over his powers.'

'I just don't see that he's a threat to us, Your, um, Amazingness.'

'Then you're an even BIGGER fool than I thought!' Habeas thundered. 'Don't you know that, for centuries now, the Cheese Whizzes have been prophesising the coming of a boy – namely **The One** – who would gather all the Cheese Whizzes into an army to defeat me?'

'With respect, the Cheese Whizzes are a dying order. Their numbers have dwindled and they are now scattered all over the world.'

'He is The One!' screamed Habeas. **'I know it!'**

From one of the thousands of TVs arrayed on the wall in front of him, Habeas heard a computerized voice say:

'FIVE HUNDRED POINTS!'

He narrowed his eyes.

'What on EARTH is Esther Okobi *doing*?' he asked.

'It, um, looks like she's just killed one of Valdor the Remorseless's Giant Raptor Birds,' Beddy Byes said nervously. 'By, um, shooting a bolt of lightning – from her hand.'

'Is that *him*,' Habeas asked, 'sitting behind tha rock?'

Beddy Byes approached the screen to get a bette look.

'It, um, appears to be,' he said.

'Who designed this nightmare?' Habeas asked.

'It was Ethan Marcus,' Beddy Byes replied. 'He's on of our finest programmers, sir.'

'ONE HUNDRED POINTS the computerized voice said.

Habeas picked up his phone and pressed zero fc reception.

'Good evening, Morag,' he said. 'Is Ethan Marcu still in the building? Oh, that's excellent news. Can yo ask him to come and see me in my office? Immediatel yes. Or sooner, if possible. Thank you.'

'FIVE HUNDRED POINTS!'
Habeas replaced the receiver.

'Sir,' said Beddy Byes, '*Night of Terror* is one of ou most popular nightmares, especially among childre About forty thousand of them experience it every night

'And yet,' said Habeas, 'this boy just marches in ther

14

and shows this girl that she has absolutely NOTHING to be frightened of!'

'Sir, it's just one nightmare. It's just –'

'He is The One, Beddy Byes. The son of Cynthia Adams – your old . . . girlfriend.'

'She was never my girlfriend,' Beddy Byes said defensively.

'No, you were *just good friends*,' Habeas said, making quotation marks with his fingers. 'Until she cruelly tossed you aside for the boy's father – a village cheesemonger. Isn't that right?'

'Yes, Your Excellentness.'

'Back when you were plain old Maurice Mackle.'

'*Morr-eece*,' said Beddy Byes, correcting his pronunciation. '*Morr-eece* Mackle.'

'And I picked you out of the gutter – and gave your life purpose.'

'You did, sir. And I am most grateful.'

'THEN SHOW IT!'

There were three sharp knocks on the door.

'Come in!' Habeas called.

The door opened and into the room walked a shortish young man with dark curly hair, wearing large black-framed glasses, a blue-and-white checked shirt, a red bow tie and red braces to hold up his trousers.

'Ethan Marcus!' Habeas said in a voice that suggested he was pleased to see him. 'Working late tonight, were you?'

'I work late every night,' Ethan told him. 'Not that I'm complaining.'

'That's excellent,' Habeas said, 'isn't it, Beddy Byes? A happy workforce is a productive workforce, I always say! Ethan, can you please describe for me what you see happening right now on screen number 1,374?'

Ethan located the screen. Then his jaw fell open and his face whitened visibly.

'I don't . . . believe it,' he gasped.

'Whether you believe it or not is immaterial to me,' Habeas told him. 'Describe what's happening.'

Beddy Byes watched a thin sheen of sweat appear on Ethan's forehead.

'That little girl,' Ethan said, walking nearer to the screen, 'she's breathing fire – and incinerating absolutely everything in her path. It looks like she's about to . . .'

'Continue,' urged Habeas.

'. . . defeat Valdor the Remorseless,' Ethan spluttered.

'And complete . . . the game.'

They watched as little Esther Okobi aimed a mouthful of flames at Valdor, who melted like a marshmallow held too long over the fire.

'But that's impossible,' said Ethan.

'Clearly not,' Habeas said. 'Go and clear your desk.'

'Wh-wh-what?' Ethan gibbered.

'Beddy Byes,' said Habeas, 'can you please explain to this young man what I'm trying to tell him?'

Beddy Byes fixed Ethan with a look.

'He's saying you're fired,' he told him. 'I'll need your security pass.'

'B-b-but . . .' Ethan tried to speak.

'I think I'll have a trapdoor fitted,' said Habeas. 'That way, when I'm finished with people, I don't have to continue looking at them. The door is behind you. I suggest you use it.'

'Yes, sir,' said Ethan, who had heard all the stories about Habeas and his infamous rages. He backed his way quickly towards the door.

Habeas turned his attention to Beddy Byes.

'The Adams boy is only getting started,' he said, rising to his feet. 'He will grow stronger and stronger. And then he will come for me.'

He stepped out from behind his desk.

'Sir,' said Beddy Byes, attempting to reason with his boss, 'if you look at the growth projections for the next twelve months –'

'I DON'T CARE ABOUT YOUR BLASTED PROJECTIONS!' Habeas roared, picking up the flipchart and throwing it across the room.

'I WANT THAT BOY DESTROYED! AND IF YOU DON'T DO IT, YOU TOO WILL BE CLEARING YOUR DESK!!!'

SOME VERY EXCITING NEWS

'Aldrin, can you hear me? Aldrin, come in! Over.'

Sisely's voice was coming from underneath Aldrin's bed.

'Come in, Aldrin! Can you hear me? Over.'

The walkie-talkies had been her idea. She needed a quick and easy way to get in touch with her friend once he'd completed a mission, and her mum said she was too young to have a smartphone.

Aldrin reached under the bed and picked up his receiver.

'Morning, Sisely,' he said.

There was silence on the other end.

'Sisely,' Aldrin said, 'can you hear me?'

'Aldrin, how many times do I have to tell you?'

Sisely harrumphed. 'You're supposed to say "over" when you've finished speaking. Over.'

'Why?' Aldrin wondered. 'Er, over.'

'Because it's the correct protocol when you speak to someone on a two-way radio. It's to make sure that when one person is talking, they don't get talked over. Over.'

'Sisely, do you *have* to be such a stickler for the rules?' Aldrin asked with a smile.

'Ahem.'

'Over.'

'There's a right way and a wrong way to do things. Now tell me, how did it go? Over.'

'Let's just say that Esther Okobi isn't going to be scared of Valdor the Remorseless and his Giant Raptor Birds any more. Her nightmares are well and truly over. Over.'

Esther's mum and Sisely's mum were in the same yogalates class and sometimes they went for coffee together. Sisely had overheard Esther's mum say that her daughter experienced regular nightmares and was often too frightened to sleep in her own bed.

'Another successful mission!' Aldrin declared. 'Over! Over.'

'And what about the Queso de Cabrales?' Sisely asked. 'Over.'

Queso de Cabrales was a blue cheese, made in Spain, which was mild with a spicy aftertaste. According to the dream journal that Aldrin's mum left him before she died, it was the best cheese to eat if you wanted to help change the outcome of a computer-game nightmare.

'Worked just like she said it would,' Aldrin declared. 'Although I feel awful this morning. Over.'

The journal was written in French, a language that Aldrin didn't speak, but that Sisely spoke fluently, which was why he'd entrusted the book to her.

'According to your mum, three-and-a-half ounces of aged Provolone will fix a Queso de Cabrales hangover,' Sisely told him. 'Over.'

'I'll ask Dad if I can have some for my breakfast,' Aldrin said. 'Over.'

At that exact moment, Aldrin's dad, Doug, called up the stairs from the shop below:

'ALDRIN?'

'YES, DAD?' Aldrin yelled back.

'CAN YOU COME DOWN HERE A MOMENT? BELINDA AND I HAVE SOME VERY EXCITING NEWS!'

'**I'LL BE RIGHT DOWN!** I wonder what that's about. Over.'

'He's probably asked Belinda to marry him,' Sisely said in her usual matter-of-fact way. 'Over.'

'No WAY!' Aldrin exclaimed. 'Over.'

'They've been going out on dates for nearly three months now,' Sisely reminded him. 'It's bound to happen eventually. Over.'

Aldrin loved his dad's assistant, but he wasn't sure he was ready for her to become his stepmum just yet.

'Sisely,' Aldrin said, 'can I ask you a question? Over.'

'What is it? Over.'

'Do you think I'm . . . doing enough? Over.'

'What do you mean? Over.'

'I mean, with my power. Esther is the first person I've helped in, what, two weeks? It's just that sometimes it feels like I'm winning battles – but not the war. I just feel like I have this amazing superpower –'

'It's NOT a superpower!'

'Hey, I didn't say "over". I have this amazing superpower – but it feels like I'm not using it to its full potential. Over.'

'So what do *you* think you should be doing? Over.'

'I don't know – having BIGGER adventures.

Something more exciting than the usual run-of-the-mill nightmares – scaring away giant spiders or helping people down from great heights. I'm just a bit, well . . . bored. Over.'

'Aldrin, you have to play things by the book. That's why your mum left you her dream journal in the first place. Over.'

'**ALDRIN!**' Doug called up the stairs again. '**DID YOU FALL ASLEEP AGAIN?**'

'**NO, I'LL BE RIGHT DOWN, DAD!** Sisely, I have to go. I'll talk to you later. Over and out!'

Aldrin slid out of bed. He walked over to the corner of the room where his pet frog was just waking up.

'Hello, Silas,' he said, picking him out of the tank. 'Time for your morning exercise.'

Aldrin placed him on the floor so that he could stretch his legs. Then he went downstairs.

The shop had only been open five minutes and Belinda was already losing her patience with a customer. As it happened, it was Agatha Rees-Lane, the nutritionist, healthy-eating campaigner and neighbourhood busy body, who once hated cheese so much that she tried to force the closure of the shop. But, ever since Aldrin entered her nightmare to save her son, Sebastian, from drowning in a river of nacho cheese, she had warmed to the strange boy and his jolly dad. Now, she popped into Doug's cheese shop, *C'est Cheese*, regularly to make the most of Doug's free-tasting policy.

'Could I try some of the Queso Manchego?' she asked.

Belinda stared hard at her across the counter. Though she'd been working hard to improve her customer-relations skills, she wasn't above putting someone in their place if she felt they were taking a liberty.

'You've already had some of the Queso Manchego,' she pointed out.

'Yes, but I've forgotten how it tastes,' Agatha told her.

'Well, I'm not surprised,' Belinda **huffed**. 'You've had the Landaff. You've had the Isle of Mull. You've had Westcombe. You've had the Loch Arthur. It's no wonder you can't tell owt from owt.'

Belinda shaved another thin slice of Manchego from the block and handed it to Agatha.

'And that's all you're having,' she snapped. 'It's not a flipping charity we're running.'

Meanwhile, Doug was struggling to carry an enormous wheel of Parmigiano Reggiano across the shop floor to the cutting block.

'Dad, let me help you with that,' Aldrin said.

'It's OK,' Doug assured him. 'I can manage.'

He dumped the wheel on to the wooden block and blew on his enormous walrus moustache.

'Whew!' he said. 'It *is* rather heavy, though! Ninety-two pounds, would you believe? Well, ninety-two-point-five, to be precise!'

Agatha turned her head and noticed Aldrin for the first time.

'Oh, it's you!' she said, smiling at him fondly through a mouthful of butter-coloured cheese. 'The odd child who was in my dream!'

'Er, I wasn't *in* your dream,' Aldrin reminded her. 'You had a dream *about* me, remember?'

'Yes, that's right,' she said, 'but it felt so . . . *real!*'

'Are you gonna buy summat or not?' Belinda asked impatiently.

'No, I think I'm going to leave it,' Agatha said, turning to leave. 'I've just discovered that I'm rather full.'

'Yeah, full of our cheese!' Belinda called after her.

'A few months ago, she were trying to close us down! Now, she's trying to eat us out of stock! Are you all right, Aldrin? You look poorly, love.'

Doug and Belinda still knew nothing of Aldrin's superpower – or the awful cheese hangovers he experienced after entering other people's nightmares.

'I'm just a bit hungry,' Aldrin said.

'We've got some nice Gouda,' Belinda suggested. 'That's if Agatha Whatsit hasn't eaten it all.'

'Yes, it's delicious,' Doug agreed.

Aldrin adored Gouda, especially its nutty taste and grainy finish. But, right then, what he needed was the spongy texture and ever-so-slightly beefy flavour of . . .

'Aged Provolone,' he said.

'Well, you know what you want better than anyone,' Doug replied, picking up a knife. 'As it happens, I've got some here. Arrived yesterday. Twelve months old.'

'About, um, three-and-a-half ounces should do the trick,' Aldrin said. 'By the way, what was it that you wanted to tell me?'

'Oh, yes!' Doug said, his eyes brightening. 'Belinda and I have an announcement to make!'

Aldrin watched as a look passed between the pair – he was almost sure his dad was blushing.

'We wanted *you* to be the first to know,' Belinda told him.

'Know what?' Aldrin asked, trying to steal a look at Belinda's left hand to see if it wore an engagement ring. Unfortunately, she was wearing plastic gloves, which meant he couldn't tell.

'Aldrin,' Doug said, 'Belinda and I . . .'

'What?' asked Aldrin again.

'. . . are arranging a cheese festival! Here in Tintwistle!'

'Oh,' Aldrin said, quietly relieved. 'That is, um . . . exciting news.'

'It'll only be small to start off with,' Doug added. 'But we're hoping in time that it'll come to be as big as the London Festival of Cheese!'

'Wow!' Aldrin smiled.

The London Festival of Cheese had once been the oldest and most colourful cheese festival in the world, with hundreds of cheesemakers coming from all over Europe to sell their wares. It featured all sorts of weird and wonderful cheese-related spectacles, such as exhibitions and even world-record attempts. And it always finished with the traditional Cheese Rolling event, in which a wheel of Double Gloucester was thrown down Fox Hill in Crystal Palace – London's steepest street – and hundreds of people risked life and limb to race it to the bottom.

Unfortunately, after more than a century in existence, the festival had come to an end because of waning interest – and had now been reimagined as the London Festival of Strawberries.

'We've had five hundred of these printed,' Belinda said, handing Aldrin a flier. It said:

Anything They Can Do, We Can Do Feta!

Artisan Cheese FestiVal.
21 April.
Farmers' Market, Tintwistle.

Aldrin felt a wave of excitement pass over him. Because he knew from Mrs Van Boxtel, his English teacher and fellow Cheese Whizz, that the London Festival of Cheese was also where dozens of Cheese Whizzes, just like them, came together each year to discuss how to bring down the evil Habeas Grusselvart.

Aldrin decided he would talk to her about it in school tomorrow. Perhaps she could persuade them to come to Tintwistle!

'Look at that smile on his face!' said Belinda.

'I think it might be my feta joke!' Doug suggested. 'Or the fact that I made the V in "festival" look like a block of cheese!'

But that wasn't the reason. Well, maybe a little bit. Mostly, though, Aldrin was smiling because he was giddy at the thought of meeting others who shared his strange superpower.

'*Anything they can do, we can do feta!*' Aldrin said. 'Brilliant!'

Doug handed his son exactly three ounces of aged Provolone. Aldrin bit into it – and immediately the pain in his head began to lift.

INTRODUCING . . .
THE ODDBALLS!

'WOW!'

Aldrin's eyes popped when he saw it. It was the first edition of the brand-new comic book that Harry and Frankie had created and he had it in his hands! Aldrin read the title out loud:

'*The Oddballs?*'

'Well, what else would we have called it?' said Harry.

They were sitting in the school cafeteria, eating their lunch.

'It's the one thing that ALL superheroes have in common,' Frankie announced. 'They're often considered outsiders in real life. That's why people think they're weird.'

Sisely looked at Aldrin over the top of her Maths book.

'I'm not **THAT** weird!' he said as he popped the lid of his lunch box.

'Think about it,' Harry said. 'Clark Kent, Tony Stark, Natasha Romanova, Peter Parker, Bruce Wayne, Harleen Quinzel, David Banner, Ororo Munroe – they're ALL a bit **odd** in their own ways. But they're brilliant too.'

Aldrin looked round at his friends. 'The oddballs' *was* how many of the students in St Martin's referred to them. They weren't odd, though – they were just different from most kids. But they were all brilliant in their own way too.

Harry was short for his age, with a pudding-bowl haircut, glasses that were as thick as swimming goggles and an asthma inhaler that he sucked on whenever he felt out of breath. But he could draw cartoon characters better than anyone Aldrin had ever known.

Frankie was as bald as a snooker ball, the result of alopecia that had started after he fell from a tree when he was five years old. And he had a tendency to tell fibs, outrageous fibs – for instance, that he visited Mars one Bank Holiday weekend. But he had a wonderful imagination and could make a boring old school day *incredibly* exciting with his tales of heroism and daring.

Sisely was extraordinarily clever for a kid her age. She was fluent in five different languages, could solve the most complicated mathematical problems in her head and had a photographic memory, which meant she only had to read something once to remember it forever. But Sisely wasn't what one might call a sociable person. She didn't know how to make chit-chat, like commenting on the weather or the latest celebrity gossip. She hardly ever laughed – or even smiled. And, as Aldrin knew from personal experience, she tended to just blurt out things that could hurt your feelings, even though that wasn't her intention. But she was fiercely loyal to her friends.

What made Aldrin an oddball was his complete and utter devotion to cheese, especially the ones that were –

'**OH MY GOD!**' the school principal, Mr Maskell, suddenly shouted across the cafeteria. '**WHAT IS THAT REVOLTING SMELL?**'

– well, a bit **whiffy!**

All round Aldrin, the other children were covering their noses and mouths with their hands. Mr Maskell made his way over to Aldrin's table.

'Is it your lunch again?' he asked.

'I think it might be,' Aldrin confessed. 'My dad put

some Cados in my lunch box. It's similar to Camembert,
except –'

'Except it stinks!' said Mr Maskell.

'Yes, sir.'

'Well, I won't tell you what it smells like to *my* nose.
Suffice to say, I originally thought the smell was coming
from the toilets. Put the lid back on that lunch box. I'm
adding Cados to the banned list.'

Yes, the principal had drawn up a **list of smelly**

cheeses that Aldrin was prohibited from eating while on school premises.

Mr Maskell walked away.

'ODDBALLS!' one of the older students shouted unkindly in the direction of the table. But Aldrin and his friends looked at each other and exchanged a wry smile. They *liked* who they were. They *liked* being oddballs. Aldrin's mum had always told him that there would be pressure on him in life to look the same as everyone else, to act the same as everyone else, to like the same things as everyone else. But daring to be different, she said – that took *real* courage! Being yourself was just about the most **heroic** thing that anyone could do.

Someone fired an apple across the cafeteria at them.

'Oi, stop that!' shouted Sebastian Rees-Lane, Agatha's son – the former school bully turned Head Prefect.

The apple knocked over Sisely's glass, spilling her milk across the table. Aldrin managed to whip the comic book away with what he liked to think were superhero-like reflexes.

'That was lucky!' he said. 'This is going to be a collector's item one day!'

'Do you really think so?' Harry asked, pushing his glasses up his nose with his finger.

'Absolutely!' Aldrin assured him. 'First issues always get auctioned off for loads of money, don't they?'

'That's true,' Harry said. 'My dad has the very first comic that Superman appeared in – and he says it's worth more than his house!'

'So how many copies are you going to print?' Aldrin asked.

'We were thinking maybe a hundred,' Frankie said. 'We're going to ask the newsagent's in the precinct if they'd be interested in stocking it.'

'You could set up a stall,' Aldrin suggested, 'at the Tintwistle Cheese Festival.'

'What's the Tintwistle Cheese Festival?' Frankie asked.

'Dad and Belinda are organizing it. I'll ask him for you if you like.'

'Really?' Harry said. 'Thanks, Aldrin.'

'Hey, I just want to be able to say I knew you two *before* you were famous,' Aldrin told him, admiring the artwork on the cover.

It featured a young boy, who bore a striking resemblance to Harry, right down to the glasses with the thick lenses and the asthma inhaler, which dangled from the belt of what appeared to be a safari suit. The boy was wrestling a fearsome-looking crocodile and had the beast in a headlock. In big block capitals, the cover announced: **'THE CROCODILE HUNTER!'** and then underneath: 'The Origin Story of a New Breed of Hero!'

Aldrin opened the comic and flicked through the pages. There were all sorts of stories inside. There was a daredevil named – funnily enough – Frankie, who travelled round America in a camper van, attempting death-defying stunts for money. There was a female super-spy called the Chameleon, who could change her skin colour to blend into any background. And there was the Big Top Five – a group of circus performers, including a knife-thrower, a juggler, a clown, an acrobat and a lion-tamer, who used their skills to solve crimes all over Europe.

'I can't believe you drew ALL of these!' Aldrin said admiringly.

'Hey, I just did the artwork,' Harry said modestly. 'It was Frankie who came up with all the story ideas.'

'They're actually based on things that REALLY happened to me,' Frankie said, 'like the time I jumped across the Grand Canyon in my mum's car.'

'You didn't jump across the Grand Canyon in your mum's car,' Sisely said, not even bothering to look up from her book this time. Frankie ignored her. Aldrin smiled.

'Here,' Frankie said. 'There's a story inspired by you as well, Aldrin.'

'Is there?' Aldrin asked.

'Yeah, you remember the time when we both had the same nightmare? I was stuck up a tree with all them crows surrounding me! You climbed up and you rescued me!'

'Oh, yes, that, um, sounds vaguely familiar, all right,' Aldrin said.

'I even wrote a story about it,' Frankie reminded him, 'for Mrs Van Boxtel's class. You remember? About a boy who can enter into other people's nightmares?'

'Oh, yes,' Aldrin said. 'It's definitely ringing a bell.'

'I mean, it's obviously a fantasy,' Frankie said. 'Couldn't happen. Not like the time at the zoo when I jumped into the lion enclosure – not a thought for me own personal safety – to rescue that kid who was about to get eaten.'

'You didn't jump into the lion enclosure,' Sisely

sighed, still not looking up from her book. Aldrin smiled again.

'It's right at the back,' Frankie said, continuing to ignore Sisely. 'The last strip in the comic.'

Aldrin turned to the back. The story was spread across two pages and was entitled 'Nighty Knight'.

'Nighty Knight?' Aldrin asked.

'Yeah, that's the name of the superhero,' Harry told him. 'Nighty because –'

'He wears a nightie?' Aldrin asked.

'No, because he does all his work at night,' Harry laughed. 'And Knight because, well, he rescues people from bad dreams.'

'Oh, right,' Aldrin said. 'That's, um, very clever.'

Aldrin looked at the character Harry had drawn. Nighty Knight was a tall, handsome boy, with blond hair, a square jaw and biceps like bowling balls. And he wore black ninja-style pyjamas, with half-moons and stars on them.

'He looks nothing like me,' Aldrin said, not even trying to hide his disappointment. 'I thought you said he was inspired by me?'

'Well, obviously, he's not going to *look* like you,' Harry laughed.

'Why not?' asked Aldrin. 'The Crocodile Hunter looks like you!'

'Look, don't take this the wrong way,' said Frankie, 'but I couldn't imagine *you* doing the things that Nighty Knight does. In this one, he fights a dragon!'

'You really couldn't imagine me fighting a dragon?' asked Aldrin.

He'd fought a dragon last month!

'Yeah, no offence,' said Harry, 'but I don't think you'd be *anyone's* idea of a superhero, Aldrin!'

'Oh, thank you very much!' Aldrin said. 'And, um, does Nighty Knight have an arch-enemy at all?'

Sisely looked up and eyed him warily.

'An arch-enemy?' Frankie asked.

'Yes, someone he must do battle with and defeat,' Aldrin explained, 'in order to save the world.'

Aldrin was thinking about Habeas Grusselvart. There was hardly a minute of the day when he *wasn't* thinking about Habeas Grusselvart.

'If Nighty Knight can enter people's nightmares,' Aldrin said, 'perhaps his enemy should be the person who *creates* those nightmares.'

'Why would anyone want to *create* nightmares?' Harry asked.

'To control the world through fear and unhappiness,' Aldrin explained.

Sisely gave him a furious shake of her head to try to shush him. Aldrin knew he was saying too much, but he was on a roll now.

'And maybe your hero has fought this enemy before,' he continued, 'but the fight was a draw. And he knows he has to confront him again – if he wants to save the world from the evil Habeas Grusselvart!'

Aldrin noticed that Harry and Frankie were staring at him with their mouths wide open, while Sisely put her head in her hands in despair.

'Who's Habeas Grusselvart?' Harry asked.

'Oh, er – he's no one,' Aldrin said, suddenly remembering where he was. 'I, er, just made him up.'

A NEW MISSION

Mrs Van Boxtel pointed to the whiteboard with her long stick.

'Now, boysh and girlsh,' she said, 'you will shee that I have written shome wordsh here. Can we all shay them together pleashe?'

The class read them aloud as she pointed to each one in turn:

'Radar . . . Kayak . . . Racecar . . . Level . . . Reviver . . . Civic . . . Madam . . .'

'Exshellent!' she said. 'Now, can anyone tell me what theshe wordsh have in common?'

Sisely's hand shot up.

'Perhapsh,' Mrs Van Boxtel said, smiling, 'we will

give shomebody elshe the opportunity to anshwer, Shishely.'

Aldrin and the rest of the class stared hard at the words.

'They're all spelled the same backwards as they are forwards!' Harry blurted out.

'That ish very good, Harry! Sho what do we call a word that ish shpelled the shame backwardsh ash it ish forwardsh?'

'It's called a palindrome!' Sisely said.

'That ish correct,' Mrs Van Boxtel smiled. 'Now, can anybody elshe think of a palindrome that ish NOT written on the board?'

Mrs Van Boxtel was not like any other teacher at St Martin's. With her thick tweed skirt, her fur-lined ankle boots and the enormous perm that sat on her head like a giant silver cloud, she looked like Aldrin's idea of a grandmother. She came from the Netherlands, which was why she spoke so differently, pronouncing her **s's** as **sh's**.

But it was her, well, *oddness* that made her classes so enjoyable.

'Noon!' shouted Harry.

'Yesh!' the teacher said, adding the word to the

board. 'Noon ish a palindrome! Anyone elshe?'

Mrs Van Boxtel also had a secret that only Aldrin and Sisely knew. She too was a Cheese Whizz and had the power to enter other people's nightmares, even though she seldom used it now because of her advanced years.

'Sho,' she said, 'I'm going to give you shome homework to do during the Easter holidays.'

Everyone groaned.

'Thish will be fun,' she promised. 'I want you to write an entire shentenshe that ish shpelled the shame backwardsh ash it ish forwardsh.'

'A whole sentence?' said Harry. 'But that's impossible.'

'Murder for a jar of red rum,' Mrs Van Boxtel replied.

The class fell silent as they thought about the words:

Murder for a jar of red rum . . .

mur der fo raj a rof redruM . . .

She was totally right!

'Will there be a cash prize for the best one?' Frankie asked.

'No, there will not!' Mrs Van Boxtel laughed. 'I am an old lady – and, shadly for me, I am not made of money!'

The bell sounded to end the class.

'Aldrin and Shishely,' she said, 'can you shtay behind pleashe?'

Aldrin and Sisely remained at their desks while everyone else left. Mrs Van Boxtel closed the door.

'Aldrin,' she announced, 'I have shomething for you.'

She reached into her handbag, then placed a photograph on his desk. It was of a boy, about six years old, with pasty skin and blond shoulder-length hair.

'Hish name ish Otto,' she explained.

'His name is a palindrome,' Sisely declared.

'Yesh, it ish,' said Mrs Van Boxtel. 'Otto Fineshtra ish a boy in Germany. He ish the godshon of my shishter, who tellsh me that he ish having awful nightmaresh almosht every night.'

'What are these nightmares about?' Aldrin asked, picking up the photograph.

'He dreamsh that hish brother'sh toysh come to life,' she explained.

'Five ounces of Pont l'Évêque,' Sisely declared, like a doctor prescribing medicine, 'and three ounces of Rosso di Lago.'

'I'll do it tonight,' Aldrin said, slipping the photograph into the inside pocket of his blazer. 'Mrs Van Boxtel, can I ask you a question?'

'Of courshe,' she said.

'Well, my dad and Belinda are organizing a cheese festival in Tintwistle.'

'How wonderful!' the teacher said.

Aldrin started to ask a question: 'Do you think . . . ?' and then he paused.

'Do I think what?' Mrs Van Boxtel asked.

'Do you think the Cheese Whizzes would come?'

'Come? You mean to Tintwishtle?'

'Yes. You told me that they used to meet every year at the London Festival of Cheese, which doesn't exist any more. But Dad thinks the Tintwistle Cheese Festival could be even bigger. So do you think they might meet here instead?'

'I have no idea,' Mrs Van Boxtel replied. 'Shadly, I have losht touch with mosht of the other Cheeshe

Whizshes. Many of them, like your mother, are no longer with ush.'

'But there must be *someone* you can contact,' Aldrin said. 'You could tell them about the festival – invite them here.'

'Aldrin,' Mrs Van Boxtel said, smiling patiently, 'you are doing wonderful work, helping all of theshe people.'

'But I want to meet *other* Cheese Whizzes,' Aldrin said. 'I want to talk to people who share my superpower.'

'It's not a superpower,' Sisely argued.

'Well, whatever it is,' Aldrin said, 'if I meet people who have the same ability as me, I might be able to find out more about what it is I'm supposed to be doing.'

'*Thish* ish what you're shupposhed to be doing,' Mrs Van Boxtel reminded him. 'Helping people to undershtand that their nightmaresh are nothing to be shcared of.'

'But I can't help but feel that there must be more to it than just . . . *that*.'

He was thinking about Habeas yet again – how he wanted to find him and stop him once and for all.

'Look,' Mrs Van Boxtel said, 'leave it with me. I will try to contact one or two of my old Cheeshe Whizsh friendsh and mention thish feshtival to them.'

'Thanks, Mrs Van Boxtel,' Aldrin said excitedly. 'It's happening in two weeks – the last day of the Easter break.'

'Like I shay to you,' Mrs Van Boxtel told him, 'I cannot promishe anything.'

And it might have been Aldrin's imagination, but in that moment he could have sworn he saw a strange look pass between Sisely and Mrs Van Boxtel.

NO MORE EXCUSES

'I thought you might be interested to know,' said Beddy Byes, 'that the Creative Department are now working on a whole new series of nightmares, including one involving a horror snowman –'

'BORING! BORING! BORING!' shouted Habeas from behind his desk. 'Why does **EVERYTHING** you say have to be so **BORING**? How long have you been my assistant now, Beddy Byes?'

'I think it's something in the order of eighteen years. Eighteen years, three months, two weeks and, um, five days, to be precise.'

'And I'm starting to feel every single one of them. What are we going to do about the Adams boy? Have you come up with a plan yet?'

'Not yet, sir, but I'm still working on –'

Just then, there was a knock on the door.

'COME IN!' Habeas bawled.

The door opened and he found himself staring at a vaguely familiar face.

'Who is this person?' Habeas asked. 'And why do I feel like I've met him before?'

'His name is Ethan Marcus,' Beddy Byes reminded him. 'And I believe you fired him last week.'

'Oh, yes – creator of the so-called *Night of Terror*!' Habeas recalled. 'I thought you took his security pass from him.'

'I'm the best computer programmer you have,' Ethan said. 'You think I can't find a way to override the security system in this building?'

'Beddy Byes, show this person out, preferably through one of the upper windows.'

'Just before you do,' Ethan said, taking a step forward, 'I thought you might be interested in seeing this!'

With a dramatic flourish, he placed a piece of paper on the desk in front of his former boss. Habeas studied it for a moment.

'*Anything They Can Do, We Can Do Feta*,' he read.

'Is that supposed to be some kind of joke?'

'Yes, it's a pun,' Ethan said.

Beddy Byes eyed him warily.

'A cheese festival in Tintwhistle?' Habeas read, then he repeated the word 'Tintwistle' like it had triggered a memory for him. 'This is the boy's father, isn't it?'

'Yes, Doug Adams,' Ethan confirmed. 'Apparently, he thinks it'll become bigger than the London Festival of Cheese.'

'This is most impressive work,' Habeas purred. 'Beddy Byes, do you remember when you used to impress me?'

'I . . . I . . . I . . . certainly do,' Beddy Byes said, tripping over his words. 'And I . . . I . . . I . . . hope to again, sir.'

'So why didn't you tell me about this? **YOU ARE PAID TO BE MY EYES AND EARS! YOU SHOULD HAVE KNOWN ABOUT IT!'**

'I'm s-s-s-sorry, sir.'

'WE KNOW THE CHEESE WHIZZES MET IN SECRET EVERY YEAR AT THE LONDON FESTIVAL OF CHEESE TO PLOT MY DESTRUCTION! WHAT IF THEY MEET IN TINTWISTLE?'

'They *are* meeting in Tintwistle,' Ethan cut in.

'You know that for a fact?' asked Habeas.

'I have an informant – inside the order. I know when they're meeting, and I know where.'

'What did you say your name was again?' Habeas asked.

'Ethan,' came the reply. 'Ethan Marcus.'

'Well, Ethan Marcus, you have just redeemed yourself in my eyes. You're un-fired!'

Habeas smiled, a plan formulating in his mind. 'I've had an idea,' he said. 'For how we can stop the boy. Beddy Byes, leave us.'

'What?' Beddy Byes asked.

'I wish to speak to Ethan alone,' Habeas told him. 'Now, get out.'

Beddy Byes stared at his boss. He'd never been dismissed like this before.

'Something wrong?' Habeas asked.

'Er, no,' said Beddy Byes, and he left the room.

Habeas ordered Ethan to sit down on the other side of the desk.

'You know,' he told him, 'I see a very big future for you here.'

'Er, thanks,' said Ethan. 'So what's this idea of yours?'

'All in good time.' Habeas smiled. 'But first I think it's about time I paid young Aldrin another visit!'

STAY OUT OF OTHER PEOPLE'S NIGHTMARES

Aldrin had rarely seen his dad so excited.

'Belinda posted something about the festival,' Doug said. 'On the, um, internet thingamy.'

'Do you mean social media?' Aldrin asked.

'Yes, exactly!' said Doug. 'We've had interest from cheesemakers *and* cheesemongers all over Europe – France, Italy, Spain, Germany, Ireland, Switzerland, Greece.'

'That *is* exciting,' Aldrin agreed. 'Dad, can Frankie and Harry sell their new comic book at the festival?'

'Of course they can!' Doug said, then he picked up issue one of *The Oddballs* from Aldrin's study desk. 'Is this it?'

'Yes,' said Aldrin. 'Harry did all the drawings himself.'

'Well, he's very talented,' Doug observed as he turned the pages. 'Who's Nighty Knight?'

'Oh, he's a superhero who can, um, *enter* other people's nightmares.'

'Enter other people's nightmares?' Doug repeated, screwing up his face. 'Why would he want to do that?'

'So he can show people that they've nothing to be frightened of,' Aldrin explained.

Doug shook his head. 'Dear oh dear – where *do* you boys get your imaginations?' He chuckled to himself, then he placed the comic book back on Aldrin's desk. 'Oh, I have your supper here – just as you ordered!'

He reached into the pocket of his green-and-white-striped apron and placed two small packages on the desk next to Silas.

'The Pont l'Évêque is especially good,' he said. 'It's as soft as dough.'

'Thanks, Dad,' Aldrin said.

'Is that homework you're doing?' Doug asked. 'Aren't you supposed to be on holiday?'

'It's sort of homework,' Aldrin explained. 'Mrs Van Boxtel wants us to come up with a palindrome. It's a word that's spelled the exact same way backwards – except we have to find an entire sentence like that. It's very tricky. I'm going to give it up for tonight.'

'Well, I'll be up for a couple of hours yet. There's a lot of things to organize ahead of the cheese festival.' He hesitated for a moment,then said: 'You, erm, do like Belinda, don't you, Aldrin?'

'Of course I do!'

'That's good. Because I'm very fond of her. I mean, I know she's not your mum, Aldrin, but she makes me very happy.'

'I know, Dad.'

'Anyway, I'll let you get some sleep. Oh, and Aldrin?'

'Yes, Dad?'

'Maybe stay out of other people's nightmares tonight, will you?'

'What?' Aldrin asked, shocked.

'I'm talking about Nighty Knight! From the comic book!'

'Of course!'

They said goodnight the way they always did.

'*Sweet dreams* –' Doug said.

'**– are made of cheese,**' Aldrin added.

'***Who am I* –**'

'**– to diss a Brie?**'

'Night, son.'

'Night, Dad.'

When Doug left, Aldrin looked into Silas's tank.

'Night, little friend,' he said.

He changed into his pyjamas, then he reached inside the pocket of his blazer and took out the photograph that Mrs Van Boxtel had given him. He picked up the two cheese parcels and climbed into bed.

He unwrapped the Pont l'Évêque and breathed in its creamy, slightly garlicky aroma. He bit into it. It was soft and sticky and it clung to the back of his teeth. He chewed it while he focused on the photograph of Otto Finestra, his thin features, pasty complexion and long blond hair.

Before he'd even swallowed it, he opened the Rosso di Lago, which was similar in texture, but smelled like fresh-cut grass. He popped it into his mouth, then he put the photograph down and he closed his eyes, picturing Otto's face in his mind.

He chewed the Pont l'Évêque and the Rosso di Lago until they turned into a mass of salty, buttery, grassy, garlicky gloop in his mouth.

And *very quickly* . . .

without even realizing . . .

that it was happening . . .

his eyes started to feel . . .

very,

very

heavy . . .

And then . . .

he was suddenly . . .

out

for

the . . .

OTTO FINESTRA'S NIGHTMARE

Aldrin found himself in a darkened room. As his eyes adjusted, he could see that the walls were covered in posters of racing cars and racing-car drivers.

'OUCH!' he suddenly exclaimed.

The floor was strewn with toys, and he'd stepped on a plastic giraffe.

Aldrin saw an empty bed, its covers thrown back. There was also a wardrobe and a chest of drawers.

'Otto?' he whispered. 'Otto, are you in here?'

Aldrin could hear the faint sound of sobbing. It seemed to be coming from inside the wardrobe. He tapped lightly on the door.

'Otto,' he said in a gentle voice. 'Is that you in there?'

There was no reply.

'Otto,' he said. 'I'm going to open the door now, OK?'

Aldrin pulled the handle downwards and the door creaked open. Standing there, huddled in the corner, was the boy from Mrs Van Boxtel's photograph.

'*Wer bist du?*' he said, his eyes wide with surprise.

Aldrin didn't speak German, but 'Who are you?' was usually the first question people asked when he popped up unexpectedly in their nightmares.

'My name is Aldrin Adams,' Aldrin said.

'*Sprechen sie Deutsch?*' the boy said.

Brilliant, Aldrin thought. He had no German and, from the sound of it, Otto had no English.

'OK,' said Aldrin. 'What are you frightened of?'

'*Skelett!*' the boy said.

'Skelett?' Aldrin echoed.

'*Skelett!*' the boy said more urgently now.

'The problem,' Aldrin explained, 'is that I don't know what that word actually means.'

'*Skelett!*' the boy shouted, looking over Aldrin's shoulder now. '*SKELETT*!!!'

Aldrin slowly turned his head. And that was when he discovered **EXACTLY** what the word meant.

In the middle of the bedroom floor stood . . . a **SKELETON**!

It was about six feet tall – toys that came to life in nightmares were almost *always* life-sized – and had FOUR arms, and at the end of each one, gripped by a set of bony fingers, was a curved sword!

'Why can't kids play with *nice* toys?' Aldrin sighed.

The skeleton's bones rattled horribly as it stepped forward, swinging all four swords with the skill of a samurai.

'Otto,' Aldrin asked, 'do you have something I might use as a –?'

But, before he could finish his sentence, the skeleton swung a sword at him. Aldrin ducked and performed a forward roll to escape the blow. Then he spotted a drumstick on the floor. He picked it up and held it in front of him like a sabre.

The skeleton advanced, bones clattering and all four arms swinging their weapons in a circular motion. It lunged wildly at him with one of its swords. This time, Aldrin took a step to the side and aimed the drumstick at one of its two right arms. It shattered at the elbow and the sword fell to the floor with a heavy **CLANK**.

But the skeleton kept coming and Aldrin backed away as it continued to stalk him round the bedroom.

It aimed the next blow at Aldrin's head – and Aldrin was forced to duck to avoid it.

'*Auf gehts!*' shouted Otto, which Aldrin presumed was an expression of encouragement.

Aldrin swung the drumstick, but the skeleton blocked the blow, then lifted a sword high, before bringing it down hard, narrowly missing Aldrin and embedding the blade in the top of Otto's chest of drawers. Before it could pull it out, Aldrin kicked out at the skeleton's arm, snapping it off.

There were now just TWO swords to worry about!

'If you, er, fancy giving me a hand here,' Aldrin told Otto, 'I wouldn't say no to some help!'

But Otto remained exactly where he was.

Aldrin and the skeleton performed circuits of the bedroom, the skeleton occasionally lunging, Aldrin either jumping out of the way or using the drumstick to parry the blow.

'YOU SEE?' he shouted to Otto. **'IT'S JUST A TOY – IT'S NOTHING TO BE –'**

And that was when **DISASTER** struck!

Not looking where he was going, Aldrin stepped on a toy racing car and suddenly lost his footing. He staggered backwards, his legs disappearing from underneath him, and a second later his head hit the floor hard.

He was momentarily **dazed**. By the time his head cleared, the skeleton was standing over him, bearing down on him with his two remaining swords poised to deliver the final, **FATAL** blow!

Aldrin realized that he'd dropped his drumstick. He felt around the floor for it, but it wasn't there! He watched in horror as the skeleton lifted both swords above his head!

Aldrin closed his eyes, ready for the worst!

And then . . .

. . . nothing happened!

Aldrin opened his eyes again. The skeleton had stopped! It was frozen to the spot, swords raised, but unmoving.

'What the –?' Aldrin said aloud.

Then he spotted Otto, who had crawled out of his hiding place. He pushed the skeleton and it fell forward on to its face. Aldrin noticed that the door of the battery compartment was open . . .

And in Otto's hand was a giant AA battery!

'*Danke,*' Otto smiled.

It sounded like he was saying thanks.

'Well, thank you too!' Aldrin replied. 'Go on. It's safe to go back to bed now.'

Aldrin watched Otto get under the covers, then he waited to see some Neufchâtel, or some Délice de Bourgogne, or some Tomme de Savoie – a sign that would tell him he was about to wake up in his own bed.

But he didn't. He remained in Otto's room, trapped inside the boy's dream. This had only ever happened to him once before. It was the time he came face to face with –

But he didn't allow himself to finish the thought.

He felt a sudden compulsion to open the bedroom door. When he did, he expected to see a landing stretching out in front of him. Instead, he found himself standing outdoors . . . staring down a pier.

And at the end of it stood a familiar figure.

He was a tall, powerfully built giant of a man, with a pale complexion, a wild mane of black curly hair, hooded eyes, a crooked nose, dark sideburns that ran down to his chin and a long black coat, which was buttoned right to his neck, with the collar standing up.

Even from a distance of two hundred feet, Aldrin recognized him . . .

It was Habeas Grusselvart!

'Long time, no see,' Habeas said tauntingly.

Aldrin started walking towards him, then he broke into a run, then a sprint. As he reached him, Aldrin stretched out his hands to grab his evil enemy – but he went straight through him like he wasn't even there!

Habeas laughed his wicked laugh:

'MWAH-HA-HA-HA-HA-HA-HA!'

Aldrin turned and stared at his foe. Then he started swinging his fists at him – first his left, then his right. But the punches sailed through him and it quickly dawned on Aldrin that it was just a hologram!

'COME AND FACE ME!' Aldrin shouted. **'COME AND FACE ME, YOU COWARD!'**

'As you wish,' a voice behind him said, then he felt two firm hands on his back and he was shoved face down on the ground.

He rolled over. Habeas – the *real* Habeas – was standing over him. He placed a boot on Aldrin's chest and he laughed again:

'MWAH-HA-HA-HA-HA-HA-HA!'

Aldrin attempted to stand, but Habeas pressed down hard with his foot.

'You're going to regret that!' Aldrin vowed through his clenched teeth.

'What are you going to do?' Habeas asked in a mocking voice. 'Call for your mummy – like you did the last time?'

Aldrin had used the magic words 'Knockdrinna Snow', the name of a particularly special goat's cheese Camembert, to summon his mother's help, just as Habeas was about to skewer his Adam's apple with a fondue fork. But it was a trick he could only perform three times in total.

'No,' Aldrin replied. 'I'm more than capable of fighting my own battles!'

'Oh, please!' said Habeas. 'You're not facing a battery-powered skeleton now, Adams!'

'You have nothing to offer the world except unhappiness,' Aldrin told him, 'and I'm going to STOP you!'

'You?' Habeas laughed. 'You're just another Cheese Whizz, trying to save the world one nightmare at a time!'

'Otto won't be scared of that skeleton again.'

'No, but I'm still out there in the world – and you know not where – manufacturing new nightmares for five thousand people every week. So what if you help one or two people here or there?'

'Five thousand people per week?' Aldrin asked with a sense of deflation.

'Even if I stopped creating new nightmares tomorrow,' Habeas told him, 'it would take you FOREVER to catch up! You're wasting your life, Aldrin!'

Then his mouth twisted into an ugly smile. 'Just like Cynthia wasted hers!' he said scornfully.

'DON'T YOU TALK ABOUT MY MOTHER!' Aldrin raged. With both hands, he swept Habeas's boot off his chest, then he jumped to his feet.

Habeas, smiling, backed away. Aldrin put his head down and made a bull's rush at him, leading with his head, at the same time shouting:

'DON'T YOU *DARE* TALK ABOUT MY MOTHER'

But, as Aldrin reached him, he felt himself being tripped, then falling forward again. But when he landed this time it wasn't on the pier. It was in his bedroom.

He felt that common dream sensation of falling from a height, then he woke up with a pain in his head so severe that he could barely open his eyes.

A DROP IN THE OCEAN

'Aldrin, can you hear me? Aldrin, come in! Over.'

Aldrin sat up in the bed and reached for his walkie-talkie.

'Mooorning, Sssisssely,' he mumbled into it. 'Ooover.'

'You sound terrible,' she said. 'Four slices of Red Leicester will fix that, according to your mum's dream journal. Over.'

'Thanks, Sisely,' he said, laying his head on the pillow again. 'Over and out!'

'Wait a minute,' she said. 'You didn't tell me how it went. Over.'

'Went?'

'Otto's nightmare. What happened? Over.'

'I met him,' Aldrin said. 'Over.'

'Who?' asked Sisely. 'You mean Otto? Over.'

'No,' said Aldrin. 'Well, yes, I did meet Otto. It turns out he was terrified of this toy skeleton with four arms. That part of the night went to plan. But then . . . I met Habeas and –'

'You met Habeas?' Sisely interrupted.

'Hey, I didn't say "over" yet.'

'I'm sorry, I'm just a bit . . . shocked. What happened? What did he say? Over.'

'He told me I was wasting my life – just like my mum wasted hers. Over.'

'You're not wasting your life. You helped a little boy overcome his nightmares last night – didn't you? Over.'

'But, again, that was just *one* person! Habeas laughed at me. He said he was creating five thousand new nightmares every week – while I'm trying to save the world one nightmare at a time. And he's right, Sisely. What I'm doing is just a drop in the ocean. Over.'

'But what else *can* you do? Over.'

'I need to find him. Not in the world of dreams, where he can do what he wants – but out there, in the real world, where I can fight him on equal terms. He must have a secret lair somewhere – all supervillains have a secret lair – where he creates these nightmares. If I can destroy that, then I can stop him. Over.'

'But how are you going to find this lair? Over.'

'With the help of the Cheese Whizzes, of course. Over.'

'But you don't *know* any Cheese Whizzes – apart from Mrs Van Boxtel. Over.'

'She's going to invite them to Tintwistle for the festival. Over.'

'No, I was there, Aldrin. She said she'd try, but she couldn't promise anything, remember? Over.'

'I have every faith in her, Sisely. Anyway, I'd better go. I'm supposed to be working in the shop today – and I suppose I'd better eat some cheese. Over and out.'

Aldrin put his walkie-talkie back on his bedside table, swung his feet out of the bed and made his way downstairs.

'Red Leicester?' Belinda exclaimed when he told her what he wanted. 'For breakfast?'

'Yeah, I just have a craving for it this morning,' Aldrin explained.

Doug chuckled.

'It was one of Cynthia's favourites,' he said.

'Was it?' Aldrin asked.

'Oh, yes,' Doug told him, placing the block of cheese on the wooden cutting board, 'especially first thing in the morning. How much of this do you want?'

'I was thinking, I don't know, maybe *four* slices?' Aldrin replied.

'That's what she always had!' Doug said, bringing the wire down on the block. 'Honestly, there's so much of your mum in you, Aldrin, it's uncanny.'

As he savoured that smooth, almondy cheese, with its surprisingly sweet aftertaste, he thought about what his dad said. The man was right. Aldrin and his mum had so much in common – and far, far more than Doug even realized.

Aldrin missed his mum every day, but never more than he did at that moment. Habeas Grusselvart had touched a raw nerve. He'd told him something that he already suspected, that he could – and *should* – have been doing more. His mum would have understood the frustration he felt at this moment. His mum would have understood his confusion.

Because, at some point in her life, she must have felt all those feelings herself.

10

FLASHBACK

Cynthia was late. Cynthia was *always* late. No matter how early she got out of bed, she never seemed to have enough time to get to where she needed to be.

But this morning she couldn't afford to be late because this was a VERY important day for her. She had borrowed her dad's car and was on her way to London for a job interview. But this wasn't just any job interview – she was on her way to Farlowe's Cheesemakers, where its legendary owner, Aline Lacombe – *the* Aline Lacombe! – was going to interview her for a job as an apprentice cheesemaker.

When Cynthia had left school at the start of the summer, her father had told her to follow her dreams. Cynthia had always adored cheese, and so when she saw the advert for the apprenticeship she couldn't imagine anything else she'd like more in the world than to work there – which explained her anxiety about being on time this morning.

She was so concerned about not being late that she failed to notice the young man with the pointy nose and glasses, who was waiting to cross the road up ahead . . . or the giant puddle just in front of him.

Cynthia ploughed through it at full speed . . .

WHOOOOOOSH!!!!!!

. . . soaking the man from head to toe!

Shortly afterwards, Cynthia was sitting in the reception area of Farlowe's Cheesemakers.

'Madame Lacombe is running a little bit behind schedule today,' Madame Lacombe's secretary explained. 'You'll be called shortly.'

Cynthia sat down to wait. Moments later, the door opened and in walked a young man in a light-grey suit that was *saturated* with filthy brown rainwater.

'Oh, dear!' said Cynthia. 'You're soaked to the skin! Is it raining?'

'It was YOU!' the young man said, remembering Cynthia's face.

'I beg your pardon!' she replied.

'You ***splashed*** me!' he told her. 'In your car! I was waiting to cross the road!'

'Oh, I'm terribly sorry!'

'I'm here for a job interview – and look at the state of me!'

'A job interview?'

'Yes – for the apprentice cheesemaker's role.'

'Oh,' said Cynthia, realizing they were there for exactly the same reason. 'I see.'

'But I'm *never* going to get it now!' the man said. 'Not looking like this!'

But Cynthia had an idea.

'My dad asked me to collect his dry-cleaning this

morning,' she said, jumping to her feet. 'I have one of his suits in the boot of the car. You look about the same size as him.'

As she rushed towards the door, the secretary called her back:

'Madame Lacombe will see you now!'

'I'm sorry,' Cynthia told her. 'I just have to get something from the car first.'

'Madame Lacombe does not like to wait,' the secretary told her in a severe voice. 'Lateness is something she does not tolerate in others.'

Cynthia could go ahead with the interview and let her rival for the job face Madame Lacombe in his dirty, rain-sodden clothes, or she could go outside to fetch the clean suit – and risk losing the job to him.

It didn't take her long to decide what was the right thing to do.

'I won't be long,' she said, pulling her car keys from her handbag.

A minute or so later, she returned and handed the clean clothes to the young man. While he disappeared into the gents' toilets to put them on, Cynthia told the secretary that she was ready for her interview now.

'For you, there is no interview,' the woman said.

'What?' Cynthia asked.

'I told you,' the secretary replied. 'Madame Lacombe does not like to be kept waiting.'

'But I was only gone for a minute!'

'Good day to you.'

At that moment, the young man emerged from the toilets, wearing Cynthia's dad's suit.

'It fits!' he declared with a smile, then he sensed the cold atmosphere in the room. 'What's wrong?'

'Oh, it's nothing,' said Cynthia.

'Why haven't you gone in for your interview?' he wondered.

'Madame Lacombe does not wish to see her,' the secretary told him, 'because she was late.'

'She wasn't late,' the young man tried to explain. 'She just popped out for a moment to help me.'

'Are you Maurice Mackle?' the secretary asked.

'Yes,' said the young man, 'but it's pronounced *Morr-eece*.'

'Madame Lacombe will see you now, *Morr-eece*.'

'No,' said Maurice. 'She *must* see this lady first – sorry, what's your name?'

'Cynthia,' said Cynthia.

'She must interview Cynthia first,' Maurice insisted.

'Otherwise, I don't want the job.'

The secretary stared at him in disbelief.

'Madame Lacombe is the most famous cheesemaker in the **entire world**!' she reminded him. 'You have the opportunity to learn from the woman who has been described as the *Mozart of cheese*! And you are prepared to walk away from that?'

'Absolutely,' he said, turning round and heading for the door.

'*Morr-eece*, don't be a fool,' Cynthia called after him.

'I'm going,' he announced.

'*ATTENDEZ!*' a voice suddenly shouted in a French accent. '*ATTENDEZ!*'

Cynthia and Maurice turned. There, standing in the doorway of her office, was an elderly woman, short of stature, with a slightly sour face and silver hair pulled back into a bun.

It was Aline Lacombe.

She and her secretary spoke to each other in French, which neither Cynthia nor Maurice understood. Then she fixed Maurice with a stern look and said, 'Do you wish to be my apprentice or not?'

'Yes, of course I do,' he told her, 'but only if the competition is fair. The only reason Cynthia was late was because she saw that I was soaked to the skin, then she went out to her car to get me a clean suit. She did it out of kindness, even though we're both going for the same job – and now you won't interview her. I've wanted to be a cheesemaker since I was five years old. But, if that's how things work in Farlowe's, then it's definitely *not* where I want to be!'

Madame Lacombe's features suddenly thawed – and she smiled.

'You know,' she said, 'every year I hire just one apprentice to learn the art of how to make cheese. But this year, for the first time ever, I am going to take on two.'

Cynthia and Maurice exchanged confused looks.

'Come with me, both of you,' Madame Lacombe said. 'I hope you can you start right away because there is so much to learn!'

'But don't you want to interview us?' Cynthia asked.

'I already know everything I need to know about you,' Madame Lacombe told her. 'And already I have the feeling that you will be the **greatest apprentices** that Farlowe's has ever had – and the **very best of friends**.'

11

THE TINTWISTLE CHEESE FESTIVAL

'Roll up! Roll up!' Doug called, sounding like a carnival barker. 'Guess the weight of this enormous wheel of Parmigiano Reggiano and win yourself a year's supply of cheese from *C'est Cheese!*'

He was dressed like a town crier from the days of old, in a long pillar-box-red Edwardian frock coat, a three-cornered hat, black slip-on shoes with enormous silver buckles and white breeches that were tucked into white knee-high socks. And he was ringing a handbell.

'That's right, ladies and gentlemen, boys and girls,' he announced, 'a year's supply of cheese will be *yours* – if you can guess the exact weight of this wheel of *scrumptious* Italian cheese!'

On the table behind him sat the wheel of cheese that Aldrin had seen his dad struggling to carry in the shop. It was as big as a motorcycle tyre.

'Can I try to lift it?' asked Mr Gaskin, the local postman.

'Can you heck as like!' snapped Belinda. 'You're to guess by *looking* at it! And you look with your eyes, not your hands!'

Aldrin smiled to himself. Inside, though, he felt sad. In the past two weeks, he had heard not a word from Mrs Van Boxtel and it looked like there would be no secret meeting of the Cheese Whizzes after all.

Just at that moment, Aldrin saw Sisely walking through the crowded market to the *C'est Cheese* stall.

'Hi, Sisely,' he said glumly. 'How has your Easter been?'

'Fine,' she said. 'Did you come up with any sentences that are spelled the same way backwards?'

'Er, no,' Aldrin said. 'I spent the entire two weeks waiting for Mrs Van Boxtel to ring. But she never did. I tried phoning her, but she didn't answer. I even called at her flat, but she was never home.'

'She did tell you not to get your hopes up.'

'I know – but I'm still disappointed.'

Sisely then turned to Doug.

'How is the cheese festival going, Mr Adams?' she asked. 'My mum said I should make more of an effort at making small talk.'

'It's going wonderfully well.' Doug smiled. 'And thank you for asking, Sisely. There are cheesemakers here from all over Europe – and lots of fun exhibits. As a matter of fact, Aldrin, you and Sisely should go off and explore. And don't forget to go and see Madame Bluessauds.'

'What's Madame Bluessauds?' Sisely wondered.

'It's a collection of life-sized sculptures of famous people,' Doug explained, 'all made from Gorgonzola! Also, somewhere around here, the people who produce that delicious Bilbault's Gruyère that you love, Aldrin, are attempting to make the largest toasted-cheese sandwich in the world! Oh, and at six o'clock don't forget that the festival ends with the Cheese Rolling on Lambert's Hill!'

'OK,' said Aldrin, struggling to get excited.

'Just before you go,' Doug said, 'Sisely, would you like to guess what this wheel of Parmigiano Reggiano weighs?'

'And you're not allowed to touch it!' Belinda added. 'I'm only saying because some folk, who shall remain nameless, have been taking liberties. Mr Gaskin were one of them – not that I'm one to point the finger.'

Sisely walked up to the table and stared at the large straw-coloured wheel. Aldrin could almost hear the cogs of her mind turning as she took in its depth and diameter. Finally, after a silence lasting almost a minute, she said:

'Ninety-two-point-five pounds.'

Doug's mouth fell open.

'Eh?' said Belinda, sounding like she, too, could

scarcely believe what she'd heard.

'Ninty-two-point-five pounds,' Sisely repeated.

Out of the side of his mouth, Doug whispered to Aldrin:

'You didn't tell her, did you, son?'

'No, Dad,' Aldrin assured him. 'That's just Sisely. She's a genius.'

Belinda picked up the clipboard on which more than sixty other festival-goers had scribbled their guesses. 'You don't want to change your answer to summat else, do you?' she asked. 'Like fifty-point-six pounds? Or seventy-five-point-three pounds?'

'Ninty-two-point-five pounds,' Sisely repeated, taking the clipboard from her, then writing the figure underneath the other guesses.

'Well, if you *do* win,' Belinda said churlishly, 'a year's supply of cheese – if you'd bothered to check the small print – means one block per week. It don't entitle you to march into the shop every morning and clean us out of stock.'

That cheered Aldrin up – even if only for a moment.

'I'm sure she understands that, Belinda,' he said. 'Come on, Sisely, let's go and see if can we find Frankie and Harry. See you later, Belinda. See you later, Dad.'

The Tintwistle Cheese Festival was a roaring success. The farmers' market was absolutely thronged with people, many of them speaking in different languages – French, Italian, Spanish, German, Greek as well as, of course, English.

And the air was thick with the **smell** of the cheeses they'd come to buy and sell – buttery Havartis, and milky mozzarellas, and eggy Bries, and meaty Manchegos, and grassy Taleggios, and salty Cheddars, and pungent Parmesans, and salty blues.

Everywhere that he and Sisely wandered, there was something interesting to see. They stood and watched a man in a blue-and-white-striped T-shirt juggling EIGHTEEN balls of Edam, each one the size of a grapefruit. Aldrin and Sisely clapped and cheered along with the rest of the crowd.

Then Aldrin spotted a large group of people queuing to have their photograph taken with an enormous caramel-coloured cow.

'**It's ISLA!**' Aldrin shouted, suddenly forgetting his disappointment.

'Who's Isla?' Sisely wondered.

'Have you never heard of Isla's Orange Cheddar? It's made in Fife in Scotland. Well, *she's* the cow on the packet! I can't believe I'm going to meet *the* Isla!'

Sisely rolled her eyes – for someone who considered himself a superhero, Aldrin could be very immature at times, she thought. But still, she agreed to pose with him next to Isla, then waited with him for the Polaroid photograph to be developed because she was learning that that was the kind of thing that friends did for each other.

Once they'd collected the picture, they moved on, Aldrin still smiling wistfully and talking about his brush with fame.

Soon they found the stall where Harry and Frankie were selling their comic book. There was an older boy standing with them, flicking through a copy of *The Oddballs*. He was about seventeen, with a suntanned complexion and blond hair, which was cut in a floppy style that was fashionable among surfers. He was wearing board shorts, flip-flops and a garishly loud multicoloured Hawaiian shirt, and had a skateboard under his arm.

'You put this together yourselves?' he asked, sounding very impressed.

'Yeah, Harry here did all the drawings himself,' Frankie told him.

'And Frankie came up with all the ideas,' Harry added.

'Dude,' the boy said, shaking his head, 'this is like something you'd buy in a comic store.'

'Er, thanks,' said Harry.

'How much are you selling this for?'

'A quid,' Frankie replied.

'Are you kidding me?' came the reply. 'You should be selling it for five times that!'

'Really?' Harry asked. 'Do you think?'

'Absolutely,' the young man said, handing him a five-pound note. 'The name's Archie, by the way. I'm a HUGE comic-book fan.'

'Oh, right,' said Harry. 'I'm a big fan myself.'

'Yeah, I gathered that! Some of these characters! The Crocodile Hunter! Nighty Knight! They're amazing!'

Harry and Frankie flushed with pride.

'Oh, Archie,' Harry said, making the introductions, 'these are my friends Aldrin and Sisely.'

Archie nodded and smiled at them.

'Aldrin. Sisely. It's nice to meet you, dudes,' he said.

'Er, yeah, you too,' said Aldrin.

Sisely said nothing. She was still thinking up palindromes in her head.

Archie put his skateboard on the ground, then pushed off.

'Your change,' Harry called after him.

'Keep it!' Archie shouted over his shoulder. 'And stop selling it for a quid – it's worth five!'

'OK, let's call it a day,' Harry declared, 'and check out the rest of the festival.'

'Brilliant!' said Frankie, rubbing his hands together. 'I want to see the world's biggest toasted-cheese sandwich.'

Aldrin started to get excited again. But then he remembered his disappointment with Mrs Van Boxtel – and he felt his stomach sink once more.

12

THE BRIE BLIND TASTE CHALLENGE

'It's over this way,' Harry said, consulting his festival map.

Aldrin, Sisely and Frankie followed him through the crowded market until they arrived at a large stage surrounded by people. Aldrin's eyes goggled at the sight before them. There were two giant-sized pieces of bread, each one as big as a super-king mattress, laid one on top of the other. And in between them was a layer of Gruyère that was as thick as Aldrin was tall.

'Look at it!' Aldrin said, at the same time unconsciously licking his lips. 'Can you believe the SIZE of it!'

'How are they going to toast it?' Harry wondered.

A man wearing a heat-resistant hazmat suit and a fishbowl helmet stepped up on to the stage. He was holding what looked like a long rifle, connected by a hose to a backpack.

'It's a flame-thrower,' Frankie announced. 'I should know – I faced enough of them during my days as a spy.'

'You've never been a spy,' Sisely reminded him. 'You're a twelve-year-old boy.'

But Frankie was right – at least about the flame-thrower. The crowd was ordered to step back, then, a few seconds later, the man in the hazmat suit started aiming a **JET OF FLAMES** at the top of the bread.

Almost instantly, the air was filled with the smell of hot toast. A few seconds after that, the Gruyère started to melt down the sides of the bread and it was replaced by the more deliciously overpowering smell of grilled cheese.

Then a woman climbed the steps onto the stage. With a retractable tape measure, she took the length of the sandwich, then the width, then the depth. And then, in a voice bursting with excitement, she declared:

'Ladies and gentlemen, boys and girls – we have a **NEW world record!**'

A huge roar went up.

'OK, after that, I am STARVING!' Aldrin told his friends as the crowd dispersed.

Just then, he heard a man's voice calling: 'Who will take the Brie Blind Taste Challenge? Come on, ladies and gentlemen, boys and girls – a volunteer, please!'

Aldrin's hand **SHOT** into the air.

'I'll take it!' he shouted.

The man conducting the Brie Blind Taste Challenge was a tall, thin man with a bald head, a thick moustache, the ends of which curled upwards, and a slightly military bearing. And he spoke in a posh voice.

'I say, what's your name, chappie?' he asked.

'It's Aldrin,' Aldrin answered. 'Aldrin Adams.'

'Jolly good. OK, step this way, won't you?'

He conducted Aldrin up four steps on to another stage and told him to sit down at a table. On it, there were six paper cups, under each of which, the man explained, there was a piece of cheese. He said he wanted Aldrin to tell him what Brie it was from a list of options.

'How does that sound to you, chappie?' the man asked.

'Bring it on!' Aldrin told him.

A crowd of onlookers gathered.

'OK, first things first,' the man said. 'I'm going to blindfold you.'

'Blindfold me?' Aldrin asked. 'Why?'

'Because it's called the Brie *Blind* Taste Challenge! And by switching off the most dominant human sense – namely, that of sight – you will taste and smell the cheese better.'

'If you say so,' Aldrin shrugged.

The man stood behind him and pulled a blindfold over his eyes before tying it at the back.

Aldrin heard Harry shout: 'Good luck, Aldrin!'

'OK, here comes the first one,' the man said, lifting cup number one to reveal a small piece of silky butter-coloured cheese with a white-grey paper rind. He placed it in Aldrin's hand. 'Tell me what cheese you think that might be. I'm going to give you four options.'

'I don't need any options,' Aldrin told him. 'I'm sure I'll know it.' He sniffed it, then popped it into his mouth. He chewed it for ten seconds, then said:

'Oh, it's a bit of Marin French Crème.'

He heard the man gasp.

'Marin French Créme!' he declared. 'By Jove, he's absolutely right! How on earth did you know that?'

'I could tell from its creaminess,' Aldrin said, 'and the slight taste of Greek yogurt from the cheese itself.'

The crowd laughed.

'It looks like we've found ourselves something of an expert!' the man said. 'Or was it just beginner's luck? I'm going to give you the next one.'

The man lifted cup number two and handed Aldrin a second piece. Again, Aldrin sniffed it.

'Smells of damp,' he observed. 'A bit mushroomy actually.'

He popped it into his mouth and rolled it around on his tongue.

'There's a slight taste of lemon curd off it,' Aldrin said. 'In which case, I would say it's probably . . . La Bonne Vie?'

'CORRECT!' the man told him.

There were cheers from the crowd. Aldrin's confidence was really up now.

'Give me the other four together,' he said.

The man laughed. He lifted each cup in turn and placed the four remaining pieces of cheese into the palm of Aldrin's hand. Aldrin dropped them, one by one, into his mouth.

'The third one is Alouette,' he said, speaking with his mouth full, which his mum definitely would NOT have approved of. 'The fourth one is . . . Président. The fifth one is definitely Dietz & Watson. And the sixth one isn't a Brie at all. It's Camembert Le Châtelain, and I think you put it in there to try to trick me!'

'Saints alive – the chap is right on ALL counts!' Aldrin heard the man declare. 'I've never seen anything like it! Ladies and gentlemen, boys and girls, please put your hands together to show your appreciation for a young chap who truly, TRULY knows his cheese!'

With the blindfold still covering his eyes, Aldrin smilingly acknowledged the applause from the crowd. And then suddenly he heard a voice whisper in his ear:

'I know who you are, chappie – and I know what you can do.'

Aldrin froze. The hairs on his neck standing to attention.

'Don't be afraid,' the man said in a calm voice. 'I'm

a Cheese Whizz, the same as you. There's a meeting taking place tonight.'

'Where?' said Aldrin in a barely audible whisper.

'I can't tell you that yet – for security reasons, you understand. Is it your intention to stick around for the Cheese Rolling?'

'Yes,' Aldrin said.

'Jolly good show. Then I shall meet you afterwards – in front of Madame Bluessauds. And tell NOBODY!'

13

A BIG CHEESE ROLL

'Explain it to me again!' Sisely said.

They were standing with a crowd of several hundred people at the top of Lambert's Hill at the back of the farmers' market, staring down a grass slope that was steep enough to ski down.

'A wheel of Double Gloucester is rolled down the hill,' Aldrin said, 'and everyone races after it.'

'But the slope has an approximate gradient of forty per cent,' Sisely pointed out, 'which means that the cheese will reach a maximum speed of sixty miles per hour on its way down.'

'We'll have to take your word for that,' said Harry.

'What I mean is that nobody has a chance of *beating* the cheese.'

'That's not how the race is decided,' Frankie told her. 'The winner is the first person to reach the bottom and pick it up.'

'Well, I still say it's stupid,' Sisely insisted. '*And* dangerous. And I don't see the actual point of it.'

'There doesn't have to be a point to *everything*,' Aldrin told her. 'Cheese rolling is just an ancient custom, Sisely – some people even say it dates back to Roman times. It's a bit of fun, that's all.'

'*Please* tell me *you're* not thinking of doing it!' she said.

'Definitely NOT!' Aldrin scoffed. 'I'm not COMPLETELY insane!'

Aldrin had more important matters on his mind than charging down a steep hill after an uncatchable cheese, much as he loved Double Gloucester. He was about to meet up with a group of people who shared his superpower. He couldn't have been more nervous – or excited.

He didn't mention the meeting to Sisely. He knew he should – she was his sidekick after all. But the stranger had warned him to tell absolutely nobody about it and presumably that included his non-Cheese Whizz friends.

'Well, I'm DEFINITELY doing it!' announced Frankie, then he started performing stretching exercises.

Aldrin couldn't help but smile. He remembered a time when Frankie was terrified of heights – but not since Aldrin had helped to rescue him from the recurring nightmare in which he fell from a tree.

Doug suddenly appeared in the middle of the crowd, holding a wheel of Double Gloucester the size of a beach ball.

'OK, everyone,' he said. 'Are . . . we . . . ready?'

'Wait a minute,' said Aldrin. 'Just let me get out of the way before –'

But he didn't get to complete his sentence. And Doug couldn't hear him anyway over the excited clamour of the crowd. He teed up the competitors:

'Ready . . . Set . . .'

'WAIT!' shouted Aldrin.

'GO!' shouted Doug, tossing the cheese into the air.

Suddenly, Aldrin was swept forward by the crowd of people chasing the wheel of cheese as it bounced down the hill. And not just Aldrin either. Harry had also failed to step out of the way in time and now he, too, found himself caught in the same human avalanche as it crashed down the hill.

They had no choice but to run with the others, gaining momentum with every second.

Aldrin's legs were moving WAY too fast for him, and very quickly the inevitable happened . . .

He FELL.

Suddenly, he found himself careering head over heels down the slope. And he was gripped by the fear that he would break an arm, or a leg, and have to miss the meeting of the Cheese Whizzes.

He tumbled . . .

. . . and tumbled . . .

. . . and tumbled some more . . .

. . . until he eventually landed in an undignified heap at the foot of the hill.

As he lay on his back, looking up at the sky, Aldrin did a quick mental audit of his limbs. Miraculously, nothing seemed to be broken. He sat up. Bodies of the other racers were strewn all around him. People were climbing to their feet, dazed but delighted to have got through it alive and not too badly injured.

Aldrin spotted Harry. He was sitting a few feet away, reaching for his glasses, which had fallen off. But he still laughed.

'That was AMAZING!' he said.

'It was!' Aldrin agreed.

'WE HAVE A WINNER!' he heard his dad announce.

Then he noticed Frankie being hoisted on to the shoulders of the crowd. And in his hands was the wheel of Double Gloucester. Frankie held it aloft like it was the World Cup. And Doug proclaimed: 'THE FIRST -EVER TINTWISTLE CHEESE-ROLLING CHAMPION IS . . . FRANKIE FIDDERER!'

'Wow!' said Aldrin. 'He'll talk about this moment for the rest of his life.'

'Yeah,' Harry agreed. 'And because of his reputation for telling fibs no one will ever believe him!'

But at least, for once, there were hundreds of witnesses to Frankie's moment of heroism. They crowded round him then to offer their congratulations. Aldrin noticed Sisely making her way towards Frankie with a scowl of disapproval on her face. Aldrin took advantage of the confusion to slip quietly away, then back up the hill towards the appointed meeting place.

When he reached Madame Bluessauds, he saw two men in long brown coats packing the giant cheese sculptures away in a series of crates, before loading them into a refrigerated truck.

But there was no sign of the well-spoken stranger who'd conducted the Brie Blind Taste Challenge and told him to come here. After twenty minutes, Aldrin's excitement began to give way to despair again.

Then he heard his name called in a sort of hushed whisper:

'Aldrin! Psssttt!'

He spotted him, poking his head round the back end of the refrigerated truck.

'I'm sorry about all the intrigue,' the man said. 'As you can understand, the secrecy of the order is absolutely paramount.'

'What's your name?' Aldrin asked, hurrying across with a furtive look over his shoulder.

'Wilbur,' the man said, offering him a handshake. 'Wilbur Leveson-Gough. And it's rather spiffing to make your acquaintance. So tell me, chappie, do you want to meet more of our kind?'

'Absolutely,' Aldrin said. 'More than anything else in the world!'

14

THE ONE

'This is the place,' Wilbur announced.

They'd stopped outside Pizza the Action on Duke Street, close to the farmers' market.

'The Cheese Whizzes are meeting *here*?' Aldrin asked. 'I love their four-cheese pizzas! Although I usually just eat the four cheeses and leave the rest.'

'We booked the vacant room upstairs,' Wilbur said, 'on the understanding that there'd be no questions asked!'

Wilbur opened the door and led Aldrin up the red-carpeted stairway. A door at the top opened into a large room that was filled with people. No one noticed Wilbur and Aldrin slip in and sit down three rows from the back.

Someone was speaking. Aldrin recognized him as the man in the blue-and-white-striped T-shirt whom he'd seen juggling balls of Edam.

'I'm sorry to have to say it,' the man was saying in a doleful voice, 'but we are losing the battle. There simply aren't enough of us – and Habeas Grusselvart's resources are limitless.'

Wilbur leaned towards Aldrin's ear.

'That's Arthur Ladd,' he whispered. 'He's a former coal miner from Northumbria. Retired now, of course.'

'I saw him juggling eighteen balls of Edam!' Aldrin told him.

'Oh, yes, that's his party piece,' Wilbur said. 'Rather impressive, isn't it?'

Arthur continued his downbeat assessment of how the Cheese Whizzes were faring in the fight against Habeas Grusselvart.

'We're wasting our time trying to take him on in the dreamworld,' he said, echoing Aldrin's own thoughts. 'He's making nightmares quicker than we can respond. What we need to do is find him in *this* world.'

Aldrin felt the urge to shout, **'I agree!'** but he felt a tap on his shoulder. He turned round. When he saw who was sitting behind him, he let out an involuntary

gasp. It was Archie – the boy in the Hawaiian shirt with the skateboard, who was so impressed by Harry and Frankie's comic book.

'Sorry, dude,' he said in a hushed voice. 'I didn't mean to startle you.'

'*You're* a Cheese Whizz too?' Aldrin whispered.

'Yeah,' the boy said, then a look of recognition fell across his face. 'Oh, now I get it! *You* must be the inspiration for Nighty Knight!'

'Yeah,' said Aldrin, 'but Harry and Frankie don't know about my secret.'

'Right,' said Archie, nodding his head. 'Anyway, it's nice to meet you again.'

Aldrin looked round the room then. He counted forty-three people in total. He couldn't believe that ALL of them shared his superpower – *and* his secret.

A tiny woman with a pretty face and short dark hair stood up then.

'I sink zat Arthur is quite correct,' she said in a thick French accent. 'Habeas Grusselvart is winning ze war and we are failing – miserably. Ze only hope we have of stopping him is to find his base of operations, where he creates zees nightmares – and destroy it!'

'Who's that lady?' Aldrin asked Wilbur.

'That's Maxine Joli,' Wilbur explained. 'An archaeologist from Marseilles. Her great-grandfather was the legendary Didier Durand – the most famous Cheese Whizz of them all. Did fifteen thousand missions in his lifetime. Capital chap, by all accounts.'

From the other side of the room came the screech of chair legs on the floor as another woman climbed to her feet. She wore tight-fitting motorcycle leathers and loads of make-up, especially around her eyes.

'More of this old guff!' she said. She had a strong London accent. 'Find 'is base of operations? And 'ow do you propose to do that when no one's come close to findin' 'im in five hundred years? Includin' your precious great-grandfavah!'

'That's Estelle Giddens,' Wilbur whispered. 'Not my cup of tea. An excellent Cheese Whizz, but she's always trying to take over. Not to be trusted.'

'How DARE you speak about ze great Didier Durand in zis way?' Maxine responded angrily.

'Yeah, whatevah, love,' said Estelle. 'All I'm sayin' is that it's the same fing every flippin' year. You stand up and say we 'ave to find 'Abbeas, then we nevah do – cos we're runnin' arahnd the place like a bunch of 'eadless chickens.'

'Ah, yes,' said Maxine wearily, 'zis again!'

'What we need,' Estelle continued, 'is a leader.'

There were mutters of agreement throughout the room.

'And every year,' Maxine replied, 'I tell you ze same thing. Ze Cheese Whizzes have never had a leader.'

'Well, maybe that's why we're bangin' our 'eads against a brick wall!'

'And let me guess – *you* wish to put yourself forward as ze leader?'

'I'd make a pretty good leader.'

'I agree!' someone shouted.

'Ha!' Maxine laughed. 'Zis is just about power for you! You would destroy ze Cheese Whizzes, just to feed your ego!'

A loud argument broke out then between those who supported Estelle and those who didn't.

'SILENCE!' a man shouted in a loud voice. Then he climbed to his feet. He was a giant of a man with an Irish accent, and he wore a brown three-piece suit and an eyepatch. 'We're not going to achieve anything if we allow ourselves to become divided like this. Look, I've said it before and I'll go on saying it, we don't have the numbers to beat the enemy – either in the

dreamworld *or* the real world. We have to find more Cheese Whizzes. There must be hundreds of thousands of people out there who don't know they have the gift.'

Suddenly, Wilbur cleared his throat to get the attention of the room. All eyes turned to look at him – and the boy seated beside him.

'*On* that very subject,' he said, 'may I introduce you all to Aldrin Adams?'

Silence fell like a blanket over the crowded room.

'You are Cynthia's boy?' Maxine asked.

'Er, yes,' Aldrin said, then he turned to Wilbur. 'Are you saying you knew my mum?'

'Some of us did,' Wilbur replied.

'So you knew I was her son,' Aldrin said, 'when I volunteered for the Brie Blind Taste Challenge?'

'Of course I did!' Wilbur told him. 'You're the absolute double of her!'

'For several months now,' said Maxine, 'zere have been rumours zat Cynthia's son has been active.'

'Active?' Aldrin asked.

'Zat you have been entering ze nightmares of uzzer people.'

'Well, it's true,' said Aldrin. 'I've done it quite a few times now.'

In response to that, there was much kerfuffle – muttered comments and nodding heads.

The Irishman fixed him a look with his one uncovered eye.

'The name is Cormac de Courcy,' he said, 'and I, too, knew your mother, Aldrin – just as I know your father.'

Of course, Aldrin thought. Cormac de Courcy had a cattle farm in West Cork and he made some of the tastiest Cheddar in the world.

'The reason that we are all so surprised,' he said, 'is that the power to enter other people's nightmares is unheard of in someone as young as you.'

'I know,' Aldrin said. 'My mum told me.'

At that, Cormac's face brightened.

'Ah, Nel's been looking after you, has she?' he asked. 'You know, I'm actually surprised not to see her here today.'

'What?' Aldrin said. 'Are you saying Mrs Van Boxtel *knew* you were meeting?'

'*Of course*,' Cormac replied. 'As soon as your dad told me about the cheese festival, I phoned everyone – including her.'

'When?' Aldrin wondered.

'Must have been two weeks ago,' Cormac replied.

Aldrin was shocked. Why had she kept it from him?

'I have a question for ze boy,' said Maxine. 'How did you discover your powers?'

'By total accident,' Aldrin confessed. 'But my mum left me her dream journal, which explains what cheeses work best for which dreams. And, by the way, you're right about Habeas winning the war. He told me he's creating nightmares for five thousand people per week!'

There were gasps.

'What do you mean,' Cormac de Courcy asked, 'when you say . . . *he* told you?'

'He *told* me,' Aldrin said casually, 'in a dream I entered.'

'You have met Habeas Grusselvart?' asked Maxine, her face long and drawn.

'No, you 'aven't,' Estelle said. 'The boy's makin' up stories.'

'I'm not,' Aldrin told her. 'I've met him twice, as a matter of fact. The first time, we ended up having a sword fight with fondue forks. Then, a couple of weeks ago, I met him again. That's when he told me about the five thousand nightmares per week. Why are you all looking at me like that?'

'It's just that none of us has ever seen him,' Arthur

said. 'I think I'm right in saying that, am I?'

All around the room, heads nodded.

'What, never?' asked Aldrin.

'No,' Wilbur confirmed. 'We don't even know what he looks like.'

'He never reveals himself to us,' said Maxine. 'And, if he has revealed himself to you, it can mean only one thing. He fears you.'

'Fears me?' Aldrin repeated. 'I don't think so – he laughed in my face and told me I was wasting my time.'

'So?' said Maxine, looking round at the other shocked faces. 'Are we all sinking ze same thing? Zat he is . . .'

Aldrin could feel the weight of everyone's eyes on him.

'**The One,**' said Cormac.

Estelle stared bitterly at Aldrin. 'I don't believe it for a minute,' she said. 'We've been waitin' five 'undred years for The so-called One – I don't even believe he – or she – exists.'

'The One?' Aldrin asked. 'What do you mean by The One?'

But no one answered him.

Wilbur stood up. 'I am starting to think that it was

perhaps a mistake to bring the chap here,' he admitted. 'Aldrin, I think you should leave right now.'

'Let's not be too hasty,' said Arthur. 'We need to find Habeas Grusselvart. And he's the only one in this room who know what he looks like.'

'So 'e says,' said Estelle.

Wilbur shook his head. 'He's not our responsibility,' he said. 'Cynthia asked Nel Van Boxtel to watch over him. If he really is The One, there must be a reason why she hasn't told him. I'm sorry, chappie, you're going to have to leave.'

Aldrin stood up to go.

'But what do you mean by The One?' he asked.

'It's not our place to say,' Wilbur told him. 'You'll have to speak to Nel yourself.'

I will DEFINITELY be doing that, Aldrin thought as he left the meeting. That woman had a LOT of explaining to do.

15.

PART OF THE FURNITURE

Beddy Byes drove his white van into the car park of the Codfather Packing Company and reversed it into the loading bay. He switched off the engine and got out, then he knocked three times on the metal shutter. It was opened by a man in white overalls.

'Another load?' he asked. 'Where's this one come from?'

'A shop in Hull,' Beddy Byes answered, throwing open the back doors of the van to reveal a kaleidoscope of different-coloured cheeses. 'Get it unpacked before it stinks out the van.'

This was one of the many responsibilities that Beddy Byes had taken on since he came to work for Habeas Grusselvart's nightmare-generating enterprise. Whenever he heard of a cheesemonger's closing, he approached the owner and offered to take the remaining stock off their hands.

It was his boss's desire, after all, to own *all* the cheese in the *world*! Which was insane, of course. But then all supervillains have their crazy obsessions – and Beddy Byes was quite prepared to go to Hull and back to indulge Habeas's power-hungry whims.

He took the lift to the fourth floor and stood on the viewing platform. Through a window, he looked down on the vast warehouse where all the cheese was discarded. Millions upon millions of tons of Cheddar, Gouda, Gruyère, Brie, Emmental, Edam, feta and Roquefort were piled high in a **stinking, decomposing** mountain of slurry.

The room was sealed to prevent the smell from leaking out – for one whiff of that rotting sludge pile would be sufficient to knock a person unconscious. And so noxious was the gas generated by this rancid mound of gunge that a single spark would have been enough to blow the entire factory sky-high!

Beddy Byes watched three men, wearing oxygen masks and protective clothing, shovel the new cheese on to the putrid heap.

And in his heart, for once, he felt . . . nothing.

He and Habeas had often stood on this viewing platform and stared in silent awe at this malodorous monument to his boss's vanity. It was Habeas's favourite room in the entire factory, and sometimes they even ate their lunch while gazing down on it.

'Do you think I'll ever own it all?' Habeas sometimes asked.

'Absolutely,' Beddy Byes would answer, 'Oh Strong and Beneficent One!'

But now he rarely saw the evil overlord to whom he'd dedicated more than eighteen years of his life. The sad truth was that Habeas had little or no interest in him any more.

He crept along the corridor to Habeas's office and stood with his ear to the door. Habeas and Ethan were talking in urgent whispers. They were plotting something big for the Adams boy – although *what*, he was unable to hear.

'Beddy Byes?' Habeas called teasingly. 'Is that you listening at the door again?'

Beddy Byes opened it and shuffled in, muttering apologies. Habeas and Ethan were sitting side by side in two armchairs, just like Habeas and *he* had done in happier times.

'I wanted to let you know,' Beddy Byes said, 'that I've just returned from Hull, Your Majesticness. I collected almost half a tonne of liquidated stock from yet another cheesemonger who found out the hard way that no one wanted his –'

'Beddy Byes, I've missed you!' Habeas blurted out.

'What?' asked Beddy Byes, unable to believe what he was hearing.

'I said I've missed you!'

Beddy Byes couldn't help but crack a smile.

'I've missed you too,' he said, 'Oh Wise and Handsome One!'

'There was a time,' Habeas reminded him, 'when you were part of the furniture around here.'

'I was, Your Greatness.'

'Well? Would you like to be again?'

'Yes, sir. Oh, yes please, sir!'

'Here you are then,' Habeas said, nodding at the floor in front of him.

'I beg your pardon?' Beddy Byes replied.

'A part of the furniture,' Habeas said. 'Get down on all fours in front of me there. I want to use you as a footstool.'

'Look at his face!' Ethan laughed.

Beddy Byes had no choice but to comply. He got down on his hands and knees and crawled in front of his boss. Then he felt Habeas's heavy boots in the middle of his back.

'Yes, it's good to rest the old puppies,' Habeas said, 'after a day of plotting the downfall of the Adams boy. Ethan, put your feet up – there's room here for two.'

ANSWERS

'Mr Owl ate my metal worm,' Sisely said.

Everyone in the class laughed.

'Mishter Owl did what?' Mrs Van Boxtel asked.

'Mr Owl ate my metal worm,' Sisely repeated.

The teacher wrote the words in large capital letters on the whiteboard.

'What a wonderful shentenshe!' she said. 'Now, tell me, boysh and girlsh, ish it what we would call a palindrome?'

'Yes!' Frankie shouted.

'Yesh, it is!' the teacher agreed. 'It ish a fantashtic exshample of a palindrome! Well done, Shishely. Sho doesh anybody elshe have one?'

'Do geese see God?' shouted Harry.

'Do geeshe shee God?' Mrs Van Boxtel repeated as she wrote the words on the board. 'It ish an intereshting question – but ish it a palindrome?'

'Yes,' said Sisely, 'it's a palindrome.'

'Yesh, it is!' agreed Mrs Van Boxtel. 'Well done, Harry! Exshellent work! Aldrin, did you think of one?'

'No,' he said in a crabby voice. He was still annoyed at her – and at Sisely for that matter.

'Well,' said Mrs Van Boxtel, 'can you perhapsh think of one now?'

'Friends don't lie to each other,' Aldrin said.

'Friends don't . . . lie to each other,' Mrs Van Boxtel repeated, not even bothering to write the words on the board. 'What doesh everybody think? Ish *thish* a palindrome?'

'No,' Sisely said straight away. 'It's not.'

'No, it ishn't,' agreed Mrs Van Boxtel, at the same time admonishing Aldrin with a look. 'It ishn't even closhe to one.'

'Was it a car or a cat I saw?' Sisely said.

'Wash it a car or a cat I shaw?' repeated the teacher. 'Let ush shee if *thish* ish one, shall we?'

When the class ended, Sisely turned round in her

seat and said: 'That *wasn't* very mature of you.'

'Aldrin and Shishely,' the teacher said, 'pleashe wait behind after classh.'

When the other boys and girls had left the classroom, Mrs Van Boxtel walked down to where Aldrin and Sisely were sitting.

'Sho I had a call yeshterday,' she said, 'from my old friend, Wilbur Leveshon-Gough. He tellsh me that you met.'

'Yes, we met!' Aldrin said irritably. 'And he took me to the meeting of the Cheese Whizzes.'

'Yesh,' she said. 'That wash mosht unfortunate.'

'Why didn't you *tell* me about the meeting?' Aldrin asked.

'Becaushe I am trying to protect you, Aldrin. That ish what your mother ashked me to do – above everything elshe.'

Aldrin looked at Sisely then.

'So did *you* know as well?' he asked. 'That the Cheese Whizzes were coming to Tintwistle?'

'Yes,' she admitted, 'I did.'

'I ashked Shishely to keep an eye on you at the feshtival,' said Mrs Van Boxtel, 'to make sure that you did not shlip away.'

'I did my best,' Sisely added. 'But then after the Cheese Rolling I got distracted for two seconds and you disappeared.'

For the first since they'd become friends, Aldrin felt betrayed by her.

'You knew that the Cheese Whizzes were in town,' he said to her, 'and you kept it from me.'

'I could say the same thing about you,' Sisely replied.

'What did they mean,' Aldrin asked, turning his anger on Mrs Van Boxtel, 'when they said that I might be The One?'

'I have absholutely no idea,' said Mrs Van Boxtel, turning her head away.

'I'm *entitled* to know,' Aldrin fumed.

The teacher let out a long exhalation of breath.

'For hundredsh of yearsh,' she said, 'the Cheeshe Whizshesh have been predicting the coming of one who would have the power to deshtroy Habeash Grusshelvart forever.'

'And they think it might be . . . *me*?' Aldrin asked.

'Like I shay,' Mrs Van Boxtel told him, 'it ish jusht a shtory.'

Aldrin remembered the conversation he'd had with his mum in a nightmare some months earlier. She'd been trying to tell him something before he woke up.

'My mum believed I was The One,' Aldrin said, 'didn't she?'

'Your mother thought it wash true,' Mrs Van Boxtel said, nodding slowly. 'Yesh.'

'Arthur Ladd said that I'm the only Cheese Whizz who has ever seen Habeas Grusselvart.'

'It ish clear that Habeash alsho believesh that you are the one shent to deshtroy him.'

'Don't you see?' Sisely suddenly cut in. 'That's why Mrs Van Boxtel is trying to protect you.'

'What?' Aldrin said. 'By keeping me away from the other Cheese Whizzes?'

'You are shtill jusht a boy,' Mrs Van Boxtel reminded him. 'You are not ready to confront him yet.'

'I can defeat him,' Aldrin said. 'Especially if I'm The One. Hey, maybe *I'm* supposed to lead the Cheese Whizzes!'

'The Cheeshe Whizshesh have never had a leader,' said Mrs Van Boxtel.

'Well, Estelle Giddens thinks that's what's holding us back.'

'You do not want to lishten to Eshtelle. She ish not to be trushted.'

'So what are we going to do? How do we beat Habeas Grusselvart?'

'We keep doing what we can – undoing hish evil work whenever the opportunity preshentsh itshelf.'

'What, saving the world one nightmare at a time?'

'That ish all we can do.'

'Habeas is laughing at me, Mrs Van Boxtel. He's laughing at all of us.'

'Sho let him laugh. You might think the work you are doing ish not important, Aldrin. Or you might think it ish not enough. But every pershon you help ish one lessh pershon who ish having nightmaresh.'

'I'm sorry, but I just feel like I'm –'

'What?'

'– *better* than that.'

'Oh, grow up, Aldrin,' Sisely told him.

Aldrin scowled and stood up. 'Well, like Mrs Van Boxtel said,' he said as he stomped out of the classroom, 'I'm still just a boy, aren't I?'

17

FLASHBACK

Cynthia and Maurice were having the time of their lives.

Madame Lacombe taught them about hundreds of different cheeses and how they were made. They learned how to milk cows, goats and sheep, and they carried the milk in buckets, still warm, from the milking shed to the kitchen.

Cynthia loved this part of the process, when it was possible for the milk to become any one of the thousands of varieties of cheese that existed in the world. It all depended on what you did to it next. You could add vinegar or citric acid, from a lemon or a lime, to create delicious ricotta or mascarpone. Or you could add living bacteria to it to create the even tastier Stilton or Gorgonzola.

Madame Lacombe spoke to them only in French, which they learned to speak fluently, along with all the other lessons they picked up from her.

She showed them how to add something called a coagulant to turn the liquid into a 'curd', or gel. She taught them the correct way to cut up the curd, then wash it in water, drain it and shape it into a wheel. Then she showed them how to 'age' or 'mature' the cheese, which essentially meant controlling how it went off.

For Maurice, *this* was the most exciting part, for it was the rotting process that gave so many cheeses their distinctive flavour, colour and texture. For instance, Roquefort, one of the world's favourite blue cheeses, was taken to the caves of Roquefort-sur-Soulzon, in southern France, where it was exposed to a special mould found in the soil there over the course of eight weeks. That's why it was full of blue spores!

How many people in the world, Madame Lacombe often asked, understood any of the weird and wonderful ways in which plain old milk was turned into the most delicious food in the world? Not many, she said.

To Madame Lacombe, cheesemaking was a privilege and an art, no different from painting or classical

music. And Cynthia and Maurice discovered the joy of it together. They became not only work colleagues, but the firmest of friends, just as Madame Lacombe said they would. Two young friends who, on their days off, explored the great city of London together.

Maurice was kind and sweet and sensitive. Cynthia was clever and fun and adventurous. And they brought out the very best in each other. They were inseparable.

But there was another side to Maurice, Cynthia

noticed. There were times when his mind seemed like it was elsewhere. It was as if he was dragging a great big boulder of sadness around with him.

Cynthia mentioned it to him one morning while they were milking one of Madame Lacombe's Jersey cows.

'Are you OK?' she wondered. 'You seem miles away.'

'Can I tell you something?' Maurice asked. 'Can I confide something in you?'

'Of course you can, Morr-eece,' she answered. 'We're best friends, aren't we?'

'I have these nightmares,' he told her.

'Nightmares?' Cynthia asked – because it was a subject that she happened to know a LOT about. 'What kind of nightmares?'

'I have this recurring one,' he said, 'where I'm the last living thing left on the planet.'

'The last living *thing*?' Cynthia asked – because it was a new one on her. 'I don't understand, Morr-eece.'

'I'm walking around and the streets are deserted,' Maurice explained. 'I go to the cinema and there's no one there. I go to the park – no people. And not only no people – no birds, no dogs, no trees. Nothing else alive.'

'That sounds awful,' Cynthia sympathized.

'It's the loneliest feeling in the world,' Maurice told her. 'Then I wake up and think, what if that were really to happen? What if I ended up all alone in the world?'

'You'll never be alone in the world,' Cynthia assured him. '*We'll* always be friends.'

Maurice made an attempt at a smile, but he seemed unconvinced.

As it happened, Cynthia, too, had a secret. She was in possession of a very strange, supernatural ability. If she ate cheese before she went to sleep, then thought really, really hard about someone, she could gain entry to their nightmares.

It had been almost a year since her father had sat her down at the kitchen table and revealed the secret of her power to her. She was a Cheese Whizz, he told her – just like him!

She had only used her power about a dozen times. But that night, after Maurice told her about his nightmare, she took a piece of smoked halloumi to bed with her. And, when she started to feel sleepy, she thought really, REALLY hard about her friend, picturing his kind face as she chewed the cheese and it turned into a giant glob of bitter, salty mush.

And *very quickly* . . .

without even realizing . . .

that it was happening . . .

her eyes **started to feel** . . .

very,

very

heavy . . .

And then . . .

she was suddenly . . .

out

for

the . . .

She found herself walking through Trafalgar Square in London. But it wasn't the Trafalgar Square she knew, because there were no buses and no cars. There were no people rushing to and from work. There were no people going for lunch, or sightseeing, or feeding the pigeons. The streets were desolate.

The only sound that could be heard was the sound of silence – and it was deafening!

Just then, Cynthia did spot someone. It was Maurice. He was sitting alone on a bench on the side of the street, looking about as miserable as it was possible for someone to look. She called his name:

'MORR-EECE!!! MORR-EECE!!!'

And she waved at him as she crossed the road to where he was sitting.

Maurice snapped out of his dreamlike trance.

'Cynthia?' he said – like she was the last person in the world he expected to see.

'How are you?' she asked.

'I'm –' he started to answer. But then he said, 'What are you doing here?'

'I was just passing,' she told him.

'But I've had this nightmare hundreds of times,' he told her, 'and you've never been in it.'

'Sorry to disappoint you – but I'm here now.'

'I'm not disappointed,' he said. 'It's just that I'm usually the only one here. That's my nightmare, you see – that I'm the last living thing on the planet.'

Cynthia sat down beside him.

'You're not the only one who sometimes feels that way,' she said. 'Lots of people get sad for no apparent reason. And, when they do, it's difficult for them to see and hear and smell the world around them. But listen, Morr-eece!'

'What am I listening to?' he asked.

'Do you hear pigeons?'

'No.'

'Listen closely!'

Maurice closed his eyes.

'Yes,' he said after a moment. 'I *can* hear pigeons! Where are they?'

'They're over there, look. Those children are throwing bread to them.'

Maurice laughed.

'I see them!' he declared. 'I see them!'

'And do you see that bus driver over there?' Cynthia asked. 'Look, he's giving that man a piece of his mind for parking his van in the bus lane!'

'Yes!' Maurice laughed. 'And the language he's using!'

'It could turn the air blue!' Cynthia agreed. 'And look over there! There's a teacher taking her class on a school trip to the National Gallery!'

'I see them!' Maurice said. 'I see them!'

Suddenly, the world around him was filled with people rushing here and there, getting on with the business of the day. There was talking and shouting and laughing and arguing. There was noise and there were smells and there was colour.

Maurice sat back and watched it, like a man who had suddenly gained the ability to see.

'Just remember,' Cynthia told him, 'none of us is EVER truly alone.'

At work the following day, Maurice didn't mention Cynthia's cameo role in his nightmare. He carried on as if nothing had happened.

It was two mornings later, while he was sticking a thermometer into a giant bucket of curd to take its temperature, that he finally said something.

'I had my nightmare,' he told her, 'three nights ago – except this time *you* were in it!'

'Was I?' Cynthia asked innocently.

'Yes,' Maurice said, smiling. 'But the funny thing is, well, it felt so . . . real!'

18

NEMESWISS

'What was wrong with you today?' Harry asked Aldrin when school was finished. 'I didn't see you smile once. That's very unlike you.'

'I couldn't think of a stupid palindrome,' Aldrin lied. 'That's all.'

'I couldn't come up with one neither,' said Frankie. 'Although *I* was busy, of course, what with my heroics at the Cheese Rolling on Saturday.'

'Harry,' Aldrin said as they stepped outside, 'can I ask you a question? You know superheroes better than anyone, right?'

'I've read a lot of comics in my life!' Harry acknowledged.

'Why are they never happy?' Aldrin asked. 'I mean

in their day-to-day, non-superhero lives.'

'I don't know,' Harry said. 'I suppose it's because they have such a **HUGE** weight of responsibility on their shoulders.'

'Exactly!' Aldrin said. 'I mean, they're constantly thinking about saving the world, aren't they?'

'Yes,' Harry agreed, 'but, no matter how much they do, the threat to the world still exists – because the enemy is still out there.'

'There's also another thing,' Frankie added. 'In real life, they're frustrated. Because they have these amazing powers, but they can't tell anyone about it. So they always feel underappreciated.'

'Hey, speaking of superheroes,' Harry said, 'Frankie came up with an idea for a new character.'

'That's right,' Frankie added. 'He's called . . . the Bounce! His bones are made of rubber! Means he can fall out of trees, or off mountains, or out of aeroplanes – and he never breaks a bone. Show him, Harry.'

Harry reached into his schoolbag and pulled out a drawing.

'This is what the Bounce is going to look like!' he said.

Aldrin smiled. He was wearing *the* most AMAZING

superhero costume – made entirely of bubble wrap!

'**Wow!** I absolutely LOVE the suit!' Aldrin told them.

Harry and Frankie headed home then, while Aldrin walked in the direction of Burnett Road with a heavy heart, thinking about Sisely and Mrs Van Boxtel. He couldn't shake the suspicion that they were keeping even more secrets from him.

He was passing the skatepark when he spotted a familiar figure wearing a Hawaiian shirt and attempting a laser flip on his board.

'Archie!' Aldrin shouted. 'Archie!'

Archie spotted him, picked up his board and walked over to the railings.

'I didn't know you lived around here,' said Aldrin.

'Yeah, all my life,' said Archie. 'Hey, we haven't been formally introduced, by the way. The name's Archie McMenemy.'

He stuck his hand through the bars and Aldrin shook it.

'Aldrin,' he said. 'Aldrin Adams.'

'Well, I know who you are now!' Archie said. 'Dude, you caused a LOT of excitement at the meeting!'

'Did I?' asked Aldrin.

'Yeah, I mean, you've actually SEEN Habeas Grusselvart!'

'Twice.'

'Twice – I forgot! So come on, as the only man or woman alive who has ever laid eyes on the world's most evil supervillain – what does he look like?'

'Oh, he's, um, tall. Very tall, in fact. And muscular. He's got pale skin. Black curly hair, like a lion's mane. A crooked nose. Sideburns down to his chin. And he wears a long black coat, buttoned right up to the neck, with the collar standing up.'

Archie nodded as he listened.

'It's funny,' he said, 'I thought he'd be, I don't know, a blob sitting on a throne – like Jabba the Hutt!'

'No.' Aldrin laughed. 'He looks like a normal human being – well, except obviously evil. Can *I* ask *you* a question?'

'Sure – go ahead.'

'*Am* I The One?'

'The One?'

'Yeah, like everyone was saying – at the meeting.'

'There's no such thing as The One!' Archie said.

'Oh,' Aldrin replied, struggling to hide his disappointment.

'No, what I mean is, when people talk about The One, they're really talking about NemeSwiss.'

'NemeSwiss?'

'Yeah, NemeSwiss is the name of a superhero who –' Archie said, but then he seemed to regret having said anything. 'Look, maybe Mrs Van Boxtel should be telling you this stuff.'

'Mrs Van Boxtel didn't even tell me that the Cheese Whizzes were meeting in Tintwistle!'

'Well, she's probably trying to protect you.'

'But I don't *need* protecting.'

'Aldrin, it's like Maxine Joli said, if Habeas has revealed himself to you, he clearly fears you. And you can bet he's out there right now, plotting your downfall.'

'Please, Archie,' Aldrin begged him. 'You have to tell me!'

'OK,' he said with a reluctant sigh. 'One hundred years ago, a Cheese Whizz from Ethiopia named Lufassi Samatta prophesised the coming of a boy who would bring an end to Habeas Grusselvart's centuries-old reign of terror. That boy would be called NemeSwiss.'

'Why NemeSwiss?' Aldrin asked.

'Because it's like nemesis – meaning the agent of

someone's downfall,' Archie explained, 'but with Swiss on the end, just to make it sound more cheesy!'

'NemeSwiss,' Aldrin repeated – he liked saying it. 'NemeSwiss.'

'According to Lufassi Samatta, NemeSwiss would have supernatural abilities far beyond those of the average Cheese Whizz.'

'What kind of abilities?'

'Well, Cheese Whizzes like me can only enter into one person's nightmare at a time. NemeSwiss, if the prophecy is to be believed, will have the power to enter into the nightmares of thousands and thousands of people – at the same time.'

'Wow!' Aldrin exclaimed.

'The average Cheese Whizz has to think about a person really, really hard while eating cheese to enter into their dream. But NemeSwiss just has to think of a particular nightmare – being attacked by giant ants, for instance – and he can enter into the dream of everyone in the world who is experiencing that nightmare at that time.'

'So you're saying *I* can do that?' Aldrin asked.

'Well, we don't know that you're NemeSwiss yet, do we?' said Archie. 'And there's only one sure-fire way of actually finding out if you are or not.'

'How?'

'What are you doing tonight? Do you have a nightmare to go to?'

'Er, no,' replied Aldrin.

'So why don't you give it a go?'

'I will.'

'OK, at eleven o'clock tonight, think about being chased by giant ants.'

'And what cheese should I eat while I'm thinking about it?'

'According to Lufassi, NemeSwiss could access his powers by eating any cheese at all.'

'What about some Crottin de Chavignol?'

'Perfect.'

'OK,' said Aldrin, already feeling a rumble of excitement in his tummy. 'I'm going to do it! I'm going to do it tonight!'

19

A VERY EXCITING NIGHT

Aldrin lay on his bed with his hands behind his head and Silas perched on his chest, and he wished away the minutes until it was eleven o'clock.

'Tonight is going to be a VERY exciting night,' he told his little friend. 'You see, it turns out that I was right. Sisely and Mrs Van Boxtel *have* been holding me back. I don't expect you to understand any of this, little pal, but there's a very distinct chance that I'm a superhero named NemeSwiss and I've been sent to save the world from Habeas Grusselvart.'

The response from Silas was predictable enough: *RRRIbbit . . . rrRIBBIT . . . RRRIbbit . . .*

'Like I said,' Aldrin said, 'it's hard to believe, but there you have it.'

He checked the time. It was five minutes to eleven.

'I think we'll put you to bed now,' Aldrin said. 'And I'm going to need you to be extra quiet for me tonight, OK?'

RRRIBBIT . . . RRRIBBIT . . . RRRIBBIT . . .

Aldrin kissed Silas on the top of his head, then returned him to his tank. As he did so, he heard Sisely's voice coming from under the bed:

'Aldrin, can you hear me? Aldrin, are you there? Over.'

RRRIBBIT . . . RRRIBBIT . . . RRRIBBIT . . .

'Yes, I can hear her, Silas,' Aldrin said. 'I'm just trying to think here.'

'Aldrin, can you hear me?' she repeated even more

urgently. 'Aldrin, are you there? Over.'

But he was still furious with her. She had read his mum's journal from cover to cover. She must have known about Lufassi Samatta and the legend of NemeSwiss, just as she knew about the meeting of the Cheese Whizzes in Tintwistle.

'Aldrin, can you hear me?' she said, sounding desperate now. 'Aldrin, please, I need to talk to you. Over.'

Aldrin bent down and pulled the walkie-talkie out from under the bed. He turned it over, stuck his thumbnail into the little lever that opened the battery compartment, then he pulled out the battery.

Sisely's voice died in an instant.

He climbed into bed and picked up the little parcel of goat's cheese from the top of his bedside table. He unwrapped it and held it to his nose, unable to resist its delectable, toasted-hazelnutty smell.

He checked the time. It was exactly eleven o'clock. He bit into the cheese. It was dry and chewy in his mouth. He closed his eyes gently and he pictured in his mind a giant ant walking towards him.

He chewed the Crottin de Chavignol until it turned into a mass of salty, milky, nutty pulp in his mouth.

And *very quickly* . . .

without even realizing . . .

that it was happening . . .

his eyes **started to feel** . . .

very,

very

heavy . . .

And then . . .

he was suddenly . . .

out

for

the . . .

20.

THE GIANT ANT NIGHTMARE

Aldrin found himself standing in what appeared to be a jungle. It was hot – unnaturally so. He could feel the sweat pouring from his forehead into his eyes. All around him there were trees with leaves that were as big as he was tall. Overhead, he could hear the trilling of exotic birds – and then, in the distance, something else.

It was a sort of loud murmur, the way a football crowd might sound if you were standing outside the stadium. But it seemed to be growing louder and it seemed to be getting closer. And then, all at once, the thick undergrowth in front of him parted and a boy, wearing pyjamas, emerged from it, screaming:

'RUN! RUN FOR YOUR LIFE!'

Aldrin jumped to one side to let him run past. Then seconds later, he was followed by a girl in a nightdress, shouting:

'THEY'RE COMING! THERE'S THOUSANDS OF THEM!!!'

Then they started coming thick and fast – a stampede of people, all dressed for bed, and all running to escape from some unseen danger, their faces stricken with fear. There were too many people to count. They gushed past Aldrin like a torrent of water – thousands of them, it seemed to him – until the torrent finally slowed to a trickle.

The last person through the undergrowth was an elderly man in a dressing gown, who grabbed hold of Aldrin's arm and implored him to run:

'THEY ARE ON THE MARCH! THEY ARE EATING EVERYTHING IN THEIR PATH!'

Aldrin laughed in the man's face.

'They're just insects,' he tried to assure him. The giant ants that Aldrin had pictured were about an inch-and-a-half long – the same size as his index finger. 'They're perfectly harmless.'

'PLEASE YOURSELF!' the man said – then he took off after the others.

Aldrin didn't run from the danger. He did what the superheroes in Harry's comic books did – he ran towards it. Well, he walked, looking down at the ground for the ants, fearful only of stepping on them.

He thought to himself, *Imagine being frightened of a few –*

But he didn't get to finish the thought. Because, in that moment, the earth beneath his feet shook.

BOOMP!

Then, a second later, it happened again . . .

BOOMP!

. . . sending a shudder up through his body, from his toes to the top of his head. Then the BOOMPs became louder and more urgent:

BOOMP! BOOMP! BOOMP! BOOMP! BOOMP! BOOMP!

It sounded like . . . an army on the march!

But an army of what? Aldrin wondered, still examining the floor of the forest. Surely a few hundred ants the size of his index finger couldn't make a noise like –

Aldrin heard the sound of wood splitting as the trees in front of him parted. The BOOMPs were suddenly accompanied by a new sound – chomping!

CHOMP! CHOMP! CHOMP! CHOMP! CHOMP! CHOMP! CHOMP!

Aldrin had a very bad feeling about this.

He looked up . . .

. . . and he gulped!

Because standing in front of him was a giant ant – and it wasn't the size of his index finger . . .

It was the size of an elephant!

It stared down at Aldrin with eyes as big as beach balls. Then its antennae began to wave from side to side – trying to decide whether this boy was a predator or prey.

Aldrin began to back away. And, as he did so, another ant – this one even bigger than the first – appeared next to the original one. Then another. Then another. Then another.

Aldrin decided that the time for bravery was past – now it was time to run like the wind!

He took off like an Olympic sprinter as the ants resumed their march:

BOOMP! BOOMP! BOOMP! BOOMP! BOOMP! CHOMP! CHOMP! CHOMP! CHOMP! CHOMP!

Aldrin ran so fast that he soon caught up with the rest of the fleeing crowd.

'HOW MANY OF THEM ARE THERE?' he asked the elderly man, who was still at the back.

'MILLIONS!' the man yelled back. 'THEY'RE MARCHING IN A COLUMN TEN ANTS WIDE – AND THREE MILES LONG!'

BOOMP! BOOMP! BOOMP! BOOMP! BOOMP! CHOMP! CHOMP! CHOMP! CHOMP! CHOMP!

'OK,' Aldrin said, 'JUST KEEP RUNNING AND WE'LL BE –'

That was when he heard his name called.

'Hey, Aldrin!' a voice said in a calm and measured way.

He looked to his right – and there stood Archie, leaning against a tree, wearing sunglasses and a big smile, without an apparent care in the world.

'Archie!' Aldrin exclaimed. 'What are you doing here?'

Archie removed his sunglasses and put them on his head.

'Dude,' he said, 'it *is* possible for two Cheese Whizzes to enter the same nightmare, you know? Wait a minute, the old lady didn't tell you about sequencing either?'

'Sequencing?' Aldrin asked.

'Yeah, if two Cheese Whizzes eat exactly the same cheese and think about exactly the same thing at exactly the same time, they can enter someone's dream together. It was discovered by an Irish Cheese Whizz named Theo Redmond – fifty or sixty years ago.'

'Something *else* that Sisely and Mrs Van Boxtel kept from me.'

'The only problem is that I won't be able to influence what happens in any way. I can only observe. But then you're not going to need me. You're NemeSwiss after all!'

'Right,' Aldrin said.

BOOMP! BOOMP! BOOMP! BOOMP! BOOMP! CHOMP! CHOMP! CHOMP! CHOMP! CHOMP!

'So what's the play?' Archie wondered.

'The *play*?' Aldrin repeated.

'Yeah,' said Archie, 'as in what are you doing now?'

'I was, erm, running away,' Aldrin confessed.

'Running away?' Archie asked – he sounded aghast. 'Why?'

'When you mentioned giant ants, I thought you meant, well, giant ants. I didn't think you meant GIANT ants!'

'So how big are they?'

'Each one is the size of an **ELEPHANT!** And there's a column of them marching this way that's apparently THREE MILES LONG!'

'So?' asked Archie.

'So?' Aldrin repeated. 'Can you not hear that?'

BOOMP! BOOMP! BOOMP! BOOMP! BOOMP! CHOMP! CHOMP! CHOMP! CHOMP! CHOMP!

'Of course I can hear it!' Archie said. 'But you're NemeSwiss, dude! You can't run away!'

'Can't I?' Aldrin asked.

'All these people are counting on you,' Archie reminded him.

It was the last thing that Aldrin wanted to hear.

'There's about five thousand people here,' Archie told him. 'This is ALL OF THE PEOPLE IN THE WORLD who are having a nightmare about being chased by giant ants right now! And you have to show them that they've nothing to be afraid of!'

BOOMP! BOOMP! BOOMP! BOOMP! BOOMP! CHOMP! CHOMP! CHOMP! CHOMP! CHOMP!

'Can I do that *while* we run?' Aldrin asked.

'No,' said Archie. 'You're not *going* to run.'

'What *am* I going to do then?'

'You're going to stand here with me and you're going to think.'

The ants were almost upon them now.

BOOMP! BOOMP! BOOMP! BOOMP! BOOMP! CHOMP! CHOMP! CHOMP! CHOMP! CHOMP!

'What do ants hate?' Archie asked.

'Er, I don't know,' Aldrin replied.

'Come on – think!'

Aldrin suddenly remembered something.

'When I was younger,' he said, 'we had an ant infestation in the shop – and my mum sprinkled vinegar on the floor. It drove them away.'

'There's your answer then,' Archie told him.

BOOMP! BOOMP! BOOMP! BOOMP! BOOMP! CHOMP! CHOMP! CHOMP! CHOMP! CHOMP!

'It's going to take a pretty big bottle of vinegar in this case,' Aldrin pointed out. 'Unless –'

'Unless what?' Archie wondered.

'Unless I make it . . . *rain* vinegar!' Aldrin said.

'Now you're using your brain!' Archie told him.

'I mean, can I actually *do* that?' Aldrin asked.

'You're a superhero!' Archie declared. 'You can do ANYTHING!'

Aldrin looked up at the sky above them. He raised his two arms with the palms of his hands turned heavenwards.

'VINEGAR RAIN FALL,' he shouted at the clouds, 'AND REPEL THIS ARMY OF ANTS!'

BOOMP! BOOMP! BOOMP! BOOMP! BOOMP! CHOMP! CHOMP! CHOMP! CHOMP! CHOMP!

'Er, that was maybe a *tad* overdramatic,' Archie laughed, 'but it should do the trick!'

Aldrin felt a drop of something touch his lips. It tasted sour. He felt more drops fall on his face and forehead.

And the clouds above them burst!

Suddenly, the vinegar was falling on them like it was coming from a fire hose. The smell of it was overpowering – then something truly extraordinary happened.

BOOMP! BOOMP! BOO–

The march of the ants stopped.

The thousands of people who were fleeing noticed

that the earth had stopped shaking and they stopped running. They turned round, shielding their eyes and pinching their noses to avoid the stinging, foul-smelling rain.

'THEY'RE TURNING BACK!' a voice shouted.

It was true. The noise started again . . .

BOOMP! BOOMP! BOOMP!

But this time it was receding . . .

Boomp! Boomp! Boomp!

. . . into the distance.

boomp . . . boomp . . . boomp . . .

. . . until it couldn't be heard at all.

Aldrin closed his eyes and the rain stopped falling.

'What happened?' a voice in the crowd asked.

'That boy,' Archie said, pointing at Aldrin. 'He made vinegar fall from the sky!'

'He saved us!' the elderly man declared. 'He saved our lives!'

The crowd cheered and roared and lifted Aldrin off his feet and put him on their shoulders.

'What's your name?' he was asked as the people carried him around in grateful triumph.

'His name,' said Archie, 'is NemeSwiss! And he's the greatest superhero of them all!'

Aldrin smiled to himself, savouring the adulation of the crowd. Then, a few seconds later, he was back in his bed, staring at his *Fromages de France* poster and trying to gather his bearings. And strangely – miraculously, even – he discovered that he had no cheese hangover . . . at all!

21

'THAT'S . . . NOT POSSIBLE!'

Beddy Byes was working late. Beddy Byes was *always* working late.

He had figures and spreadsheets and pie charts to look over. The Creative Department was waiting for him to sign off on hundreds of new ideas for nightmares and Beddy Byes had to study each one in detail before giving it his approval.

And then, on top of all the other demands on his time, there was the need to keep feeding that monument to his boss's greed and vanity – his mountain of decomposing cheese. Beddy Byes spent at least two hours of every week scouring the pages of *Cheese News* magazine, looking for snippets of gossip about cheesemongers that might be in financial difficulty.

That very night, he'd read about **Cheese Louise**, an artisan cheese shop in Higher Dinting, which was about to close its doors after more than thirty years in business. He scribbled down the name on a scrap of paper.

It was after midnight when he finally packed up to leave. As he passed Habeas's office, he noticed that the door was ajar. Nervously, he stuck his head round it. Habeas was standing in front of his **WaLL of Torment**, so caught up in his thoughts that that he failed to notice his Personal Assistant and Vice President of Global Operations.

'Good evening,' Beddy Byes said, 'Your Highnessness . . . ness.'

'HAVEN'T YOU EVER HEARD OF KNOCKING?' Habeas roared, jumping with fright.

'I-I-I'm deeply sorry,' Beddy Byes wittered. 'I saw the d-d-d-door was open and I –'

And then he stopped. On a screen, right in the middle of the **WaLL of Torment**, he could see Aldrin Adams doing something that he never expected to see.

There was a long, snaking column of giant ants that were as big as elephants – and it was about to devour a crowd of several thousand terrified men, women and children, who were attempting to run away. Then he saw the Adams boy look up at the sky, with his arms raised. Then the clouds overhead burst. Beddy Byes watched in stupefied wonder as the army of giant ants turned away and the crowd cheered and lifted Aldrin on to its shoulders in joyous relief.

'**That's . . . not possible!**' Beddy Byes blurted out.

Habeas pulled a small remote control from the pocket of his long black coat and pointed it at him. Suddenly, the ground beneath Beddy Byes' feet opened up and he felt himself falling through the floor. He landed with a painful THUMP.

Habeas stared down at him from the hole above.

'I've just had that trapdoor fitted!' He grinned. 'And you are the first to use it!'

'I WAS WORRIED!'

Sisely looked furious. Sisely *was* furious.

'You didn't answer my calls,' she said, glowering at him across their table in the cafeteria.

'Calls?' Aldrin replied with mock innocence. 'What calls?'

'On the walkie-talkie! I was *trying* to contact you!'

'Oh, *that* thing! I switched it off.'

'You switched it OFF? Why?'

'I was tired. Wasn't in the mood to talk.'

'I was worried,' she told him, 'when you didn't answer.'

'Well, you didn't need to be,' Aldrin said flippantly. 'I'm more than capable of looking after myself. I'm the one with the superpower, remember?'

'It's NOT a superpower,' she insisted.

'Isn't it, though, Sisely?' He challenged her with a stare. '*Isn't* it?'

Did she know that his true identity was NemeSwiss? His mum must have mentioned it in her dream journal. Did Mrs Van Boxtel tell Sisely to keep that from him too – in the belief that she was *protecting* him? And was that why Sisely was always so keen to tell him that this ability he possessed wasn't a superpower?

'So what did you want?' he asked. 'Why were you looking for me?'

'I had a job for you,' she told him.

'Well, what is it?'

Sisely pushed a small envelope across the table to him.

'It's a girl,' she said, 'who's having bad anxiety nightmares.'

'What, ONE girl?' he asked, unable to hide his disappointment. 'And what are these nightmares about?'

'She's lost in a crowded shopping centre and she can't find her mother.'

This was SO far *beneath* him! Last night, he'd

rescued several thousand people from an army of ginormous ants. And now he was being asked to, what, hold a little girl by the hand and take her to the lost and found office?

'What's wrong?' Sisely asked.

'It's just not very exciting,' he said.

'It might not be exciting to *you*,' she pointed out, 'but that doesn't mean it's not terrifying for her.'

'Yeah, whatever,' Aldrin said, picking up the envelope and slipping it into the inside pocket of his blazer.

'Caciocavallo,' Sisely told him. 'For crowd dreams. That's according to your mum's journal.'

'And you've read every page of it, haven't you, Sisely?' Aldrin said in an accusing tone.

'What do you mean?' asked Sisely.

'I'm just saying, you're the only one who knows all the secrets it contains.'

Sisely stared at him for a moment, then went back to reading her physics book.

Aldrin popped the lid of his lunch box and braced himself for the smell. He needn't have. It was Emmental for lunch today, and it didn't really smell of anything.

A moment later, Harry and Frankie arrived.

'We need to come up with an enemy for the Bounce,'

Frankie was saying. 'He's got to have someone to fight, hasn't he?'

'I was thinking about a character called Echidna,' said Harry. 'He's Australian and he's half-human and half-hedgehog. And his entire body is covered in sharp spikes, which makes him the Bounce's mortal enemy.'

'That's brilliant,' Aldrin declared, subtly watching Sisely for her reaction. 'I mean, every superhero has to have a . . . *NemeSwiss*.'

He placed a heavy emphasis on the last word. Sisely looked up from her book. Her eyes were wide with surprise.

'A what?' she asked.

'A nemesis, Sisely,' Aldrin replied. 'It's the agent of someone's downfall. I thought you would have heard of that word before, no?'

'That wasn't the word you used,' she said.

'Yeah,' Frankie said, 'I think you said "nemeswiss", Aldrin.'

'Did I?' Aldrin asked innocently.

'Yeah, that's what I heard too,' said Harry. 'Typical of you, Aldrin – always thinking about cheese!'

Frankie had an idea then.

'Here,' he said, slapping his own forehead. 'We

should change Nighty Knight's name . . . to NemeSwiss!'

'Why?' asked Harry.

'Because he was inspired by the dream I had where Aldrin rescued me from the tree,' Frankie explained. 'And Aldrin loves cheese!'

'NemeSwiss!' Harry said, staring into the mid-distance. 'I love it!'

'I love it too,' Aldrin agreed. 'It's a proper name for a superhero – isn't it, Sisely?'

Sisely looked up at him again.

'Is everything OK?' he asked her pointedly.

'I have no idea what you're talking about,' she said.

23

FLASHBACK

Cynthia was a very busy young woman. Between learning the ropes at Farlowe's and her by now regular adventures in the world of nightmares, cheese had taken over her life.

In the two years since she had helped Maurice deal with his fear of loneliness and rejection, she'd entered the nightmares of more than two hundred people and helped change the endings for them.

It was almost a full-time job in itself.

She knew all about Habeas Grusselvart. Her father had told her about his evil plan to try to control the world through fear and unhappiness, and she made it her business to try to undo as much of his work as she could manage.

She listened out for stories of people experiencing bad dreams. When she talked to friends, casual acquaintances or work colleagues, she always tried to steer the conversation round to nightmares. Often, people volunteered stories about their own night terrors in which they were falling from a height, or being bitten by a dog, or drowning in the sea, or lost in a maze, or being chased down a deserted street.

And Cynthia would try to help them. She wasn't always successful the first time. Sometimes, she had to go back four or even five times before she managed to bring a nightmare to a happy conclusion. For the best possible results, it was a case of finding the right cheese for the right dream and this could only be discovered through a process of trial and error.

For example, it took her a full year to find out that Limburger was the most effective cheese to eat to influence the outcome of a clown nightmare. She discovered that Gouda was the best cheese for drowning nightmares and that Queso de Cabrales worked best for computer-game nightmares. For any nightmare involving a maze, it was Camembert Rustique, while any kind of English Cheddar worked for nightmares that involved being chased.

She decided to start keeping a dream journal. She bought a giant ledger, two inches thick, with a red cover, in which she recorded all her nocturnal adventures – the missions that had been successful and the missions that had failed. She wrote down everything in French, partly because it was the language in which Madame Lacombe insisted on speaking to them and Cynthia wanted to improve her grasp of it. But also, because it wasn't her first language, when she wrote down her secrets in French, she felt like she was recording them in code.

She learned to be patient. Every nightmare was a puzzle to be solved and sometimes it took time to figure out the right cheese.

If she ate the wrong cheese, the nightmare was fuzzy and she couldn't do anything to influence the outcome. But the right cheese made the dream vivid and gave her the power to change how a nightmare ended.

She discovered that a small amount of mozzarella

or Edam would allow her to access someone's dream as an observer. It allowed her to enter, check out the lie of the land and then consider her next move.

Over time, she developed an instinct for it. Like a golfer knows the right club to use for every tricky shot, so Cynthia gained an understanding of what cheese, or combination of cheeses, would work for which nightmare. Smoked halloumi was very good for nightmares involving loneliness – but she discovered that it was even more effective if she halved the amount of halloumi and added in some herbed Brie.

In the back of the ledger, she started to keep a glossary. In alphabetical order, and in French, she listed every kind of nightmare she could think of, then next to each one she added the name of the cheese, or combination of cheeses, that worked best, as well as the amount to be eaten.

She also wrote down the best cheese or cheeses to be consumed as a cure for the terrible hangovers that inevitably followed each and every cheese nightmare.

After two years, Cynthia's dream journal was bursting with her discoveries and observations, many of which were scribbled on scraps of paper and multicoloured Post-it notes that peeked out from between the pages.

She kept it locked away in the drawer of her dressing table.

One morning, Maurice called at the little flat that Cynthia was renting on the King's Road in Chelsea. Madame Lacombe was keen for them to learn every aspect of the business and had decided that it was time for them to go out into the field. Their job was to try to persuade shops and supermarkets to stock Farlowe's cheese, and Maurice arrived in a large refrigerated van, which was packed with cheeses of just about every variety.

When he rang the bell, Cynthia was still getting ready. She invited him up and told him to make himself a cup of tea in the kitchen. Madame Lacombe wanted them to look their best while they were representing Farlowe's and had supplied them both with brand-new suits. Cynthia was admiring the cut of hers in the mirror when she remembered with a flash of horror that she'd left her dream journal on the table.

She ran into the kitchen to find Maurice flicking through it with a look of shock on his face.

'*Qu'est-ce que c'est?*' he asked – they were in the habit of sometimes speaking to each other in French outside work.

'How DARE you read my diary!' Cynthia shouted.

'I'm sorry,' he told her. 'I saw my name – on a Post-it note that was sticking out. I shouldn't have . . . Cynthia, what *is* this?'

'It's nothing,' she said.

'*Seagulls – Saint Agur Blue*,' he read. '*Falling from a height – Gouda*. What's going on? What's this about?'

For a moment, Cynthia considered telling him to mind his own business. But Maurice was her friend. The best friend she'd ever had.

'You've written about the nightmare I used to have,' he said. 'The one where I'm the only living thing on the planet. And beside it it says, "smoked halloumi and herbed Brie". Cynthia, what's going on?'

Cynthia wanted to tell her friend the truth. But she remembered something her father had said to her when he first told her about her power – that whomever she shared her secret with would become a target for Habeas.

'Morr-eece, I can't tell you,' she explained. 'I really want to – you're my best friend in the world – but it might put you in danger.'

'I don't care about the danger,' he told her truthfully. 'I'm worried about you, Cynthia. Please tell me – I'm begging you! What is this book for?'

'You'd better sit down,' Cynthia sighed.

Maurice pulled up a chair.

She took a deep breath and prepared to unburden herself of her secret.

'Morr-eece,' she said, 'I have a very unusual supernatural ability . . .'

24

AN UNEXPECTED VISITOR

It was Saturday morning and Aldrin was in his favourite place in the entire world – behind the counter of *C'est Cheese*.

He was chewing on a thin wedge of Roomano Pradera, a four-year-old Gouda that was fiery orange in colour and tasted like candyfloss.

Doug was out on the shop floor, dealing with Mrs Verner from Lyons Grove, who was attempting to return a block of cheese that had mould on it.

'It is *supposed* to have mould on it,' Doug was attempting to explain. 'It's *blue* cheese. The mould is what gives it its flavour.'

'Well, *I* don't like it,' Mrs Verner said.

'You, er, ate enough of it before you discovered that,'

Doug said, examining the cheese. 'There's only two bites left.'

'That's what Belinda said when I tried to return it yesterday,' Mrs Verner told him. 'She told me to sling me hook.'

'It's fine, Mrs Verner,' Doug said. 'I'll give you a full refund.'

'Oh, I don't want my money back,' Mrs Verner said. 'I'll have some more of the same cheese.'

'But that will have mould on it as well.'

'I'll give it another try – and, if I don't like it after a

few bites, I'll bring it back again.'

Aldrin picked up a pen and began doodling on the notepad they used to take orders. He wasn't especially good at art – not in Harry's league anyway – but he was gripped by a sudden urge to draw a costume. Well, not so much a costume as a suit – one befitting a boy with his superpowers!

He took his inspiration from the amazing bubble-wrap onesie worn by the Bounce, except where *his* was translucent in appearance Aldrin's would be banana yellow. And, where the Bounce's was full of giant bubbles, Aldrin's had dozens of black dots, big and small, that gave the impression the costume was made of Swiss cheese.

On his feet, he drew large knee-high boots, which he imagined would be red in colour, as would his elbow-length gloves, his utility belt and the eye mask that would conceal his identity from the world.

He pondered long and hard over whether he should have a cape. There was a part of him that thought capes were a bit 'Look at me!' But then all the best superheroes had them, so in the end he figured why not?

Lastly, he sketched a large N and then an S – for NemeSwiss – on the chest of the suit.

He picked up the notepad and held it at arm's length. *Not bad*, he thought. *Not bad at all.*

'Thanks, Doug,' Mrs Verner said over her shoulder.

Shortly afterwards, Belinda returned from the wholesaler's carrying a large cardboard box filled with fig jam and truffle honey and other condiments that went well with cheese.

'Here,' she said, 'I just saw that Mrs Verner leaving. I told her to sling her hook yesterday. Mould on her blue cheese!'

Doug and Aldrin said nothing. Belinda placed the box on the counter.

'Are you two going to give me a hand,' she asked, 'or are you just going to stand there with your flaming gobs open? Seriously, I'm rushed off me feet today. There's five more boxes outside in the van. I've got to stack all these on the shelves. Then I've got the orders to do for Mrs Casey's son's wedding, Mr Halpin's wine-and-cheese night and Mrs Ging's book club. Then I've got the accounts to update – all while serving folk.'

Doug smiled at her.

'I've got an idea,' he said. 'Aldrin, hand me that pen and tear me out a page from that order book, will you?'

Aldrin did what Doug asked.

'What are you doing,' Belinda asked, 'you daft thing?'

'I'm putting a sign in the window,' he told her.

'A sign? What kind of a sign?'

'A "Help Wanted" sign. I've been thinking for a while that we could do with an extra pair of hands in the shop.'

'Well, I *am* exhausted after that flipping festival.'

'There you are then! Business is booming, Belinda! We can afford to hire a new assistant!'

Doug held up the sign. It read:

Position available
for a GOUDA worker!
Apply within!

'You and your cheese puns!' Belinda said. 'You're half daft, you are!'

Doug put the sign in the window of the shop. Aldrin looked down at the superhero suit he'd sketched. It seemed a bit stupid to him now. He was about tear the page from the notepad and screw it up into a ball when the door of the shop pinged. He looked up. There, standing in the doorway of the shop, was Archie.

'That was quick!' said Doug.

'Sorry?' asked Archie.

'Are you here about the job?'

'Don't just stand there gawping,' said Belinda. 'What experience do you have in lugging boxes and telling time-wasters to sling their hooks?'

'I'm not looking for a job,' Archie said. 'I was looking for some, er, Formatge de la Garrotxa.'

'I'll serve him,' Aldrin offered.

'Oh, yes,' Doug said, 'my son knows more about cheese than anyone. Come on, Belinda, let's get the rest of those boxes unloaded.'

Doug and Belinda stepped outside the shop while Archie approached the counter, smiling.

'Hey,' he said, 'YOU were AWESOME the other night!'

'Was I?' Aldrin asked with a modesty he definitely didn't feel. 'I'm sure I wasn't! Or *was* I?'

'Yes, you were,' Archie assured him. Archie nodded to indicate the notepad next to Aldrin's hand.

'That looks, er, *interesting*,' he said.

Embarrassed, Aldrin attempted to turn it face down on the counter.

'No, I mean it,' Archie said. 'Can I see it?'

'I was just mucking around,' Aldrin told him as he pushed it across the counter. Archie looked it over, then nodded appreciatively.

'A great superhero should have an awesome suit!' he said. 'Can I have this, dude?'

'I don't mind,' Aldrin told him. 'I was about to throw it in the bin.'

Archie tore the page from the pad, folded it in two and put it in the back pocket of his board shorts. There was an awkward silence then.

'So, er, I really *am* looking for some Formatge de la Garrotxa,' Archie told him.

'Sorry,' Aldrin said, 'I forgot!'

He reached into the refrigerated counter, picked out one of the small round parcels and popped it into a *C'est Cheese* bag.

'Thanks for showing me how to use my powers,' said Aldrin. 'Mrs Van Boxtel was never going to do it – and neither was Sisely.'

'Who's Sisely?' Archie wondered.

'Oh, she's my friend – or so I thought.'

'And, what? She knows your secret?'

'I told her at the beginning, when I was trying to

figure out how I ended up in my friend's nightmare.'

'Hey, every superhero has at least one non-superhero who knows his secret.'

'She's the smartest girl I know. Except I'm beginning to wish I'd never told her.'

'Why?'

'Because she's trying to hold me back – just like Mrs Van Boxtel. She never told me about Lufassi Samatta's prophecy. And she never said anything about NemeSwiss.'

'I don't understand – how would *she* know about those things?'

'From my mum's book.'

"Ah, her dream journal! You mentioned it at the meeting in Tintwistle.'

'She wrote down absolutely everything she knew about being a Cheese Whizz.'

'That was clever of her.'

'It's because she knew I was **The One**. She knew I was NemeSwiss. She must have written that in her journal. But Sisely never mentioned it. As a matter of fact, she's always telling me that I'm *not* a superhero.'

'So why does Sisely have your mother's dream journal in the first place?'

'Oh, because it's written in French. And Sisely speaks it fluently. That and about five other languages!'

'Dude, I know you're not ready to hear this, but try to see it from her point of view. Maybe the reason she's holding you back is because she doesn't want you putting yourself in danger.'

'She doesn't think I'm ready to take on Habeas Grusselvart.'

'Well, maybe she's right, Aldrin. And maybe the old lady is right too. Habeas will have seen what you did the other night, saving all those people from those monster ants. And he'll know just how strong your powers have become. And it'll make him even more determined to destroy you.'

'Do you really think so?' Aldrin gulped.

'Absolutely,' Archie told him. 'And I don't want to frighten you, Aldrin, but everyone you've shared your secret with could be in danger too.'

25

'SHEAGULLSH!'

It was the following Friday. Sisely was absent from school. And that never, EVER happened. She hadn't missed a day of school in her life. And yet, when Mrs Van Boxtel said her name during the class register, she was met not with the usual loud, **'PRESENT, MRS VAN BOXTEL!'** but with a silence that was almost eerie.

'Shishely?' said Mrs Van Boxtel. 'Aldrin, where ish Shishely thish morning?'

'Er, why would *I* know?' Aldrin said coolly.

The truth was that Aldrin didn't care. Despite what Archie had said, he was still furious with her – *and* with Mrs Van Boxtel – for keeping the truth from him.

'Very shtrange,' the teacher said. 'Very shtrange indeed.'

Aldrin daydreamed his way through the class. He thought about the happy faces on all the people he'd saved from the army of bloodthirsty ants. He remembered the cheers, the high fives and the love he felt from the crowd. It was like something from a movie.

He thought about Archie, his new friend, who had shown him what he could do! He had shown him the true extent of the power he possessed!

'Aldrin?' Mrs Van Boxtel said.

'Er, sorry,' Aldrin replied, awakening from his daydream. 'What was the question?'

Everyone in the class laughed.

'There wash no queshtion,' she said, 'exshept perhapsh ish there shomething outshide the window that you find more intereshting than what we are talking about in classh?'

'Er, no, Mrs Van Boxtel,' he told her.

The bell sounded and all of the other boys and girls stood up from their desks.

'Aldrin,' said Mrs Van Boxtel, 'shtay sheated – there ish shomething I want to talk to you about after classh.'

Aldrin rolled his eyes. The last thing he wanted to hear was another lecture about how she was trying to protect him. He was a superhero now – he didn't need this hassle!

When the classroom had emptied, Mrs Van Boxtel said: 'Ish everything OK?'

'Absolutely,' he lied. 'Why wouldn't it be?'

'It ish jusht that you sheem very . . . dishtant today.'

'Do I?'

'Yesh – like your mind ish elshewhere.'

'No, I'm just great, Mrs Van Boxtel. Really, REALLY great.'

She stared at him, trying to figure out whether she detected a note of sarcasm in his voice.

'Are you shtill angry with me,' she asked, 'for not telling you about the meeting of the Cheeshe Whizshesh?'

The meeting of the Cheese Whizzes? That was NOTHING compared to all the OTHER things she'd kept from him.

'No,' he said. 'It's totally forgotten.'

'That ish good,' she said, 'becaushe I have another mission for you.'

She went back to her desk, then returned with a brown manila folder, which she placed in front of him. Aldrin opened it. Inside was a photograph of

an elderly man, who
was wearing squarish
glasses and a flat cap.

'Who's this dude?'
Aldrin asked.

'Dude?' Mrs Van
Boxtel repeated.

'Who's this *man*
then?' Aldrin asked.

'Hish name ish
Ernie Williamsh.'

'But who *is* he?'

'He ish jusht a man I met on a bush.'

'You met him on a bus?'

'Yesh, we got talking and he mentioned to me that
he hash theeshe terrible nightmaresh.'

'And what are these nightmares supposedly about?'
Aldrin asked.

'Sheagullsh!' Mrs Van Boxtel said.

'Seagulls?' Aldrin repeated disbelievingly.

'Yesh, sheagullsh.'

This was even lamer than Sisely's little girl lost in a
shopping centre – which he still hadn't got round to. A
grown man – frightened of seagulls!

'He told me that he ish shtanding on a pier,' she said, 'and he ish eating chipsh from a bag, then all of a shudden he ish being attacked by –'

'Seagulls?'

'Sheagullsh – exshactly.'

It didn't feel like a job worthy of a superhero! It didn't feel like a job for NemeSwiss!

'Not a problem,' he shrugged. 'I've done a seagull nightmare before. I mean, they're just birds, aren't they?'

'For you and me, they are jusht birdsh,' she reminded him, 'but for thish man, Ernie Williamsh, who hash been attacked by them before, they are very, very shcary.'

'I'm sure.'

'Of courshe, you will have to shpeak to Shishely to find out what cheeshe –'

'I don't need to speak to Sisely,' Aldrin interrupted her. 'It's Saint Agur Blue. Like I said, I've done seagulls before.'

'Perhapsh you should go to shee Shishely anyway,' Mrs Van Boxtel suggested. 'It ish very shtrange for her not to come to shchool.'

'I might,' Aldrin said, 'if I've time.'

'You know,' Mrs Van Boxtel told him, 'it ish of courshe important to be a good Cheeshe Whizsh, Aldrin. But it ish MORE important to be a good friend.'

But Aldrin wasn't listening. He stood up from his desk, closed the folder and put it into his schoolbag.

'So you will do thish tonight, yesh?' Mrs Van Boxtel asked.

'Yeah, shouldn't be any problem,' Aldrin said, 'compared to, say, stopping several thousand people from being eaten by **GIANT ANTS.**'

Mrs Van Boxtel stared at him.

'What ish that shupposhed to mean?' she asked.

'Nothing,' he said. 'I'll see you on Monday.'

26

THINGS ON HIS MIND

Aldrin couldn't relax that night. He tried to distract himself by playing the piano:

P<small>LI</small>**N<small>K</small>** . . . P<small>L</small>**O**<small>NK</small> . . . P<small>L</small>I<small>I</small>I<small>N</small>N**N<small>K</small>** . . .

Or rather sitting in front of it and randomly pressing the keys . . .

P<small>LI</small>I<small>N</small>**N<small>K</small>** . . . **P**<small>L</small><small>U</small>N**K** . . . P**L**<small>U</small>u<small>N</small>N**N<small>K</small>** . . .

. . . which is what he did when he had things on his mind.

As he jabbed at the keys, Silas crooned along from his happy place on top of Aldrin's head.

RRRIBBIT . . . RRRIBBIT . . . RRRIBBIT . . .

Aldrin didn't go to visit Sisely, even though the route home from school took him by her house. She had lied to him, just like Mrs Van Boxtel lied to him. They were holding him back from his superhero destiny.

PLINK ... PLIIINNNK ... PLONK ...

Aldrin looked at the clock. It was half past ten.

RRRIBBIT ... RRRIBBIT ... RRRIBBIT ...

'Yes, you're right, Silas,' he said. 'It probably *is* time for bed.'

Doug and Belinda were at the cinema. Aldrin wanted to wait up for his dad, but he was tired.

He stood up and returned Silas to his tank.

RRRIBBIT ... RRRIBBIT ... RRRIBBIT ...

'Yes, goodnight, Silas,' Aldrin replied.

As he changed into his pyjamas, he continued to mull things over in his mind. He was still torn. He didn't want to do the stupid seagull nightmare. Shooing away a few birds – it was so far beneath him.

But then if this Ernie Williams person was in distress . . .

RRRIBBIT ... RRRIBBIT ... RRRIBBIT ...

'Fine,' Aldrin sighed. 'I'll do the stupid nightmare.'

He went downstairs to the shop. He was surprised to discover that Doug was back. He was sniffing a half-wheel of Hafod Cheddar.

'Dad?' Aldrin said.

Doug jumped.

'Sorry, Aldrin,' he said. 'You startled me. Here, have a smell of that!'

Aldrin put his nose to the wheel. It smelled like wet soil.

'Yum,' he nodded. 'So how was the cinema?'

'Oh, you know,' Doug said. 'Wasn't my kind of movie – one of these superhero things. I find them a bit far-fetched. Superpowers and whatnot.'

Aldrin couldn't help but smile.

'So did you find anyone for the job yet?' he asked.

'Sadly not,' said Doug. 'Oh, one or two people enquired about it. I just wasn't sure that they were, well, the right fit. I'm looking for someone who's especially good with the customers.'

'A sort of good cop to Belinda's bad cop.'

'Someone with a sunnier disposition, shall we say. Although don't tell Belinda I said that.'

They laughed.

'You, um, do like her, don't you, Aldrin?' Doug asked.

'Belinda?' Aldrin said. 'Of course I do! I love her!'

'I just want you to know that, well, just because she and I are – I suppose you could call it – *dating*, it doesn't mean I've forgotten about your mum. I still think about her – all the time, in fact.'

'I do too, Dad.'

'I just don't want you to think that I'm being somehow unfaithful to her memory.'

'She'd want you to be happy.'

'I know she would. So have you come down for something to eat?'

'I was going to have some Saint Agur.'

'Saint Agur!' Doug said, picking up a giant wedge and carrying it over to the cutting block. 'Excellent choice!'

Aldrin and Doug both adored Saint Agur, a moist, creamy cheese, with olive-green mould and a sharp, tangy taste. Doug cut into it.

'That enough?' he asked.

'Little bit more,' Aldrin told him.

Doug wrapped the cheese in a piece of greaseproof paper and handed it to him.

'I think I'll, um, turn in now,' Aldrin yawned.

'***Sweet dreams –***' Doug said.

'**– are made of cheese,**' Aldrin smiled.

'***Who am I –***'

'**– to diss a Brie?**'

'Night, son.'

'Night, Dad.'

Aldrin returned to his room and got into bed. He took out the photograph that Mrs Van Boxtel had given him.

RRRIBBIT . . . RRRIBBIT . . . RRRIBBIT . . .

'If you're trying to tell me that I'm too good for this kind of thing,' said Aldrin, 'then you're absolutely right. Anyway, here goes nothing.'

He bit into the cheese and he looked at the photograph of the old man. Then he put the photograph down and shoved the rest of the cheese into his mouth. He closed his eyes and pictured the man in his mind – his squarish glasses and his flat cap.

He chewed and chewed until the Saint Agur had turned into a creamy, tangy pulp.

And *very quickly* . . .

without even realizing . . .

that it was happening . . .

his eyes **started to feel** . . .

very,

very

heavy . . .

And then . . .

he was suddenly . . .

out

for

the . . .

27

THE SEAGULL NIGHTMARE

Aldrin found himself in complete darkness. He reached out his hand and he touched what felt like wet paper. And the smell! What *was* that smell? It was sharp and sour and overpowering, like . . .

. . . vinegar?

He could hear muffled voices. And, when he listened closely, he could make out a conversation.

'Where's Barry?'

'Barry?'

'Yeah, mate – Barry.'

'He's eating vomit in the doorway of JD Sports.'

'He's never! That's sick, that is!'

'That's what I told him. Eat anything, he would. I said, *Eat anything, you would, Barry!*'

'Too fussy by half, you lot. What are you waiting for – someone to cook you a nice fillet steak with onions?'

'I'd eat most things, but I draw the line at vomit.'

What on earth was going on, Aldrin wondered? And where was Ernie Williams?

'Here,' the conversation continued, 'let's pop round the back of the China Express and see if that Mr Chen-ji left summat out.'

'He won't have. He don't put his bin out till Tuesday. And anyway you'll not get into it. He puts a brick on top of it now – ever since Eric made that mess with the spare ribs.'

'Here, what's wrong with you, Frank? Are you walking funny?'

'Yeah, tried to take an ice-cream cone off a kid – got a kick for me troubles.'

This was such a strange conversation, Aldrin thought.

'Here, is that a chip bag over there?'

'Looks like it!'

'Have you checked if there's owt in it?'

'No, I've only just seen it – same as you. Hang about.'

A few seconds later, without any warning, Aldrin felt himself being thrown violently into the air.

He let out a yell:

'WHOOOAAAHHH!!!!!'

Then he landed on the flat of his back with a strange squelch.

'Here,' the talk went on, 'there's summat in there.'

'Well, I saw it first.'

'Did you heck as like! I saw it before you.'

'You little liar!'

Aldrin heard a horrible ripping sound . . .

RRRIIIIIIIIIIIPPP!!!!!

And suddenly it wasn't dark any more. He could see.

And what he could see was three **ENORMOUS** seagulls bearing down on him.

No, he was wrong. *They* weren't enormous. *He* was small. He was tiny, in fact – so tiny that if he'd stood up he could have walked between any of the three pairs of legs.

But he couldn't stand up. Because he didn't have any feet. Or legs. He didn't have any arms either. And there was a very good reason for that.

It was because he was . . .

. . . **a chip!**

That's right. He was a chip – though he could scarcely believe it.

He saw the torn remains of a brown paper bag on the ground nearby and it all started to add up.

And now he had three seagulls staring down at him – with ravenous eyes!

'Er, sorry,' he gulped, 'I seem to have somehow stumbled into the wrong dream. I'm, er, just going to try and wake up.'

But, before he could, one of the seagulls made a lunge for him with his yellow hooked beak. Aldrin rolled out of the way.

'Here, I flipping saw it first,' said another of the birds.

'Means nowt,' the first seagull said. 'I were the one who tore open the bag.'

All three birds started flapping their wings and squawking:

WAAAHHHHHHKKK!!!!!!
WAAAHHHHHHKKK!!!!!!
WAAAHHHHHHKKK!!!!!!

One of the gulls picked Aldrin up with his beak and flipped him up into the air. Aldrin found himself somersaulting backwards towards his open mouth. But, before he could swallow him, he was attacked by the other two and they started fighting noisily among themselves . . .

WAAAHHHHHHKKK!!!!!!

. . . while Aldrin hit the ground with another wet splat.

Suddenly, a few feet away, Aldrin spotted a storm drain. If he could somehow drag his soggy potato body a few feet to the right, he could slip between the bars and out of their reach.

While the seagulls fought, Aldrin began to roll on his side towards the sanctuary of the drain. He'd managed to move himself about twelve inches when suddenly he felt a shadow fall across him. He looked up to see a fourth seagull staring down at him, this one with vomit dripping from his beak.

'There's a chip here,' the bird said. 'Does none of you want it?'

He dipped his neck and picked Aldrin up in his beak.

'Oooh,' said the seagull, 'it's still hot!'

'Oi, Barry!' one of the other seagulls shouted. 'That's my chip!'

But the seagull threw his head back, flicked Aldrin up into the air, then bit him in two.

In that moment, Aldrin woke up in his bed with his

head aching, his heart pounding and the sweat coming from his pores like water from a wet sponge.

'OK,' he said aloud, 'what was THAT about?'

28

A MYSTERIOUS PACKAGE

Aldrin was still asking himself the same question several hours later. He'd fallen asleep again and awoken to discover that it was already after nine o'clock. He was supposed to be working in the shop this morning. but had slept in.

He threw his legs out of the bed as Silas greeted the day:

RRRIBBIT . . . RRRIBBIT . . . RRRIBBIT . . .

'Morning, Silas,' Aldrin said as he started pulling on his clothes. 'I had *the* strangest dream last night.'

RRRIBBIT . . . RRRIBBIT . . . RRRIBBIT . . .

'No,' he said, 'it was a disaster, I'm afraid. I dreamt that I was a chip and all these seagulls were trying to eat me. Except they had human voices. I didn't even *see* this Ernie Williams dude from Mrs Van Boxtel's picture.'

Aldrin was worried. It was his first mission failure since his early days as a Cheese Whizz, when he accidentally entered into one of Silas's nightmares and dreamt that he was a frog who was about to have his legs chopped off in the kitchen of a restaurant. Ever since then, he had been in full control of his powers – until now. He tried to console himself with the thought that perhaps the Saint Agur had passed its best-before date. But he was concerned. Aldrin picked Silas out of his tank and placed him on the floor of the bedroom.

'Right, I'm off to work,' he said. 'I'll see you at lunchtime, little friend.'

Aldrin wandered downstairs. Belinda was emptying the day's float into the till while Doug was busy unwrapping the cheeses.

Comté was the cheese that Cynthia prescribed for a hangover resulting from a seagull nightmare. Aldrin took the quarter-wheel down from the shelf and he cut four generous slices off it.

'A package arrived for you,' Belinda said.

'For me?' Aldrin asked.

201

'It were on the doorstep when I arrived for work.'

Aldrin wasn't expecting a package.

'What is it?' he asked.

'I've no idea,' Belinda said. 'Your dad put it on the table for you.'

Intrigued, Aldrin headed back upstairs to the kitchen. And there, sitting on the table, was an enormous box covered in brown wrapping paper and bound up with string.

His name and address was written on it in bold, black, felt-tip capital letters:

ALDRIN ADAMS,
C/O SAY CHEESE,
47 BURNETT ROAD,
TINTWISTLE

He took the scissors from the drawer and snipped the string, then he tore open the paper. He popped open the lid of the box. When he saw what was inside, he wondered for a moment whether he might be hallucinating!

It was a banana-yellow one-piece outfit covered in black dots, big and small, which made it look like it was made of Swiss cheese. Right in the centre of the chest, there was a rubber shield bearing the letters 'N' and 'S', just like the one he'd sketched on his dad's order book.

He looked in the box again. There were more goodies inside. There was a pair of red rubber knee-high boots, as well as a red rubber utility belt. There was a pair of red elbow-length gloves and a red leather eye mask. And lastly – the classiest touch of all – there was a red cape!

It was his very own superhero suit!

Aldrin ran all the way to the skatepark, where he spotted Archie through the railings performing a heelflip on his board.

'Archie!' he called out.

'Hey, dude,' Archie said, removing his helmet.

'Was it you who gave me the suit?' Aldrin asked.

'Yeah, do you like it?'

'I love it! Thank you so much – it was so kind of you.'

'Hey, you're NemeSwiss!' Archie reminded him. 'You can't keep turning up in people's nightmares in those pyjamas of yours! A superhero has to *look* the part if he's going to *act* the part, right?'

'But where did you get it?'

'I went to a tailor and had it made. Does it fit? If the

cape is too long, I can have the hem taken up for you.'

'I haven't tried it on yet. I just put it back in the box and hid it under my bed.'

'You're waiting for the right moment to put it on, right?'

'Er, right.'

'Well, what are you doing tonight?'

'Tonight? I think Dad and Belinda are going out. I'll probably watch TV and hang out with Silas, my frog.'

'I'm talking about *tonight*,' Archie said. 'In your dreams, dude. Did the old lady give you a job to do?'

'She did. An old man called Ernie. She met him on the bus. He has this nightmare where he's eating chips and he gets attacked by seagulls.'

'Seagulls?' Archie laughed. 'Hey, I suppose even Superman had to rescue the odd cat from a tree.'

'Except I tried to go into his dream last night and he wasn't there. Instead, *I* was a chip – and all these seagulls were trying to eat me.'

'That *is* weird.'

'I was going to try again tonight.'

'Dude, do you mind me saying something to you?'

'You can say anything to me.'

'Scaring away seagulls – it's beneath you. You have

the power to help thousands of people every night. Do you know how many people dream that they're trapped in a city skyscraper that's being attacked by a Tyrannosaurus rex?'

'How many?'

'OK, I don't know the *exact* answer to that question. But it's a lot. Hey, I'm sure the old dude can put up with the seagulls for a night or two more. You could even wear your suit.'

'**Wow!**'

'Remember, just think of a skyscraper – and a giant T. rex.'

'I will.'

'And, hey, would you mind if I joined you again – just to watch . . . and admire?'

'Of course. Shall we say eleven o'clock?'

'Sounds good. What cheese?' Archie wondered.

'Can you get some Taleggio?' Aldrin asked.

Aldrin adored Taleggio, a semi-soft Italian cheese that smelled of yogurt and tasted like salty pizza crust.

'Shouldn't be any problem,' said Archie. 'I'll see you later then . . . NemeSwiss!'

29

POSITION FILLED

'Where have you been?' Belinda asked.

'I just had to, um, pop out for a minute,' Aldrin said.

'You've been gone twenty. We can't have you shirking. We're understaffed as it is.'

As Aldrin pulled on his apron, the door pinged and a woman walked in. She was around the same age as Doug and Belinda. She was wearing a white dress with a pink cardigan over it and had neat blonde hair and a pretty smile.

'Hello,' Doug said by way of greeting.

To everyone's considerable surprise, she responded in song:

'Hello! Is it Brie you're looking for?'

Doug laughed like it was the funniest thing he'd ever heard.

Belinda and Aldrin exchanged confused looks.

'It's a Lionel Richie song,' Doug explained. 'Except she's changed the word "me" to "Brie"!'

'I was told you enjoyed a pun,' the woman smiled, showing two rows of perfect white teeth. 'Cerys is the name. Cerys Filbey.'

'Welcome to *C'est Cheese*, Cerys Filbey!' Doug said, still chuckling. 'What can we get you?'

'I'm not here for cheese,' she said, her smile still on full beam. 'I'm enquiring about the job that's advertised in the window.'

'Position's been filled,' Belinda said.

'Filled?' asked Doug – it was clearly news to him.

'Yeah, that nice man who were in yesterday,' she said.

'What, the one who just got out of prison?' Doug asked.

'He did a good interview,' Belinda insisted.

'He also did ten years for armed robbery, Belinda.'

'There's none of us perfect,' Belinda told him.

'Cerys,' Doug said, 'what do you know about cheese?'

'Well,' she said, 'I know that burrata is absolutely

heavenly with soft peaches, olive oil and oregano. I know that Gorgonzola Dolce is creamy because it's aged for two months and Gorgonzola Piccante is crumbly because it's aged for six. I know that Gouda is a wonderful substitute for Gruyère and – heavens above – is that Hafod Cheddar I can smell because my mouth is positively *watering* here!'

Doug and Aldrin stared at her with their mouths agape.

'No,' Belinda said to Doug, 'she don't sound right for the job. Thanks for popping in, love – sorry you've wasted your time.'

'Are you kidding, Belinda?' Doug laughed. 'She's perfect. Cerys, how do you know so much about cheese?'

'I had my own shop for years,' she said. 'I don't know if you ever heard of *Cheezy Does It* in Cardiff?'

'What a wonderful name!' Doug exclaimed. 'When can you start?'

'I can start now if you like.' Cerys shrugged.

Aldrin handed her an apron. As she put it on, the door pinged and in walked Mrs Huskavarna from Apian Grove.

'I'm looking for some goat's cheese,' she said, looking from Belinda to Doug to Aldrin to Cerys.

'Goat's cheese,' Cerys said, offering Mrs Huskavarna a big, warm smile. 'Let's see what we have,' and she threw her eyes over the refrigerated display. 'Oh, the Selles-sur-Cher is absolutely divine! The grey-blue mould gives it a musty odour – can you smell that? It has a rigid bite, but it turns creamy in the mouth. It's a little bit salty with a persistent aftertaste.'

Aldrin, Doug and Belinda watched this performance in stunned silence.

'The other one I'd highly recommend,' Cerys continued, 'is the Sainte-Maure de Touraine, which also comes in a log. As you can see, this one is lightly dusted with ash, which helps in the maturing process, and it's usually at its peak between late April and early November, which means you're in luck! This one has a very clean, acidic taste with a slightly nutty finish. I'm going to let you try both and you can decide yourself.'

Out of the corner of her mouth, Belinda said, 'She'll not last a week. You mark my words.'

But Aldrin looked at Doug, who was visibly blushing, and one thing was immediately clear.

The man was smitten!

30

MAG! NIF! I! CENT!

'So what do you think of her?' Doug wanted to know.

'Who?' Aldrin asked.

It was ten o'clock that night and Aldrin was just about to go to bed with some Taleggio wrapped in greaseproof paper.

'Cerys, of course! What a first day!' Doug declared.

'Just be careful,' Aldrin warned. 'I think Belinda might be jealous.'

'Jealous?'

'Of Cerys. All those people telling you that she was just what the shop was missing.'

'They're absolutely right! Have you grown, by the way?'

'What?'

'You just seem, I don't know, taller. Or maybe your voice has broken. It definitely sounds deeper.'

'Does it?'

'Or maybe you just seem more confident or something. Yes, that's it. You're growing up, Aldrin. Anyway, it's getting late. I shall let you go to bed.

'*Sweet dreams* –'

'– are made of cheese,'

'*Who am I* –'

'– to diss a Brie?'

'Night, Aldrin.'

'Night, Dad.'

Aldrin went to his bedroom. He put the Taleggio on his bedside table, then he got down on his hands and knees and looked under his bed. He saw the walkie-talkie underneath, its battery still removed. He swept it aside with his hand and made a grab for the delivery box. He pulled it out and opened it.

He removed all the items and laid them out on the bed. He took off his clothes and stepped into the banana-coloured onesie. It fitted like he'd been measured for it by a tailor. He reached behind his back and he pulled up the zip. He stared at his reflection. Yellow was DEFINITELY his colour!

RRRIBBIT . . . RRRIBBIT . . . RRRIBBIT . . .

Aldrin liked to think it was a froggy compliment.

Next, he picked up the belt and fastened it round his waist.

Oh, yes, he thought. 'It's REALLY starting to come together now!'

He put the two boots down on the floor. Holding on to his bedside table for balance, he stepped into them – first the left one, then the right one.

And he suddenly felt at least two inches TALLER!

Next came the eye mask. He stretched the elastic over his head and pulled the material down over his eyes.

WOW! he thought.

He honestly wouldn't have recognized himself now!
RRRIBBIT . . . RRRIBBIT . . . RRRIBBIT . . .

'Don't worry, Silas!' he said. 'It's still me!'

He picked up the gloves and he pulled them on, stretching them right up to his elbow – first the left, then the right. He made a fist of his right hand and he drilled it into his left palm. He didn't know why. Maybe he'd seen Batman do it.

There was just one piece left . . .

The cape!

Aldrin picked it up off the bed, holding it delicately between his fingers. He noticed that his hands were trembling.

RRRIBBIT . . . RRRIBBIT . . . RRRIBBIT . . .

He threw the cape over his head and he felt the hem of it touch the back of his calves. He fastened the other end round his neck by pushing the two snap buttons together.

He stared and stared at his reflection until it felt like he wasn't seeing himself any more.

And he wasn't.

He was seeing . . . NemeSwiss!

And, even if he said so himself, he looked . . .

MAG! NIF! I! CENT!

He climbed into bed.

RRRIBBIT . . . RRRIBBIT . . . RRRIBBIT . . .

'Yes, night, Silas,' he said, then he reached for the cheese.

He unwrapped it and breathed in its delicious aroma. Then he bit into it – it felt smooth and sticky on his tongue – and he thought really, REALLY hard about a skyscraper and a Tyrannosaurus rex.

He chewed the Taleggio until it turned into a thick ball of yogurty, doughy goo in his mouth.

And *very quickly* . . .

without even realizing . . .

that it was happening . . .

his eyes started to feel . . .

very,

very

heavy . . .

And then . . .

he was suddenly . . .

out

for

the . . .

THE TYRANNOSAURUS REX NIGHTMARE

Aldrin found himself standing on a busy city street. It was quiet, except for the kind of sounds you'd usually associate with a busy city street – people talking on their mobile phones, buses zooming past, car horns honking.

He looked up. He was standing in front of a skyscraper – the same as the one he'd pictured just before he fell asleep. But there was no sign of any –

RRROOOAAAGGGHHH!!!

The noise was louder and more terrifying than anything he'd ever heard before!

And then he heard it again:

RRROOOAAAGGGHHH!!!

It set off a wave of screaming and shrieking as the normal street around him suddenly turned into . . . chaos!

People ran this way and that as the ground beneath their feet began to pound.

BOOOOOOMMMMMM!!!!!!
BOOOOOOMMMMMM!!!!!!
BOOOOOOMMMMMM!!!!!!

Then, at the end of the long avenue that stretched out in front of him, the thing hove into view – the biggest, the strongest, the most feared dinosaur of them all!

It was twenty feet tall and weighed eight tons – and it was heading his way!

RRROOOAAAGGGHHH!!!

Cars swerved to avoid the fearsome creature as it edged its way towards the oncoming traffic, snapping with its powerful jaws, tearing up the asphalt with the massive claws on its feet and flattening bus shelters, newspaper stands and hot-dog stalls with casual flicks of its long, powerful tail.

Aldrin gulped.

As it reached the skyscraper, the beast stopped, stood

up to its full height and began looking in the windows of the building. Then it tilted its head backwards and opened its enormous mouth, exposing a set of teeth, each of which was as sharp as a bread knife. It let loose another roar – and this one was truly blood-curdling:

RRROOOAAAGGGHHH!!!

Aldrin felt a hand on his shoulder. Then he heard a voice say:

'So what's the play this time?'

He turned his head. Archie was standing next to him.

'Archie!' Aldrin exclaimed. 'I don't know what to do! The thing is . . . **HUGE!**'

'It's a pretty big Tyrannosaurus rex,' Archie agreed. 'You'd better do something quickly, though. It looks like it's about to take a bite out of that skyscraper!'

'I need to get up there!' Aldrin said.

'Yes, you do!' Archie told him.

'But how?' Aldrin wondered. 'Should I go into the building and use the lift?'

Archie laughed.

'What's so funny?' Aldrin asked.

'Er, would Superman use the lift?' Archie said.

'No,' Aldrin replied, 'he'd probably . . . fly.'

'So? Fly!'

'But I *can't* fly.'

'Who told you you couldn't fly?'

'I just didn't think I was *that* kind of superhero.'

'Aldrin,' Archie said, squeezing Aldrin's shoulder, 'you can do anything! You're NemeSwiss!'

'But how do I even take off?'

'Hey, I'm sure you've seen as many superhero movies as I have.'

Aldrin raised his right hand and made a fist.

'Superman does something like this,' he said.

Then he bent his knees and straightened them again – and suddenly he took off – vertically, like a rocket ship bound for space!

'WHOOOAAAAAHHH!!!!!!' he screamed as he shot heavenwards, past the Tyrannosaurus rex's head, past the top of the skyscraper and through the clouds into the black, star-filled sky above.

'STOOOOOOPPPPPP!!!!!!' he roared. **'STOOOOOOPPPPPP!!!!!!'**

It took a few moments for him to figure out how to apply the brake. And, when he did, he found himself hovering high above the city, the

buildings looking like salt and pepper shakers below him.

'OK,' he told himself. 'Here goes!'

With his two arms stretched out in front of him, in the familiar Superman style, he dived downwards again.

Inside the skyscraper, the thousands of people who were at that moment experiencing the same nightmare were very soon transfixed by the sight of something very unexpected – a chubby, red-haired boy in some sort of superhero costume buzzing round the Tyrannosaurus rex like a really annoying bluebottle!

Aldrin flew round and round and round the dinosaur's head, saying in a mocking voice: 'Hey there, little one! Why so angry? It's not so bad! It's not so bad!'

The dinosaur was furious. It let out an angry roar:

RRROOOAAAGGGHHH!!!

It swatted at Aldrin with its arms – but a Tyrannosaurus rex's arms are very short, and Aldrin managed to remain teasingly out of range of the creature's efforts to knock him out of the sky.

'Why so mad?' Aldrin continued to taunt the beast.

'Hey, you're not so scary! All these people can see that now! You're not scary! You're like a big puppy dog, aren't you?'

The people inside the building cheered as they watched the dinosaur become more and more confused and agitated.

'Come on, puppy!' Aldrin laughed. 'You want to play, puppy? Let's play!'

In that moment, Aldrin may have grown a little too confident because what he failed to notice was the Tyrannosaurus rex's powerful tail whipping through the air towards him – and then . . .

WHAAACK!

. . . it caught him, sending him somersaulting backwards, like a fly struck mid-flight by a rolled-up newspaper, before . . .

BUUUMPF!

. . . he hit the ground!

He was dazed for moment. But his head cleared just in time for him to see the Tyrannosaurus rex standing over him, saliva spilling from the sides of its mouth and its hungry eyes trained on him.

'Nice doggy!' Aldrin said soothingly. 'Easy now!'

The creature opened its terrifying mouth and Aldrin rolled out of the way just as it snapped at him with its powerful jaws.

Aldrin got to his feet and he took off again, high into the clouds. On the other side of the city, in the distant docklands, he could see the outline of a giant crane. He flew off in that direction.

The people inside the building shouted, 'Where are you going?' and, 'Come back!'

Aldrin surprised himself at how quickly he managed to master the various aspects of flying – **turning, slowing, stopping** and **hovering**.

He reached the crane within a minute, gripped the giant metal arm of the thing and shook it violently until it snapped off.

It weighed more than a hundred tons – yet to Aldrin it felt no heavier than a badminton racquet!

He flew back to the Tyrannosaurus rex, who was once again striking terror into the people in the building.

'Hey, puppy!' Aldrin called out, showing it the metal arm. 'You want to play fetch? Will you fetch this if I throw it?'

The bloodthirsty beast was more than a little

irritated to have Aldrin back, **buzzing** round its head again, jabbing this giant metal stick at it, saying, 'If I throw it, will you bring it back? Will you bring it back, puppy dog?'

RRROOOAAAGGGHHH!!!

It swung its tail at Aldrin again – but this time it missed. And, in that moment, Aldrin had an idea.

Attached to the arm of the crane was a thick steel cable with a hook on the end. Aldrin detached it, then dropped the arm, which fell to the ground with a loud . . .

CLANK!

Momentarily distracted by the sound, the Tyrannosaurus rex failed to notice Aldrin fly up towards its face and start to wrap the cable round and round its long snout – wiring its jaw closed!

The creature flew into a rage! It started thrashing around, again attempting to use its powerful tail to swat this irritant away. But Aldrin dived down low, still holding the other end of the cable. He wound it round the creature's ankles, before flying clear.

The Tyrannosaurus rex tried to pursue him. But it couldn't move its legs. And its momentum caused it to come crashing down, face first . . .

BOOOOOOMMM!!!!!!

. . . on to the street.

The people inside the skyscraper cheered to see this prehistoric terror quite literally brought down to earth – by a boy in a superhero costume!

Aldrin hovered overhead for a moment until the creature gave up struggling and lay completely motionless.

Down below, Aldrin saw Archie giving him the thumbs-up sign. Aldrin returned to the ground. From the windows of the skyscraper, people called out:

'You saved our lives!'

And:

'Can we get a selfie with you?'

Aldrin made his way towards the once-feared monster, now trussed up like a Christmas turkey and whimpering like a hungry dog.

He patted its nose and spoke to it gently.

'There's a good dog!' he said. 'Now, are you going to let these nice people have a good night's sleep?'

Aldrin heard the sound of clapping and cheering coming from the building and the street around him.

'He's a hero!' the people shouted.

'What's your name?' a policewoman asked from the other side of the street.

'My name,' Aldrin said, placing his hands on his hips, 'is NemeSwiss!'

He lifted his chin in the air and felt his chest swell, while he continued to listen to the cheers and the applause of thousands and thousands of strangers who would never be frightened of a Tyrannosaurus rex ever again.

He noticed Archie across the street, saluting him.

A warm breeze blew and Aldrin felt his cape flutter behind him. It was the greatest feeling that Aldrin had ever known.

There was a little bit of him that didn't ever want to wake up. But then images of French cheeses began to flood his mind and soon he found himself blinking in the half-light of his bedroom.

32

FLASHBACK

It was an ordinary weekday morning and Maurice was sitting in the refrigerated van outside Cynthia's apartment.

'Morning,' said Cynthia, climbing into the front passenger seat. 'Are we ready to sell some cheese?'

'More than ready!' Maurice enthused.

Cynthia had her dream journal tucked safely under her arm.

'So,' Maurice said as he pulled out into the traffic, 'how did it go last night?'

'It all went to plan,' she told him. 'The poor little girl.'

'A monkey playing the cymbals, wasn't it?'

'I don't know why they have to make toys so scary.'

Cynthia opened her journal. 'Toys that come to life,' she said as she made the entry in her usual small and tidy hand. *'Des jouets qui prennent vie. Cinq onces de Pont l'Évêque et trois onces de Rosso di Lago.'*

'How's your head?' Maurice asked.

'It'll be a lot better after I eat this,' she replied, removing a ziplock bag containing four slices of Red Leicester from her briefcase.

They smiled at each other as they passed through Sloane Square.

Cynthia didn't regret telling Maurice her secret. He was not just her friend now – he had become her sidekick.

He was an additional pair of ears. He listened out for stories of people who suffered from recurring nightmares and he brought them to Cynthia's attention. For instance, the little girl who was terrorized nightly by the battery-powered monkey with the cymbals was his sister's goddaughter.

As well as providing her with material for her missions, Maurice offered Cynthia a supportive shoulder. She bounced ideas and theories off him. And, when she worried – as she often did – that she wasn't doing enough to thwart the work of Habeas Grusselvart,

Maurice reminded her that every nightmare she entered resulted in one more person being freed from his evil hold.

But, while he was being a friend to Cynthia, something else was happening. Maurice was falling in love with her. It had happened slowly over the course of the past year – in fact, almost from the very day she told him her secret.

There were many times when he was on the point of telling her how he felt. But his nerve always failed him. Until that morning.

They were driving along the Mall.

'Cynthia,' Maurice said out of the blue, 'I have something to tell you. It's something I've wanted to tell you for a long time.'

'Oh?' she replied.

He took a deep breath.

'I'm in love with you,' he said.

Cynthia remained quiet for a long moment.

'Morr-eece,' she said then in an apologetic tone, 'I'm very flattered, but –'

'You don't feel the same way,' he said.

'I'm sorry, Morr-eece,' she said, 'but no. And also –'

'What?' he snapped, feeling foolish for having

revealed his feelings. 'You're not going to tell me there's someone else?'

'Well, yes,' she said. 'His name is Doug.'

'Doug?' Maurice repeated. 'Who is he?'

'Please don't be like that,' she begged him. 'He's a buyer for a local supermarket chain in Norwich.'

'What?' said Maurice bitterly. 'And you actually *like* this supermarket buyer person?'

'Yes, I do,' she said. 'And he likes me. As a matter of fact, you might as well be the first to know –'

'Don't say it,' he told her, turning his head away.

'We're planning to set up a cheesemonger's together. In Tintwistle. Called ***C'est Cheese***.'

'I thought you were going to tell me you were getting married,' Maurice said.

'We might well,' she said, 'eventually.'

'How are you going to do this job *and* run a cheesemonger's?' Maurice asked.

'I'm not,' Cynthia revealed. 'I'm leaving Farlowe's, Morr-eece.'

'And what about us? What about our partnership?'

'Morr-eece,' she said, 'I'm really grateful for everything you've done for me.'

Maurice stopped the van.

'Please go,' he said quietly.

They were parked outside Charing Cross tube station.

'Morr-eece,' Cynthia said, attempting to reason with him, 'it doesn't mean that you and I can't be friends.'

'Please, Cynthia,' he said, turning his head away, unable to even look at her, 'just go.'

With her dream journal tucked under her arm, Cynthia climbed out of the van, shutting the door after her. Maurice drove away.

They never saw each other again.

Maurice never returned to work. He left the van in the car park of Farlowe's and walked away from the cheese business forever. Cynthia handed in her notice the following day, then moved to Tintwistle with Doug to open the cheesemonger's that was their pride and joy – at least until Aldrin came along.

Several months later, Maurice was back living in his mum and dad's spare room. Heartbroken, he slept all day and watched TV all night. And he began to feel the same sense of dread he had felt in his nightmares – the feeling of being completely alone in the world, which Cynthia had promised him he would never be.

And, just like the curds they once so lovingly tended

together, Maurice's feelings towards her turned more and more sour with every passing day.

Then, early one evening, just as he was coming downstairs for his dinner, there was a ring on the doorbell. Maurice answered the door. Standing there was a tall, powerfully built giant of a man, with a pale complexion, a wild mane of black curly hair, hooded eyes, a crooked nose, dark sideburns that ran down to his chin and a long black coat, which was buttoned right to his neck, with the collar standing up.

'*Eeew*,' the man said, screwing up his nose. 'You smell like bad Roquefort.'

'Who are you?' Maurice asked.

'You and I have a mutual acquaintance,' the man told him. 'I'm talking about Cynthia. She's been making quite a lot of trouble for me.'

Maurice's mouth fell open, exposing two rows of teeth that – much like the rest of him – hadn't been cleaned in months.

'Habeas?' he said. 'Habeas Grusselvart?'

'If your friend told you my name,' said Habeas, 'then she must have told you her secret. Am I right?'

'Yes,' said Maurice, 'except for the bit about her being my friend.'

Habeas already knew about their falling-out. He had a network of well-placed spies, and he made it his business to know what was going on in the private lives of a great many Cheese Whizzes.

'She's moved to Tintwistle,' Habeas said. 'Did you know that? With a man named Doug. They're running a ratty little cheesemonger's together.'

'I don't care what she does,' Maurice insisted.

'And they're engaged to be married.'

The news hit Maurice like a punch in the stomach.

'Must hurt,' Habeas said with mock sympathy, 'to have been cast aside like that. You were her sidekick, I assume? Or so she led you to believe. Did she confide in you? Rely on you for advice?'

'What do you want?' Maurice asked. 'Why are you here?'

'I want you to come and work for me.'

'Work – for *you*?'

'Why not? You don't look like you're snowed under with job offers.'

'But you're –'

'Evil?'

'Well, yes.'

'*Am* I, though? Or is that just something that Cynthia

and her kind like to put around? Let me tell you, Morr-eece, it's the Cheese Whizzes who are the *real* enemy. They want to control the world every bit as much as I do.'

'I'm sorry,' Maurice said, attempting to close the front door. But Habeas stuck one of his enormous size-twelve shoes in it.

'Morr-eece,' he said, 'I will fill that **BIG EMPTY HOLE** where your heart used to be. I will give you back your pride and your self-respect. I will give you a reason to get up every morning – and that reason will be to destroy Cynthia and her Cheese Whizz friends once and for all. Plus, the money is good. What do you say?'

Blinded by loneliness and jealousy, Maurice allowed himself to think about it. Having lost his job and the woman he loved, he had nothing left in the world.

'I'm offering you more than a job,' Habeas added. 'You will no longer be Morr-eece Mackle, the lovesick, unemployable wretch who smells of blue cheese. You will be **Beddy Byes**, my Personal Assistant and Vice President of Global Operations.'

'Beddy Byes?' asked Maurice.

'Yes,' Habeas answered. 'Do you like the name?'

For the first time in months, Maurice felt the corners of his mouth slowly turn into a smile.

'Yes,' he said, 'I do like it.'

'Good,' Habeas replied. 'Then allow me to say welcome to the firm!'

33

HUBRIS

There was something different about Aldrin the following day. Everyone at school noticed it. He walked the corridors with a brand-new confidence – you might even have called it a certain . . . **swagger**.

He helped Miss Wasser, one of the Maths teachers, to carry a heavy pile of books from her car to her office:

'Let me get that for you that, ma'am!' he said.

'Ma'am?' she replied.

He complimented Mr Fisher, the Geography teacher, on his new thornproof jacket:

'You're really rocking that tweed, Fisher!'

'Oh, um, thank you,' the teacher said.

He even attempted to introduce himself to Julie

Pertwee – the prettiest and coolest girl in the whole school.

'Aldrin Adams,' he said, sticking out his hand.

'I've seen you in the cafeteria,' she replied, looking him up and down. 'You sit at the table next to the toilets – with the other oddballs.'

Yes, Aldrin was absolutely **FULL** of himself. And not without reason. Because that morning, while he was getting dressed for school, he'd decided to wear his NemeSwiss suit **UNDERNEATH** his school uniform!

Well, he reasoned, Clark Kent always wore *his* superhero suit under his regular clothes. And, even though Aldrin's superpowers only worked in the world of dreams, he just **LOVED** the way the suit made him feel.

As a matter of fact, he'd gone to the toilets three times between classes that morning, just to undo his shirt buttons and take a peek at the NemeSwiss badge on his chest. Naturally, what he **REALLY** wanted to do was tear open his shirt the way Clark Kent did when he was turning into Superman. But he didn't want to give away his secret.

'Is there something . . . *different* about you?' Harry

asked him that lunchtime in the cafeteria.

Aldrin was munching on a piece of Queso Ibores.

'Different?' Aldrin replied modestly. 'In what way?'

'I don't know,' Harry said, 'you seem . . . *taller* or something.'

'Here, where's Sisely?' Frankie wondered. 'Isn't she having lunch with us today?'

She was back at school that morning with no explanation for her absence on Friday.

'She said she had to talk to Mrs Van Boxtel,' Harry said.

'What's that about?' Frankie asked Aldrin.

'I've no idea,' Aldrin answered.

'Hey,' Harry said, 'do you want to see the cover for the second issue of *The Oddballs*?'

'Sure,' Aldrin said.

Harry produced a piece of paper from his school bag and Aldrin cast his eyes over it. It was a picture of NemeSwiss . . . winking, while holding up a car with just his index finger! And alongside it was the headline:

NemeSwiss Has His Moment of Hubris!

'What does that word mean?' Aldrin asked.

'What, hubris?' Harry said. 'It means pride.'

'Nice,' said Aldrin.

'No, but not in a good way,' Frankie cut in. 'It's more arrogance than pride.'

'Exactly,' said Harry. 'Most superheroes have a **"Moment of Hubris"**, where their power goes to their head.'

'What, like they get carried away with themselves?' Aldrin asked.

'Exactly,' said Frankie. 'Because they can fly, or spin webs, or go invisible, they start to believe that they are better than everyone else. But what they forget is that they still *need* mere mortals to survive in the world.'

Aldrin made a mental note that he would have to avoid that particular fate. But, in the meantime, he thought he'd go and have another peek at his NemeSwiss suit.

'I'm, um, just popping to the loo,' he told his friends.

'What, again?' asked Frankie. 'That's about the fifth time today.'

'Stomach's a bit upset,' Aldrin lied. 'Back in a minute, dudes.'

As Aldrin walked away, he heard Harry say:

'Did he just call us . . . dudes?'

As Aldrin crossed the floor of the cafeteria, he spotted Sisely coming towards him. He'd been avoiding her all morning, but now it would have been too awkward *not* to talk to her.

'Sisely,' he said breezily. 'How goes it?'

'How *goes* it?' she repeated. 'What's going on with you? Everyone's saying you winked at Julie Pertwee this morning.'

'Hey, I was just being friendly.'

'And you high-fived Mr Fisher.'

Yes, along with the compliment about his new thornproof jacket, Aldrin had indeed invited him to 'hang five'.

'I just felt the moment called for it,' Aldrin said. 'I thought he looked kind of smart.'

'You've changed, Aldrin.'

'Why, thank you, ma'am.'

'I didn't *mean* it as a compliment. Mrs Van Boxtel said she gave you a mission on Friday.'

'Yeah, a seagull nightmare – yawn!'

'Did you do it?'

'I tried. Something went wrong. I was going to have another go on Saturday, but –'

'But what?'

'Something better came up.'

'And what about the girl lost in a crowded shopping

239

centre who can't find her mother?' she asked.

'Hey, I'm a busy man,' Aldrin told her. 'I'm sure I'll get around to everyone eventually.'

Sisely stared at him. This wasn't the kind, thoughtful boy she had once thought of as her best friend.

'Why aren't you answering your walkie-talkie?' she asked.

'I took the battery out,' he said.

'Why?'

'Because you lied to me, Sisely.'

'I didn't lie to you,' she insisted.

'Well, you didn't tell me the complete truth,' he reminded her. 'My mum said in her dream journal that I was The One and you decided to keep that from me.'

'Mrs Van Boxtel thought you were too **young** and too **immature** to be told!' she said. 'And she was right!'

The words **bounced** off Aldrin like bullets off an invisible shield.

'Except I'm not *just* The One,' he said, 'am I, Sisely?'

'What are you talking about?' she asked.

Aldrin leaned closer to her. In his most dramatic voice, he whispered: 'I'M NEMESWISS!'

Sisely screwed up her face in confusion.

'You're *what*?' she asked.

'Yeah, don't pretend you don't know,' he told her. 'You've read my mum's journal from cover to cover.'

'There's nothing in it about any NemeSwiss,' she said.

'It's my superhero identity.'

'Aldrin, you're *not* a superhero.'

'Oh, yes I am – even though you tried to keep it from me. But Archie told me everything.'

'Who's Archie?'

'Archie is my friend. A *real* friend. He showed me how I can help thousands of people at the same time, instead of one person per fortnight. I've saved people from ants the size of elephants, Sisely. I saved people from a Tyrannosaurus rex.'

'I don't understand any of this,' Sisely told him.

'Of course you don't!' Aldrin snapped at her. 'Because *you're* not a Cheese Whizz!'

Sisely stared at Aldrin. There was something about his body language – the way he stood, with his chest puffed out and his hands on his hips – that made her do what she did next.

She took hold of his school shirt with both hands and she ripped it open, sending the buttons skittering across the cafeteria floor.

She saw the suit. And she saw the NemeSwiss logo in the centre of his chest. And all she could do was shake her head and say:

'Aldrin Adams – what have you become?'

34

'IT'S MINE! AND I WANT IT BACK!'

Aldrin was still fuming about it later that afternoon when he went to the skatepark to meet Archie.

'What have *I* become?' he said. 'I can't believe that *she* asked *me* that! She actually ripped my shirt.'

'She WHAT?' Archie asked, picking up his skateboard.

'She tore the buttons off it!' Aldrin told him. '*And* I was wearing my NemeSwiss suit underneath!'

'You wore your NemeSwiss suit under your school uniform?' Archie laughed. 'Did anyone see it?'

'One or two people,' said Aldrin. 'Luckily, they just thought I'd forgotten to take off my pyjamas. Most people think I'm a weirdo anyway.'

'All superheroes are weirdos,' Archie reminded him, removing his helmet at the same time. 'We can't change who we are, dude. But just think about all those people whose lives you saved from that Tyrannosaurus rex last night!'

'I didn't *really* save their lives,' Aldrin pointed out.

'Hey, I saw you, standing there with your chin in the air and your two hands on your waist and your cape billowing in the wind. You *loved* how it made you feel.'

'I suppose I did.'

'Like a proper superhero, right?'

'Exactly,' Aldrin said. 'I just wish that Sisely and Mrs Van Boxtel could be happy for me.'

'Look,' Archie said, 'I've been holding off saying this, but the girl and the old lady are **jealous** of you, dude.'

'Do you think *that's* why they're trying to hold me back?'

'Even when the old lady was younger, she could only dream of having the kind of abilities you possess. You were born to defeat Habeas Grusselvart and bring to an end five centuries of fear and misery. That must be hard for her to get her head round.'

'But why would Sisely be jealous?'

'Because you're leaving her behind. It's already happening, dude. She can see that you don't need her any more.'

'Well, I sort of *do* need her,' Aldrin pointed out, 'because she has my mum's –'

And Aldrin suddenly stopped mid-sentence.

'What is it?' Archie asked.

'My mum left *me* her dream journal,' Aldrin said. 'Who are they to decide what I should and shouldn't be told?'

'I suppose when you put it like that . . .' Archie agreed.

'I mean, how DARE they?' Aldrin said, the anger rising in him. 'It's *my* dream journal!'

Aldrin turned on his heel. In his fury, he talked himself into a course of action.

'I'm going to tell her I want it back!' he said.

He stormed out of the skatepark and stomped angrily up Burnett Road in the direction of Sisely's house, Archie following at a distance.

Moments later, Aldrin was pressing the doorbell. Sisely's mum opened the door.

'Hello, Mrs Musa,' said Aldrin.

'Hello, Aldrin!' Mrs Musa replied. 'We haven't seen you for a while!'

'No,' Aldrin agreed. 'Is, um, Sisely home?'

'Just a second,' said Mrs Musa, then she called up the stairs:

'Sisely, Aldrin is here to see you!'

A moment later, Sisely came downstairs.

'I want my mum's dream journal,' Aldrin told her bluntly.

'What?' Sisely said. 'Why?'

'Because I don't trust you any more,' he told her.

'Maybe we should wait and talk to Mrs Van Boxtel,' Sisely suggested.

'I don't want to wait!' he told her. 'It's not her book! And it's not your book either! **It's mine! And I want it back!** NOW!'

Sisely's eyes began to water. She stomped up the stairs and returned a minute later with Cynthia's dream journal in her hand. She couldn't even bring herself to look at Aldrin as she handed it over. And, once she did, she slammed the door in his face.

Aldrin tucked the dream journal under his arm, turned round and walked back up the road to where Archie was waiting for him.

Archie spotted the large ledger-style book under Aldrin's arm, with all the multicoloured Post-it notes peeking out from between its pages.

'That must have been hard for you,' he sympathized.

'It was,' Aldrin agreed. 'But she's been stopping me from fulfilling my destiny.'

Archie smiled sadly like he understood. Aldrin found it so easy to talk to him.

'Hey, I want to do another mission tonight,' Aldrin said.

'What about that old dude again who's having his chips stolen by seagulls?' Archie asked.

'Nah,' Aldrin laughed. 'I think my days of shooing away seagulls are well and truly over!'

'Hey, have you ever experienced an earthquake before?' Archie asked.

'An earthquake?' Aldrin replied. 'No!'

'Do you know how many people have nightmares where the ground is opening beneath their feet and their homes and cars and families are disappearing into the cracks?'

'No. Many?'

'Hundreds of thousands, dude! Millions even!'

'OK, let's do that tonight. Eleven o'clock again?'

'Eleven o'clock. What cheese?'

'Let's try some Havarti this time,' Aldrin suggested.

'Havarti,' said Archie. '*C'est bon. À bientôt, mon ami.*'

'Wait a minute,' Aldrin said. 'Do you speak French?'

Archie shrugged. '*Un petit peu.*'

'Is that French for "yes"?' Aldrin asked.

'No,' Archie said, 'it's French for "a little bit". I studied it at school.'

This was just TOO perfect!

'Archie,' Aldrin said, 'will you look after my mum's dream journal?'

'Me?' Archie asked, half laughing. 'I don't think so, Aldrin.'

'Please!'

'Look, maybe you should talk to Mrs Van Boxtel about all of this.'

'I don't NEED to talk to Mrs Van Boxtel. You can read it and tell me what other secrets are in it! Please, Archie! You're the only one I can trust.'

Archie thought about it for a moment, then he sighed. 'OK, I'll look after it – but only until you patch things up with Sisely.'

'Havarti,' Aldrin reminded him. 'And think about

a piece of ground cracking under people's feet.'

'Aren't you forgetting something?' Archie said, nodding at the book, which was still in Aldrin's hands.

'Sorry,' Aldrin said. 'Almost forgot.'

And then he handed Archie his mother's dream journal.

35

SCREAMS

Agatha Rees-Lane was back.

'What did you say *this* one was called?' she asked.

'That's the Castelrosso,' Cerys replied pleasantly.

'Could I try some more?' she asked, helping herself to a second piece.

'Of course,' said Cerys. 'We offer unlimited free samples.'

'Unlimited!' Agatha said, skewering Belinda with a sharp look. 'Did you hear that?'

Belinda was **FURIOUS**. 'Why don't you just pull up a seat,' she said sarcastically, 'and have your flipping tea?'

'Don't mind if I do,' said Agatha, taking the chair that Aldrin used to reach the higher shelves and plonking herself down at the counter. 'Now, Cerys, tell me about the Castelrosso again.'

'Well, it smells like lobster butter,' said Cerys, 'with a slight twist of lemon.'

'Yes, it does!' said Agatha, holding it beneath her nose. 'I'm definitely getting that,' she added before stuffing it into her mouth.

'The first bite teases with the promise of sourness,' Cerys continued, 'but the flavour is of sautéed mushrooms with clotted cream. It's a cheese that manages to be at once rich and deep, but also light and delicate.'

Doug was staring at Cerys, all **starry-eyed** again.

'Hey,' said Belinda, giving him a nudge. 'Close your mouth, you.'

'I can't help it,' Doug said. 'She knows more about cheese than anyone I've met since . . .' and he stopped mid-sentence.

'Since who?' Belinda asked.

'Er, no one,' said Doug, snatching a guilty look at Aldrin.

'Oh,' said Cerys, suddenly thinking of something. 'I'd love you to try the fontina. It's mushroomy, but with a spicy fruit finish.'

Cerys disappeared into the storeroom to fetch it.

'I like her!' Agatha said.

'Yes,' Doug agreed, 'she's working out very well.'

'She doesn't try to rush you into making a choice,' Agatha added, 'like some others I *could* mention. Although I have to admit I'm not sure I want anything now. I'm rather full.'

'We'll be out of business in a flipping week,' Belinda predicted.

Suddenly, from out of the storeroom, came a series of loud, piercing shrieks:

'Aaarrrggghhh!!!
Aaaarrrrgggghhhh!!!!
AAAARRRRGHGGHHHH!!!'

'What's up with Mary flipping Poppins?' Belinda asked.

Doug ran to the storeroom to investigate, followed closely by Aldrin and Belinda, while Agatha used the distraction to help herself to a piece of the Puits d'Astier.

Cerys was standing up on a chair with a look of panic on her face. She was hysterical.

'AAAARRRRGHGGHHHH!!!'

'What's wrong?' Aldrin asked.

'THERE'S A FROG!' she screamed. **'OVER**

THERE – BEHIND THAT COOLER BOX!'

'A frog?' Belinda chuckled. 'That'll be Silas.'

Aldrin pulled out the cooler box and retrieved him.

'Sorry,' Aldrin told her. 'I must have left my bedroom door open. He likes to go on little adventures. Once, he jumped into my schoolbag and came to school with me!'

'KEEP HIM AWAY FROM ME!' Cerys shouted.

'It's just Aldrin's pet frog,' Doug tried to explain.

'I CAN'T ABIDE REPTILES!' she cried.

'Frogs are actually amphibians!' Aldrin said, holding Silas up to let her see that he was really quite harmless.

'PLEASE!' she said. 'I'M PHOBIC ABOUT ALL LITTLE GREEN THINGS!'

Doug turned to Aldrin. 'Try to keep your bedroom door closed in future,' he told him.

Aldrin noticed that Belinda was attempting to stifle a giggle.

'Imagine being frightened of a little frog,' she chuckled. 'It turns out she's not so perfect after all.'

Doug was angry with Belinda. 'It's no laughing matter!' he told her crossly. 'Can't you see that Cynthia is upset?'

The words were out of his mouth before he realized what he'd said. But Aldrin heard it. And Cerys heard it. And Belinda most certainly heard it because she was staring at Doug with her mouth hanging open.

'It's, um, Cerys,' said Cerys from on top of the chair.

'Yes, that's what I said,' Doug replied.

'No,' said Belinda. 'You called her Cynthia.'

Doug looked at Aldrin, who confirmed it with a sad nod.

'Belinda,' Doug said, 'I didn't mean –'

But Belinda wasn't of a mind to listen. Tearfully, she tore off her apron and threw it on the ground. Then she ran out of the storeroom, out of *C'est Cheese* and up Burnett Road.

A horrible silence fell on the shop, broken only by the sound of Agatha's voice, asking, 'Are you going to bring me that cheese you mentioned with the spicy fruit finish?'

THE BIG CHEESE

Aldrin got down on all fours and felt around under the bed for the box. He pulled it out and lifted the lid.

RRRIBBIT ... RRRIBBIT ... RRRIBBIT ...

Silas seemed almost as excited as he was!

He removed all the items from the box and laid them out on the bed. He changed out of his pyjamas and dressing gown and into the banana-coloured onesie with the black dots on it. He reached round and zipped it up at the back.

He picked up the red belt and he pulled it round his waist, buckling it at the front.

He put the two red boots down on the floor and he stepped into them – right foot, then left foot.

He picked up the red eye mask, pulled the elastic

round his head and correctly positioned the eyeholes at the front.

RRRIBBIT . . . RRRIBBIT . . . RRRIBBIT . . .

Then he picked up the red gloves and he pulled them on – right hand, then left hand – and he pulled them all the way up to his elbows.

And, finally – the *pièce de résistance*. He swung the red cape round his shoulders and fastened the stud buttons at the front.

He made his way over to the full-length mirror and took a long, admiring look at himself.

RRRIBBIT . . . RRRIBBIT . . . RRRIBBIT . . .

He tried out various superhero stances that he remembered from the posters on Harry's bedroom wall.

First, he put his hands on his hips. It was the same pose he'd struck after defeating the mighty Tyrannosaurus rex. No doubt about it – it was a good one.

Then he folded his arms, making his biceps look big, like he'd seen many superheroes do. He LOVED how it looked!

Then he made a fist and stretched his arm into the air, like he was about to take off! *Wow!?*, he thought.

He REALLY looked the part.

He started to hear a movie trailer voiceover in his head:

'*He's an ordinary boy with an extraordinary superpower – and only HE can save the world! Habeas Grusselvart and the forces of evil don't stand a chance against . . .*'

'WHAT ON EARTH ARE YOU WEARING?'

Aldrin's blood turned cold. He spun round. Doug was standing in the doorway of his bedroom.

'Wh-wh-what?' Aldrin stuttered.

RRRIBBIT . . . RRRIBBIT . . . RRRIBBIT . . .

'The costume!' Doug said. 'Where did it come from?'

'Oh, it's, um, my Halloween costume,' Aldrin said nervously.

'Halloween?' Doug repeated. 'Aldrin, it's May! Although I suppose it makes sense not to leave it until the last minute.'

RRRIBBIT . . . RRRIBBIT . . . RRRIBBIT . . .

'Hello, Silas,' Doug said. 'I wonder, does he have any idea how much trouble he caused today?'

'Did you manage to speak to Belinda?' Aldrin asked.

'I tried her mobile,' Doug told him, 'and then I called at her flat. She wasn't home. It was just a slip of the tongue, Aldrin.'

'I know, but she was very hurt, Dad.'

'Well, I'll wait until she calms down and apologize to her then. Who are you supposed to be?'

'Excuse me?' Aldrin asked.

'Well, I know you're not Spider-Man,' Doug said, 'because Spider-Man's costume is red! And I know you're not Superman because he wears blue! I'm trying to think of a superhero who dresses in yellow. What are those big dots, by the way?'

'Those are holes,' Aldrin explained. 'It's supposed to look like –'

'Emmental!' Doug exclaimed.

'That's right,' Aldrin told him.

'I know who you are now!' Doug announced triumphantly. 'You're . . . the Big Cheese!'

RRRIbbit . . . rrrIBBIT . . . RRRIbbIT . . .

'That's exactly who I am!' Aldrin said.

'Well, people are going to LOVE the costume,'

Doug assured him, 'although it's possible you'll have grown out of it by the time Halloween comes around – especially if you keep on eating cheese at that rate!'

Doug nodded to indicate the small hill of Havarti on Aldrin's bedside table.

'**Sweet dreams** –' Doug said.

'**– are made of cheese,**' Aldrin smiled.

'**Who am I** –'

'**– to diss a Brie?**'

'Night, son.'

'Night, Dad.'

Doug left, closing Aldrin's bedroom door on the way. Aldrin looked at Silas and breathed a sigh of relief:

'Phhhhhheeeeeeeeeeeewwwwww!!!!!!'

RRRIBBIT . . . RRRIBBIT . . . RRRIBBIT . . .

'OK, Silas,' Aldrin said, climbing into bed, 'I'm going to need you to pipe down now. Because tonight I have a mission – to save thousands, maybe even millions, of people . . . from an EARTHQUAKE!!!'

RRRIBBIT . . . RRRIBBIT . . . RRRIBBIT . . .

'Yes, Silas, I'll be careful,' Aldrin promised him. 'Goodnight, little friend.'

The Havarti smelled delicious. But then it always did to Aldrin. It was creamy yellow in colour and soft in texture and it tasted of butter and salt and walnuts.

Aldrin closed his eyes and thought about a crack appearing in a piece of dusty ground. He bit into the cheese and thought about the crack lengthening, then growing wider, until he saw the earth beneath his feet split in two. He popped the rest of the Havarti into his mouth and he chewed and chewed until it turned into a mass of salty, buttery, walnutty slop.

And *very quickly* . . .

without even realizing . . .

that it was happening . . .

his eyes **started to feel** . . .

very,

very

heavy . . .

And then . . .

he was suddenly . . .

out

for

the . . .

37

THE EARTHQUAKE NIGHTMARE

Aldrin found himself walking along a busy city street. Passers-by smiled at him in a friendly way, while others nudged each other and pointed at the boy in the yellow superhero costume zigzagging his way through the crowd.

'Hello, sir!' Aldrin said, ever the polite superhero. 'Good morning, ma'am!'

He spotted Archie sitting on a fire hydrant, reading his mum's dream journal.

'What's happening?' Archie said.

'Nothing yet,' Aldrin replied.

'Except that people are recognizing you. They're pointing you out – look!.'

'That's because I'm a boy wearing a superhero

costume and a cape,' Aldrin reminded him. 'They don't even know that I'm **NEMESWISS.**'

'They will soon,' Archie assured him. 'They DEFINITELY will soon.'

Aldrin heard the sound of whistling then – screechy, tuneless whistling. He looked around and noticed a sign swinging backwards and forwards on a rusty chain. A dark feeling of foreboding came over him.

'This is it,' Archie said, standing up. 'Are you ready?'

'NemeSwiss was BORN ready!' Aldrin told him – and it sounded even better on his lips than it had in his head.

He heard thunder then. Except it didn't come from above their heads. It came from below their feet.

People stopped walking and exchanged frightened looks. And that was when the ground began to SHAKE!

There were screams:

'AAARRRGGGHHH!!!'

There was a deafening **rumble**, followed by a terrifying **splitting** sound – and suddenly the ground opened up like a zip!

Aldrin watched in horror as the giant crack swallowed one car, then a second, then a third.

And THAT was his call to action!

He raised his fist. In a single leap, he was airborne. He looked down and he could see the cars wedged in the crack in the earth like toy cars stuck between sofa cushions.

He dived head first into the ravine and went straight to the first car. It was stuck fast between two rocks. Aldrin grabbed hold of the handle of the passenger door and tore it off.

There was a man sitting in the front passenger seat, bleeding from a cut on his forehead. He saw Aldrin leaning into the car, unfastening his seat belt for him.

'What's happening?' the man asked.

'You're having a nightmare,' Aldrin told him.

'Yes,' the man replied, like it was the most obvious thing in the world. 'But who are you?'

'I,' Aldrin said, pausing for dramatic effect, 'am NemeSwiss.'

'NemeSwiss?' the man asked. 'Surely you mean Nemesis?'

'No, it's *like* Nemesis,' Aldrin tried to explain, 'but with Swiss on the end.'

He grabbed the man by the scruff of his jacket, dragged him through the passenger door and took off with him in his arms. He flew out of the crack and deposited him on the pavement.

'I *get* it now!' the man said as his feet landed on solid ground. 'It's because your costume looks like Swiss cheese!'

'It's not a costume,' Aldrin corrected him. 'It's a suit.'

Then he ran and dived head first into the crack again. He reached the second car. He gripped the handle of the passenger door and tore it from its hinges. There was a cross-looking woman sitting in the driver's seat.

'I'm not leaving my car!' the woman insisted. 'It's brand new!'

'Talk to your insurance company!' Aldrin told her.

The earth roared again and the car shifted. The woman changed her mind. She unfastened her seat belt and accepted Aldrin's hand. Aldrin threw her over his shoulder in a classic fireman's lift and flew her to safety.

He jumped head first into the crack in the earth one last time to free the driver of the third car. But, when he tore open the door, there was a surprise awaiting him . . .

There was an entire family sitting in the car. A mum and dad in the two front seats, and their young son and daughter in the back with their pet whippet sitting between them.

'Who are you?' the mum asked.

'Look,' Aldrin explained, 'I don't have time to do the whole introduction thing every time I save someone tonight. One of you is having a nightmare and I'm here to rescue you. It's just the one, two, three, four of you, is it?'

'And Declan,' the dad added. 'The whippet.'

'Declan the whippet,' Aldrin repeated. 'Right.'

The earth shook again and the car lurched. The children in the back screamed:

'AAARRRGGGHHH!!!'

And Declan barked:

ROFF-ROFF! ROFF-ROFF-ROFF!

'OK,' Aldrin said, 'if I put your son on one shoulder and your daughter on the other, you and your wife could hold on to a leg each.'

'But what about Declan?' cried the boy.

'OK, just let me think,' replied Aldrin.

The ground lurched again. The crack widened and Aldrin watched in horror as the car slipped and disappeared into the hole in the earth.

'NOOOOOO!!!!!!' Aldrin screamed, then he shot down after it.

He managed to get himself underneath it. He put his hands above his head and stopped it from falling. Then he started flying upwards towards the surface of the earth again, holding the car, with its family of four and Declan the dog, above his head.

When he emerged from the giant rupture in the road, something had changed. As a matter of fact, a lot had changed. The city was a scene of devastation. It looked like it had been hit by a bomb. But there were no people around!

The streets . . . were deserted.

Aldrin – still holding the car above his head – hung in the air, looking around him, wondering where everyone had disappeared to. But it was when he looked up that he got the biggest shock of all.

The car . . .

. . . had GONE!

Aldrin looked down into the crack in the earth. Had he somehow dropped it?

That was when the lights went out. Daytime turned to night-time as if with the flicking of a switch. And, in the darkness, Aldrin heard laughter – **cruel, mocking laughter**, from somewhere overhead:

'MWAH-HA-HA-HA-HA-HA-HA!'

Aldrin knew that laugh. He would recognize it ANYWHERE!

Just then, a giant digital billboard lit up in front of him. And Aldrin found himself staring at the loathsomely smiling face . . .

. . . of HABEAS GRUSSELVART!!!

'Hello, Aldrin!' he said. 'Love the costume!'

'IT'S NOT A COSTUME!' Aldrin replied angrily. 'IT'S A SUPERHERO SUIT!'

This Habeas seemed to find very funny indeed because he laughed about it for almost a full minute:

'MWAH-HA-HA-HA-HA-HA-HA!
MWAH-HA-HA-HA-HA-HA-HA!
MWAH-HA-HA-HA-HA-HA-HA!'

He laughed until the tears were spilling down his face. Then he said:

'It's a *costume*, Aldrin! I should know – I had it made for you!'

'What?' Aldrin asked, confused.

'I know the original design was yours,' said Habeas, 'but I gave it to the Art Department here and they ran the whole thing up in a day.'

'YOU'RE WRONG!' Aldrin shouted. 'THIS SUIT

WAS A GIFT – FROM MY FRIEND, WHO'S A CHEESE WHIZZ LIKE ME!'

'You don't by any chance mean . . . Archie?' asked Habeas.

'YES, ARCHIE!' Aldrin answered.

'Archie works for ME!' said Habeas.

Aldrin's mouth dropped open as he watched the young man he *thought* was his friend step into the picture, grinning from ear to ear.

'Archie?' Aldrin said. 'What's going on?'

Archie put his hand to his head and tore off his floppy, blond, surfer-style hair. Aldrin couldn't believe his eyes. It was a wig! Underneath, Archie's real hair was dark and curly.

'His *real* name,' Habeas said triumphantly, 'is Ethan Marcus.'

'But you're a Cheese Whizz,' Aldrin reminded the young man in whom he'd confided so much. 'Why would you betray the order like this?'

Habeas laughed.

'He's not a Cheese Whizz!' he said. 'He's a computer programmer!'

Aldrin felt the anger welling up in him until it almost overwhelmed him. He extended his right fist and attempted to fly, but he found that he couldn't move. He was suspended in mid-air, high above the giant crack in the earth.

'You're not in control,' Habeas told him. 'Just like the time you saved all those people from that army of giant ants and the Tyrannosaurus rex.'

'You mean . . . those weren't real nightmares?' Aldrin asked, feeling crushed to the point of tears.

'I programmed the whole thing!' Ethan cackled. 'And you fell for it!'

'Why would you *do* this to me?' Aldrin asked. 'What did I *ever* do to you?'

'You ruined my video game!' Ethan told him. 'By showing a little girl how to defeat Valdor the Remorseless and his Giant Raptor Birds!'

'That was *you*?' Aldrin asked. 'You *created* that nightmare?'

'Yeah, and you destroyed it,' Ethan said accusingly,

'and you nearly got me the sack!'

Enraged, Aldrin again attempted to fly, but he remained frozen in the air.

'You're not still trying to fly, are you?' asked Habeas. 'Come, come, if you *really* had those kind of powers, don't you think that Nel Van Boxtel would have mentioned it to you? Or the Sisely girl? Surely Cynthia would have said something about it . . . in her diary.'

The full consequences of the betrayal struck Aldrin for the first time as Habeas held up his mum's dream journal.

'NOOO!!!' Aldrin screamed. **'NOOOO!!!!!'**

'I'm afraid so, Aldrin,' Habeas smiled. 'It seems I overestimated you. You handed it over far more willingly than I thought you would. And now *I* am the keeper of your mother's secrets.'

'GIVE IT BACK!' Aldrin roared. **'MY MUM LEFT IT TO ME!'**

'Let's see how you get on without it,' Habeas said, 'shall we?'

'GIVE ME BACK MY DREAM JOURNAL!' Aldrin screamed. **'GIVE ME BACK MY DREAM JOURNAL!'**

'You know, I'm becoming a little tired of your

whiny voice,' said Habeas. 'It's starting to, erm, *grate* on me! Forgive me – I know how much you and your dad love a cheese pun! I shall say goodbye and good riddance to you.'

Habeas nodded at Ethan, who pressed a button in front of him.

Suddenly, Aldrin felt himself falling through the air towards the ground, then through the crack in the earth, until he felt something hard hit his back.

He sat up quickly and realized that he was back in his bedroom. He had no cheese hangover. Of course he didn't. As Habeas said, it was just a computer simulation. But Aldrin felt a different kind of sickness – a feeling of loss that he hadn't experienced since his mum died. Through his stupid pride and his refusal to listen to the people who cared about him, he had blown his chance to save the world from fear and misery . . . and the hideous Habeas Grusselvart.

38

'DIVIDE AND CONQUER'

Beddy Byes grimaced. He looked down at the giant snow-boot cast that encased his broken ankle. He was in quite a lot of pain tonight.

He checked the time. It was after midnight and he decided to call it a day. His crutches were leaning against the side of the desk. He picked them up and used them to lever himself into an upright position, then hobbled his way out of the office and along the corridor.

He could hear laughter. It was coming from the computer room:

'MWAH-HA-HA-HA-HA-HA-HA!'

The door was slightly ajar and he stared through the narrow crack. Habeas and Ethan were sitting in two leather chairs in front of a giant computer screen. Ethan was wearing a large metal helmet that had wires protruding from every direction.

'*But you're a Cheese Whizz,*' he was saying in a mocking voice. '*Why would you betray the order like this?*'

Habeas laughed even harder:

'MWAH-HA-HA-HA-HA-HA-HA!'

'Did you see his face,' Habeas asked, 'when I told him where the costume had come from?'

'Priceless,' Ethan agreed. 'I still can't believe he fell for it.'

Fell for it? Beddy Byes thought. *Of course!* That day when he'd walked into Habeas's office and seen the Adams boy saving all those people from those giant ants! Beddy Byes *knew* it wasn't possible! Cheese Whizzes could enter only one person's dream state at a time. So Ethan must have used a computer simulation to trick him into thinking he was some kind of superhero who could save thousands of people.

It was brilliant, Beddy Byes had to admit.

'He was The One!' Habeas smiled. 'The One I've feared for centuries! You know, I almost feel *disappointed* at how easy it was to beat him!'

'What an idiot,' Ethan said.

'Yes,' Habeas chuckled. 'Whatever else he might have inherited from his mother, he certainly didn't get her brains.'

For a brief moment, the reference to Cynthia stirred up the sediment of long-forgotten feelings in Beddy Byes. He quickly banished them.

'The girl was obviously the brains of the outfit,' Ethan suggested.

'Oh, Sisely was a smart one all right,' Habeas concurred. 'That's why it was important to separate them. **Divide and conquer**, Ethan. That's the key to wiping out the Cheese Whizzes.'

There was a moment of silence then. Beddy Byes was just about to move away from the door when he heard Ethan say:

'I have something to tell you. Something I should have told you when I first came to work here.'

'Oh?' Habeas said.

'I really *am* a Cheese Whizz,' Ethan told him. 'Or at least I *should* have been.'

'Ah,' said Habeas, 'it's all beginning to make sense now. You mentioned that you had an informant inside the order.'

'My mother was a Cheese Whizz.'

'I see.'

'But even though I'm her first-born son –'

'You didn't inherit.'

'No, I didn't.'

'Because you were considered . . . unworthy.'

'Yes. And my mother was stripped of her abilities – because she wasn't pure of heart or intention.'

'You see, people say that like it's a bad thing! When you applied for a job here, you *knew* we weren't in the fish-packaging business, didn't you?'

'I knew you created nightmares here, yes. My mother figured out where your base was. But you've nothing to worry about. She hates the Cheese Whizzes now. She's already working to destroy them from within.'

'How do I know I can trust you?'

'Because I brought you Aldrin Adams.'

'Yes, you did! Ethan, how would you like to be my second in command?'

'Your what?'

'I'm offering you a job as my new Personal Assistant and Vice President of Global Operations!'

'But don't you already have a Personal Assistant and Vice President of Global Operations?'

'Yes. As a matter of fact, he's listening at the door again – aren't you, **BEDDY BYES?**'

Beddy Byes felt his blood chill. 'Er, yes, Your Fabulousness,' he said, 'I am.'

'Then you should be able to hear this,' said Habeas. 'You've been demoted!'

39

UNWORTHY

Aldrin swung his feet out of the bed. He felt around under it for his walkie-talkie. He put his hand on it and pulled it out. He pressed the button and spoke:

'Sisely, can you hear me? Sisely, come in! Over.'

There was no reply.

Then he remembered that he'd removed the battery. He felt around under the bed again and found it. He opened the battery compartment and popped it in. He tried again.

'Sisely, can you hear me? Sisely, come in! Over.'

Nothing.

Aldrin checked the time. It was almost seven o'clock in the morning. He was still wearing his superhero suit, or rather *costume* – because that was all it was after all.

He stared hard at his reflection in the full-length mirror. How could he have been such an idiot?

He tore off his red cape and threw it into the corner of the room. He kicked off his big red boots and tossed them into the corner as well, along with his ridiculous red elbow-length gloves. He ripped off his red mask with such ferocity that the elastic snapped and he added it to the pile.

He put on his school uniform, then he crept downstairs as quietly as he could, not wishing to wake his dad. He left the flat and headed straight for Sisely's house.

Mrs Musa was more than a little surprised to see him standing at the door at twenty past seven in the morning.

'Aldrin?' she said, pulling her dressing gown tighter round her. 'You do know what time it is, don't you?'

'Yes,' he said. 'I just wondered if Sisely was ready for school yet?'

'I don't think she's going to school today,' Mrs Musa told him. 'She's not feeling too well this morning.'

'Oh, erm, right,' said Aldrin.

He turned to walk away.

'She was very upset after you called here yesterday,'

Mrs Musa said. 'Did you two have a fight?'

'Sort of,' Aldrin said, turning back. 'Mrs Musa, can you please tell Sisely that she was right – about everything. And that I'm very, very sorry.'

Aldrin continued on to school. The playground was deserted when he arrived. He headed straight for the car park and sat cross-legged in Mrs Van Boxtel's parking space, waiting for her to arrive.

How could he have allowed himself to be suckered like that? He tortured himself with this question for more than an hour until Mrs Van Boxtel's tiny turquoise car came puttering through the school gates, its noisy exhaust belching black smoke in her wake.

She didn't see Aldrin sitting in her parking space – Aldrin noticed she wasn't wearing her glasses, and wondered whether she should have been driving at all – and he was forced to roll to safety as she brought her car to a shuddering halt.

She got out and saw Aldrin lying on the ground beside the car.

'What ish thish?' she asked. 'Why are you lying there?'

'Mrs Van Boxtel,' Aldrin said, climbing to his feet, 'I need to talk –'

'I shpoke to Ernie Williamsh,' she said, cutting him off.

'Ernie Williams?' Aldrin asked.

'Yesh, he ish the man who ish having the nightmare with the sheagullsh,' she reminded him. 'The man *you* promished to help – but then didn't.'

'I tried,' he told her truthfully, 'but something went wrong. I was a chip and the seagulls were trying to eat me. I'll have another go.'

'There ish no need,' Mrs Van Boxtel said. 'I did it myshelf lasht night.'

Aldrin noticed that her face was pale, there was a quiver in her voice and her hands were shaking.

'But you get sick when you do it,' he reminded her.

'Yesh,' she replied, 'but that wash a rishk I wash prepared to take to help thish man. Becaushe that ish our duty – ash Cheeshe Whizshesh.'

If Aldrin felt bad before, he felt even worse now, especially when he saw how wobbly her legs were. As she started walking towards the school building, Aldrin offered her his arm.

'Here, hold on to me,' he said.

But she batted his arm away.

'I don't need your help,' she snapped.

'Look, Mrs Van Boxtel,' he pleaded, 'I haven't been myself lately. It's just that, well, I met this boy named Archie McMenemy, who told me that he was a Cheese Whizz. He was at the meeting in Tintwistle. But it turned out that Habeas sent him. He told me that I was a superhero called NemeSwiss – and that I could enter the nightmares of thousands of people at the same time. But they were just . . . computer simulations.'

Mrs Van Boxtel stopped walking and stared at him, betraying no emotion. Aldrin then told her the **terrible twist** in the tale.

'I fell out with Sisely. Because I thought she was holding me back – just like you. I told her I wanted my mum's dream journal. And I gave it to Archie . . .'

Mrs Van Boxtel shook her head ruefully.

'Sho now your mother'sh diary ish in the handsh of Habeash Grusshelvart,' she said.

'I've ruined everything,' Aldrin said.

'And what do you want from me?' she asked. 'To feel shorry for you?'

'What?' asked Aldrin, surprised by her unsympathetic response.

'I told you that you weren't ready,' she explained. 'I shaid you were too **young** and too **immature** to handle the reshponshibility of being a Cheeshe Whizsh. And I wash correct.'

'Mrs Van Boxtel, I've ruined everything,' Aldrin confessed. 'I've lost Sisely and I've lost the book that my mum left me to explain how to use my power.'

'Perhapsh you will not need it any more. It shoundsh to me like you may have losht your power anyway.'

'What are you talking about?'

'You shay you tried to enter thish man'sh nightmare . . .'

'I did.'

'And what happened?'

'I don't know. He wasn't there.'

Mrs Van Boxtel nodded knowingly.

'What?' Aldrin asked. 'What does that mean?'

'Thish power wash given to you ash a gift,' she explained in a sad voice. 'And it can be taken back too.'

'Do you think that's what happened?'

'Shome people believe that the line of shuccesshion becomesh broken if a Cheeshe Whizsh ish not pure of heart and intention. A Cheeshe Whizsh who givesh in to hubrish ish conshidered to be . . . unworthy.'

With that, Mrs Van Boxtel turned her back on him

and headed for the school building. Aldrin stood, rooted to the spot.

Was that it? Was it over? Had he *really* lost his powers?

A moment later, he watched Harry's dad's car pull into the car park. He raced over to it. Harry barely had time to open the door when Aldrin was upon him.

'Harry!' he said breathlessly.

'Aldrin, what's wrong?' Harry asked. '**Whoa**, you look terrible.'

'Harry,' Aldrin said, tugging at his friend's sleeve, 'you have to tell me what happens next.'

'What do you mean?' Harry said.

'After the superhero has that moment of hubris. What happens then?'

'Well, in the movies, the next phase is the **"All is Lost"** moment.'

'The "All is Lost" moment? OK, that doesn't sound good.'

'It's not good. That's the point in the story – usually about three-quarters of the way through – where the hero reaches **rock bottom**. It's the moment where he's as far away as it's possible to be from achieving his goal. And the superhero has to look deep into his soul to try to find a way back.'

It wasn't even nine o'clock yet – and it was already the worst day of Aldrin's life.

40

THE GIRL IN THE PHOTOGRAPH

PLIN**K**-PLIN**K** ... PLIN**K**-PLIN**K** ... PLIN**K**-
PL**ON**K ...

That night, Aldrin was back at the piano again.

PLIN**K**-PLIN**K** ... PLIN**K**-P**LUN**K ...
P**LUN**K-P**LUN**K ...

He was jabbing the keys like he was angry – and he
was angry.

PL**ON**K ... PL**ON**K ... PL**ON**K ...

He was angry with Habeas Grusselvart, and he
was angry with Ethan. But mostly he was angry with
himself.

*PLUUU**NK** ... PLUUU**NK** ... PLUUU**NK** ...
PLUUU**NK** ...*

'Well, Silas,' he said, looking up towards his little

friend who was perched on top of his head, 'it looks like I messed up big time.'

RRRIBBIT . . . RRRIBBIT . . . RRRIBBIT . . .

'I know you're trying to make me feel better,' Aldrin told him, 'but it's true.'

PLINK . . . PLINK . . . PLINK . . .

'I let down Mrs Van Boxtel and Sisely,' he said. 'I've lost my mum's dream journal and it looks like I've lost my powers as well. And I've blown any chance I ever had of defeating Habeas Grusselvart. He beat me, Silas – and he did it easily.'

PLUNK . . . PLUNK . . . PLUNK . . .

At that moment, Doug walked into the room.

'Something on your mind?' he asked.

'Oh, er, just school stuff,' Aldrin lied.

'Mrs Musa was in the shop this afternoon. Young Sisely's mum.'

'Oh?'

'She said Sisely's not been herself lately. You two haven't had a falling-out, have you?'

'Sort of, yeah.'

'I'm sorry to hear that. Belinda and I are in the same boat, for what it's worth. She left a message this morning saying that she won't be coming back to work.'

'Dad, that's terrible.'

'Heigh-ho. The shop ran like clockwork today. Cerys saw to that – she really is wonderful with the customers, Aldrin. Anyway, hopefully Belinda will get over this jealousy of hers. ***Sweet dreams –***'

'***– are made of cheese,***' Aldrin smiled.

'***Who am I –***'

'***– to diss a Brie?***'

'Night, son.'

'Night, Dad.'

Doug went to bed, while Aldrin continued to jab at the keys and ponder his situation.

PLINK... PLINK... PLINK...

Harry said that the 'All is Lost' moment is when the superhero reaches **rock bottom**. But he also said that there is a way a back – if the hero looks deep into his soul.

PLUNK... PLUNK... PL–

Aldrin stopped hitting the keys. Because he suddenly remembered something.

He stood up from the piano, removed Silas from his head and returned him to the tank in his bedroom, and went to the kitchen. He slipped his hand into the inside pocket of his blazer and pulled out the envelope – the one that Sisely had given him.

He had barely given a thought to the little girl who was tormented by nightmares about being lost in a crowded shopping centre. It had just seemed so trivial compared to rescuing thousands of people from giant ants or a Tyrannosaurus rex.

He lifted the flap on the envelope and pulled out the photograph. And, when he did, he heard himself gasp.

Because the girl in the photograph . . .

. . . was Sisely.

In that instant, it all made sense to him. Her absences from school. Her anger with him for ignoring the mission.

And he felt responsible.

Sisely liked certainty in her life. It was why she liked maths so much – because it had rules and formulae and answers that were either **right** or **wrong**. Her need for certainty was why she liked to play things by the book.

It was also why she struggled to make friends. Because friends were unreliable in ways that numbers weren't. Friends could let you down – just like Aldrin had.

He turned the photograph over. On the reverse side, in Sisely's neat handwriting, was the word Caciocavallo. Then, underneath, it said, *One handful, grated.*

Could he do it now, he wondered? Would his powers still work? One thing was certain – he had to at least try.

He raced downstairs to the shop.

Caciocavallo was a pale, smooth-textured Italian cheese that that tasted of salt and earth and pecans. It was made in the shape of a teardrop and hung from a piece of rope to mature.

Aldrin rushed behind the refrigerated counter and stepped up on to the stool. He lifted down one of the large cheeses and took it over to the chopping board. With a knife, he cut through the hard rind. He took a large piece and he rubbed it against the grater until he'd generated a small pile. He filled his palm with it, then he closed his hand and took the stairs two at a time back up to the flat.

He changed into his pyjamas while still holding the cheese gratings in his clenched fist. As he did so, he told Silas:

'Sisely is having nightmares! She tried to tell me, but I wasn't listening!'

RRRIbbit . . . rrRIBBIT . . . RRRIbbIT . . .

'Thanks, Silas,' said Aldrin. 'Goodnight, little friend.'

Aldrin leaped into the bed and pulled the covers up to his chin.

'I'm coming to get you, Sisely!' he said.

He thought really, really hard about her, then he opened his hand and stuffed the handful of grated cheese into his mouth. He closed his eyes and he pictured his friend's face. And, as he did so, he chewed the Caciocavallo until it had turned into a ball of salty, earthy, pecany mush in his mouth.

And *very quickly* . . .

without even realizing . . .

that it was happening . . .

his eyes **started to feel** . . .

very,

very

heavy . . .

And then . . .

he was suddenly . . .

out

for

the . . .

41

SISELY'S NIGHTMARE

Aldrin found himself in an enormous shopping centre teeming with people. There were so many that he couldn't walk in a straight line. Instead, he shuffled along in an awkward ZIGZAG pattern, bumping into people and apologizing.

The lights overhead were intensely bright. And he could hear people chattering – except their voices were amplified so that it sounded like thousands of people were trying to be heard over one another.

Through the shopping centre's public address system came a woman's voice – so loud that Aldrin was forced to put his hands over his ears to protect his eardrums:

'GOOD AFTERNOON, LADIES AND

GENTLEMEN. THIS IS AN URGENT CUSTOMER ANNOUNCEMENT. A GIRL HAS BECOME SEPARATED FROM HER MOTHER.'

Aldrin stopped. *It* was *her*, he thought. It had to be. **'HER NAME IS SISELY. SHE IS WEARING A WHITE JACKET AND A RED DRESS. IF YOU SEE THIS CHILD, PLEASE REPORT TO THE SECURITY DESK ON THE TOP FLOOR.'**

Aldrin looked around him. The shopping centre had four levels. For close to an hour, he conducted a fruitless search of each one, but there was no sign of her anywhere.

Did this mean his powers were truly gone?

He was beginning to despair when he suddenly caught sight of her! She was standing on the ground floor, with her back to the window of Zara. She had her fingers in her ears and her eyes screwed tightly shut, like she was attempting to block out the world. At the top of his voice, he called her name:

'SSISELY! SIIISSSEEELLLYYY!!!'

Even with her fingers stuck in her ears, Aldrin could see a flicker of response in her face.

He pushed his way through the crowd. It took him almost a full minute to reach her. All that time, he kept calling out:

'SISELY! I'M COMING, SISELY! JUST HOLD ON!'

He eventually reached her.

'Sisely, it's me,' he told her in a soothing voice. 'It's Aldrin. I found the photograph. I'm so sorry about the way I acted.'

'It's OK,' she said, her eyes still shut and her fingers still jammed in her ears. 'This is a lot scarier than my other nightmare, where I'm sitting in an exam and I don't know any of the answers.'

He remembered Habeas Grusselvart's threat to make her night terrors more frightening.

'Sisely,' Aldrin said, 'can you open your eyes?'

Sisely shook her head.

'It's too bright,' she told him.

'Can you take your fingers out of your ears?' he asked.

'It's too loud,' she said. 'Aldrin, I want my mum!'

'We'll find her,' he promised. 'We're going to go to the security desk.'

He put his arm round her shoulder and guided her through the press of bodies until they reached the escalator that took them up to the second level. They stepped off it. Aldrin heard a voice, high above them, call out:

'SISELY! SISELY, I'M HERE!'

It was Mrs Musa – and she was standing on the fourth level of the shopping centre, looking down at them.

'Sisely,' Aldrin said, 'it's your mum!'

Sisely slowly opened her eyes and removed her fingers from her ears. They smiled and waved at each other.

'You see?' Aldrin said. 'It was just an anxiety dream.'

They made their way up another set of escalators – one more level to go. Sisely and her mum looked so happy to see each other. They were just moments away from being reunited – and *that* was when it happened . . .

Aldrin noticed a figure standing in the shadows behind Mrs Musa!

'**OH, NO!**' he said, pausing as they were about to step on to the final escalator.

'What's wrong?' asked Sisely.

She looked up to see the same figure take two steps forward. He was a tall man in a long black coat that was buttoned up to the chin.

'Is that . . . *him*?' Sisely asked.

'Yes,' said Aldrin, 'it's him.'

Habeas smiled down at Sisely, who instinctively knew that her mother was in danger.

'**MUM!**' she shouted.'**BEHIND YOU!**'

But Mrs Musa couldn't hear her. Aldrin watched her, still smiling, mouth the word, *What?*

Then he spotted that the guard rail in front of her . . .
was missing!

'**MRS MUSA!**' he screamed. '**LOOK OUT!**'

But it was too late!

Grinning an evil grin, Habeas stepped forward,
placed both hands on Mrs Musa's back and pushed her
over the edge.

Sisely screamed . . .

'**AAARRRGGGHHH!!!!**'

. . . as Mrs Musa fell through the air, her arms and
legs flailing uselessly.

'DO something!' Aldrin told himself.

And then he did something he'd been told to do only
in the case of extreme emergencies. He shouted:

'KNOCKDRINNA SNOW!'

42

A RAGING BATTLE

EVERYTHING stopped!

And not a moment too soon because Mrs Musa was just a fraction of a second away from hitting the hard tiled floor!

But now she was suspended in the air, six feet above the ground, her arms and legs frozen mid-flail.

The shopping centre was suddenly silent. All the people had disappeared. Now, it was just Aldrin, Sisely, Mrs Musa, Habeas . . . and the person whose approaching footsteps they could hear ECHOING through the otherwise empty shopping centre behind them.

Habeas shook his head and rolled his eyes.

'What kind of a superhero,' he asked witheringly, 'has to call his mum every time he's in trouble?'

No sooner had the words passed his lips than he was hit by a blast of air so strong that it blew him clean off his feet . . . and through the window of WHSmith!

There was the sound of glass shattering and a loud exclamation of:

'CURSES TO THAT WOMAN!'

Aldrin and Sisely slowly turned their heads. Standing behind them, smiling into the distance, like someone who'd just driven a golf ball three hundred yards . . . was Cynthia Adams!

'Mum!' Aldrin shouted.

'Hello, darling,' she said without looking at him.

'Mum, this is my friend –' he said, attempting to introduce her to Sisely.

'No time,' Cynthia told him. 'You two had better make yourselves scarce. This may get messy.'

She headed for the escalator up to the top floor, where Habeas was now climbing out of the window of WHSmith. He dusted himself down and, as Cynthia faced him, he nodded as if to compliment her on a good shot.

He pointed his finger at Mrs Musa, still hovering six feet above the ground – then raised it. Suddenly, Mrs Musa was lifted high into the air. Habeas withdrew his finger and she began to fall once again towards the ground below.

Instinctively, Aldrin put out his hands, creating an invisible shield just above the ground. Mrs Musa bounced off it like she'd been dropped on to a feather bed.

With her right hand, Cynthia made a throwing motion and a bolt of air tore out of her hand like a ball from a cannon. This time, Habeas dived clear in time. There was another explosion of glass and the sound of metal breaking.

Cynthia turned and looked at Aldrin.

'Darling, go down there and help Mrs Musa!' she said.

Aldrin and Sisely hurried to the ground floor, lifted Mrs Musa and laid her on the ground.

'Mum!' Sisely shouted. 'Mum, wake up!'

'She can't,' Aldrin told her. 'It's not her nightmare, remember? It's yours! She's not really here – except in your imagination!'

Still, Sisely held tightly on to her mum's hand, relieved that she was safe.

Above them, Aldrin heard another loud explosion of glass.

'Sisely,' he said, 'I'm going to go back up there to help my mum!"

He ran up three sets of escalators, taking the steps two at a time, to reach the top level.

When he got there, the battle between his mum and Habeas Grusselvart was raging. They were both firing balls of air from their hands – and all around them was a scene of mayhem.

The front of Boots was just a mass of twisted metal and shards of glass. Currys had been reduced to rubble. H&M looked like a herd of elephants had run loose through it.

Habeas watched Aldrin step off the escalator.

'Ah, Aldrin!' he smirked. 'No costume tonight?'

Cynthia, standing a few feet away, turned her head to look at her son.

'Aldrin,' she said, 'I told you to –'

Habeas used the distraction to send a ball of air ripping towards her. It caught her full in the stomach. Her legs shot up and her arms shot out and she was blown through the window of Ryman.

'NOOOOOO!!!!!!' Aldrin screamed

In his rage, he ran at Habeas. But Habeas picked him up as if he weighed nothing and tossed him like a piece of rubbish over the edge of the balcony. As Aldrin fell, he made a desperate grab for something to hold on to. He managed to grasp the edge of the floor and now he was left hanging three floors above the ground . . . by just his fingertips!

Habeas looked down at him and smiled cruelly.

'Why don't you just . . . *fly*?' he asked him.

Suddenly, Habeas was struck by another blast of

air that sent him skittering sideways across the floor and through the window of Argos. Cynthia appeared above Aldrin and tried to help him up. But Habeas reappeared and lunged at her, knocking her off her feet. Suddenly, they were rolling around on the floor, which was strewn with broken glass and tattered books and stationery.

Habeas had hold of Cynthia and Cynthia had hold of Habeas. But Habeas was physically stronger and he quickly got the better of her.

'Your boy needs to learn to stay out of other people's nightmares!' he told her, then he picked her up and threw her over the edge too.

'MUUUMMMMMM!!!!!!' Aldrin screamed.

As she fell, Cynthia scrabbled around for something to hold on to. She managed to grab Aldrin's leg and she held on to his ankle, just as Aldrin held on to the floor with his fingertips: mother and son dangling in the air with a fall of fifty feet below them.

Habeas walked over to the edge. He smiled in his usual sardonic way.

'Goodbye, Aldrin,' he said, then he stepped on Aldrin's fingers with the heel of his boot.

'AAARRRGGGHHH!!!' Aldrin screamed

as Habeas twisted his foot.

'And goodbye, Cynthia,' Habeas added for good measure. Aldrin was about to give in and let go. But then he noticed that Habeas was no longer smiling. Instead, he wore an expression of surprise – as a small hand pushed firmly on his back. It was too late for him to do anything, except to sigh:

'Just when I was beginning to enjoy myself!'

In that moment, he was shoved forward over the edge and plummeted towards the floor. As he struck it, he disappeared in a ball of smoke.

Aldrin and his mum looked up as Sisely made her way to the edge and stared down at them.

'Take my hand,' she said, 'I'll help you up.'

43

'HE FEARS YOU, ALDRIN'

'I made a complete fool of myself,' Aldrin said.

'He did,' Sisely confirmed. 'He really, REALLY did.'

They were sitting on a bench next to the gelato stand, amid the debris of the shopping centre's ruined fourth level. They'd helped themselves to ice creams. It wasn't technically stealing since the entire scene was a figment of Sisely's imagination.

'What happened?' Cynthia asked.

Aldrin couldn't bring himself to look at his mum.

'I sort of let myself be convinced that I was a superhero,' he said.

'What kind of superhero?' Cynthia said, licking her mango sorbet.

'I was called NemeSwiss!' Aldrin told her.

305

'NemeSwiss?'

'I told him there was nothing in your dream journal about any NemeSwiss,' said Sisely.

'And I refused to listen,' Aldrin admitted.

'He was wearing a superhero costume under his school uniform,' Sisely revealed. 'With a cape tucked into the back of his trousers.'

'Yeah, thanks for reminding me, Sisely,' said Aldrin. 'Habeas had it made for me. It's a long story, but there was this boy who told me that his name was Archie McMenemy and that he was a Cheese Whizz.'

'Archie McMenemy?' said Sisely. 'Er, didn't you notice that his name sounded very like . . . arch-enemy?'

'No,' Aldrin sighed. 'But now that you say it . . .'

'So what did this boy do?' Cynthia asked.

'He created a bunch of computer simulations that he told me were nightmares,' Aldrin told her. 'There was an army of giant ants. And a Tyrannosaurus rex that was attacking a building. Oh, and then an earthquake. He told me that I could save thousands and thousands of people every single night and . . .'

Aldrin heard his voice crack. Tears started spilling from his eyes. Cynthia put her arm round him and pulled him close to her.

'What is it?' she asked.

'Mum, I gave him your dream journal,' Aldrin told her. 'And now . . . Habeas has it.'

'Oh, Aldrin,' Cynthia said. 'Don't be so hard on yourself. You're still so young – and Habeas is so devious. You've only been a Cheese Whizz for a few months, remember? He's been doing this for centuries. Give yourself a break'

'But that book was my instruction manual,' Aldrin said. 'Without it, I don't know what cheese to eat for which nightmare.'

'You don't need it,' Sisely reminded him. 'I've read it. And I have a photographic memory.'

'That means you two are bonded together now.' Cynthia smiled. 'You can't fall out.'

'We won't,' Aldrin said.

Cynthia reached for Sisely's hand. 'Here's Aldrin talking about all the mistakes he's made,' she said, 'and he's forgetting about all the things he got right. Like sharing his secret with someone as smart as you.'

'Thank you, Mrs Adams,' said Sisely.

'Please, call me Cynthia. You see, I shared *my* secret with someone I thought I could trust – but it turned out I was wrong.'

'Beddy Byes,' Aldrin said, spitting out the words like they were mouldy Cheddar.

'Well, back then,' Cynthia pointed out, 'he was just plain old *Morr-eece* Mackle.'

'Well, he's Beddy Byes now,' Aldrin reminded her. 'He's evil through and through.'

'He's not evil,' Cynthia said. 'He just allowed his mind to be poisoned by bitterness. He was a very good friend to me once. I'm sure there's still good in him.'

'I seriously doubt it,' said Aldrin.

'How's your ice cream?'

'It's good. I wish they sold cheese-flavoured ice cream. Like Bouton de Culotte. Or Mont d'Or. Or Reblochon.'

'You're saying the names of French cheeses,' Cynthia pointed out.

'Oh, no,' Aldrin groaned. 'I suppose that means I'm about to wake up.'

'The Caciocavallo must be wearing off,' Sisely said.

Cynthia looked at Aldrin sadly. 'That's the second time you've summoned me to a nightmare,' she reminded him. 'You know you'll only be able to do it one more time?'

Aldrin felt a heavy weight of sadness in his heart.

'I know,' he said. 'Before I wake up, I have to ask you a question, Mum.'

'What is it?' she wondered.

'Do you really believe that I'm The One?' he asked.

'Yes, I do,' she said. 'I've always believed it – even before you were born. I knew it when I was expecting you.'

'I went to a meeting of the Cheese Whizzes,' Aldrin said. 'Wilbur Leveson-Gough told me that Habeas has never revealed himself to any living Cheese Whizz.'

'It's true,' Cynthia confirmed. 'I didn't even know what he looked like until after I died. He fears you, Aldrin. He knows that you're the one who's been sent to destroy him.'

'But how?' Aldrin asked.

'That's what you and Sisely have to figure out,' Cynthia smiled. 'Together – OK?'

And in that moment Aldrin woke up in his bed, the throbbing head and the extreme sweats back again like two old friends.

44

A LARGE, TATTERED LEDGER

'A skinny caramel latte,' said Beddy Byes, 'and an apple Danish – erm, please.'

Janice Orbison, the canteen manager at the Codfather Packing Company, looked him up and down.

'I've no apple Danishes,' she said.

Which confused Beddy Byes because he could see a large tray of them through the glass counter – sweet and sticky and fresh from the oven.

'Aren't *those* apple Danishes?' he asked, pointing them out.

'I'm saving them,' said Janice, 'for folk what work in the warehouse. They're not for them what – sorry, what exactly is it you do around here again?'

It would be true to say that the sudden demotion of

Beddy Byes had resulted in a certain loss of respect for him among the rest of the staff in Habeas Grusselvart's nightmare-generating operation.

'Just the skinny caramel latte then,' said Beddy Byes, counting out the exact change and handing it over. Janice put the money in the till. Five seconds later, she placed a cup of coffee in front of him. Beddy Byes hadn't heard the usual **spit** and **gurgle** and **hiss** of the Barista 5000 Coffee Machine as it did its thing. As a matter of fact, he could have sworn that Janice gave him a coffee that was already sitting there. When he touched the sides of the cup, it was cold.

'Something wrong?' Janice said.

'Er, no,' said Beddy Byes. 'I just wondered – could you perhaps bring it to my table for me?'

'Why?' she snapped.

Beddy Byes looked down at his giant snow-boot cast.

'I, erm, broke my ankle,' he explained.

'You don't carry things with your ankle, do you?' asked Janice.

Behind him, Beddy Byes heard sniggering. Rita Choo (Training Delivery Manager with Special Responsibility for Things that Go Bump in the Night) and Don Decadent (Training Delivery Manager with

Special Responsibility for Scary Clowns) were finding this hilarious.

'I'm using crutches,' Beddy Byes tried to explain, 'which means I don't have the use of my hands.'

'We don't operate a table service,' said Janice.

There was more sniggering behind him.

'Let *me* help you with that,' he heard a voice say.

He turned around. It was Holt Hession (Training Delivery Manager with Special Responsibility for Things that Bite and Sting).

'That's very kind of you,' Beddy Byes said.

He started making his way towards a table on his crutches. Then, behind him, he heard a . . . SPLAT! He looked round to discover that Holt had dropped his coffee on the floor.

'Oops!' The man grinned. 'Butterfingers.'

Everyone laughed.

Beddy Byes felt his cheeks kindle with embarrassment and anger. And, in that moment, he came to a decision – he was going to quit his job as Habeas Grusselvart's longest-serving agent of evil!

He slowly picked his way to the lift that took him up to the executive level. Then he hobbled along the expensively carpeted corridor to the office of the man to whom he'd dedicated more than eighteen years of his life.

He knocked. There was no reply. He pushed the door and entered, muttering apologies under his breath. But the office was empty.

He decided to scribble his resignation letter on a piece of company stationery. He searched his boss's desk for some headed notepaper. And that was when he saw it . . .

It was a large, tattered ledger, about two inches in thickness, with scraps of paper and multicoloured Post-it notes peeking out from between its pages.

He picked it up. It smelled damp and musty. On the cover was the word:

DREAM JOURNAL

With **trembling** fingers, he began to turn over the pages. He stared at the thousands and thousands of French words laid out in Cynthia's beautifully neat handwriting.

Immediately, the years fell away, and he was transported back to the happiest time of his life – his days as an apprentice cheesemonger, back when he was just plain old Maurice Mackle.

His quiet moment of reverie was interrupted by

someone kicking one of his crutches away. He fell on to the floor and Cynthia's dream journal was ripped from his hands.

'What are you doing?' he heard a voice say.

Ethan was standing over him. He was wearing a suit and tie and looked every inch the Personal Assistant and Vice President of Global Operations to the world's oldest and most heinous supervillain.

'Where . . . did you get that b-b-book?' Beddy Byes stuttered.

'That's none of your concern,' Ethan told him. 'You're no one around here now.'

Beddy Byes floundered on the floor, using his crutches to try to get himself upright again. And, as he did so, he changed his mind about quitting his job. Instead, the beginnings of a new plan began to come together in his mind.

45

LOOFASI SMADA

'I'm sorry,' Aldrin said.

It was a morning for apologies. He was standing in Mrs Van Boxtel's classroom along with Sisely.

'No,' said Mrs Van Boxtel, '*I'm* the one who ish shorry. It wash my job to watch over you, Aldrin – and I did not do thish to the besht of my ability.'

'He wouldn't have listened to you anyway,' Sisely pointed out. 'He wanted to believe that he was a superhero and NOTHING was going to persuade him that he wasn't.'

Mrs Van Boxtel laughed.

'Aldrin,' she said, 'I am shad to tell you that, deshpite your powersh, you really are nothing without Shishely'sh brainsh.'

'Thank you,' said Aldrin. 'I kind of found that out the hard way.'

Mrs Van Boxtel looked at Sisely then.

'Habeash clearly thought that by giving you thish awful nightmare, he could drive a wedge between the two of you,' she said. 'It ish eashier to defeat people when they are isholated. It ish the rule of divide and conquer. But you memorizshed absholutely everything that wash in Aldrin'sh mother'sh dream journal, yesh?'

'Everything,' said Sisely.

'Then,' she said, 'it wash not jusht Aldrin who wash guilty of undereshtimating you. Habeash wash too. Aldrin, how did you meet thish Archie or Ethan pershon?'

'I met him at the Tintwistle Cheese Festival,' Aldrin remembered. 'He was buying a copy of Harry and Frankie's comic book, *The Oddballs*. Then that night, after the Cheese Rolling on Lambert's Hill, I met him at the meeting of the Cheese Whizzes.'

Mrs Van Boxtel's expression turned grave and her face visibly paled.

'He wash *at* the meeting of the Cheeshe Whizshesh?' she asked.

'Yes,' replied Aldrin. 'Then I saw him a few days later

when I was passing the skatepark. He was doing tricks on his board. That was when he told me about Lufassi Samatta's prophecy.'

'Who?' asked Mrs Van Boxtel.

'He said he was a Cheese Whizz from Ethiopia,' Aldrin remembered, 'who predicted the coming of a boy who would destroy Habeas Grusselvart.'

'Lufassi Samatta?' Sisely asked. 'Are you sure it wasn't **Loofasi Smada?**'

'Maybe,' Aldrin answered. 'Was he mentioned in my mum's dream journal?'

'No,' she told him, 'but "Loofasi Smada" is **"Adams is a fool"** spelled backwards. I think he was having some fun with you.'

Aldrin felt so stupid.

'He mentioned another name,' he said. 'Theo something or other. He was an Irishman who discovered sequencing.'

'What's sequencing?' Sisely asked.

'It doesn't matter,' Aldrin said. 'He made it up anyway.'

Suddenly, Aldrin noticed that the old lady was staring into the mid-distance with a look of concern on her face.

'Mrs Van Boxtel,' he said, 'is everything OK?'

The teacher shook her head.

'No,' she replied. 'I think everything ish FAR from OK. How did Ethan find out where the Cheeshe Whizshesh were meeting?'

'I've no idea,' Aldrin admitted.

'Who wash he with?' she asked. 'Did you shee him leave with anyone?'

'No,' Aldrin told her. 'He was just . . . *there.*'

'What does it mean?' asked Sisely.

'It meansh that, for the firsht time in five hundred yearsh,' said Mrs Van Boxtel, 'the Cheeshe Whizshesh have been infiltrated.'

'What?' Aldrin exclaimed as a shiver ran through his body.

'Yesh, I am shad to shay,' said Mrs Van Boxtel, 'that we have a traitor in our midsht.'

46

A LETTER

Aldrin and Sisely walked home that afternoon, their heads still spinning from the revelation that the ancient order had been betrayed by one of its own.

'So who do you think it was?' asked Sisely.

'I've no idea,' Aldrin admitted. 'I mean, everyone at the meeting seemed so nice. Except . . .'

And then he paused.

'There was a woman there called Estelle,' Aldrin remembered. 'She was dressed in motorcycle leathers. She said loads of mean things. And she kept talking about how she was the one to lead the Cheese Whizzes in the battle against Habeas Grusselvart. Even Wilbur said she wasn't to be trusted.'

'Who's Wilbur?' Sisely asked.

Aldrin realized in that moment just how many secrets he'd kept from his friend.

'Wilbur Leveson-Gough,' Aldrin explained. 'He was the man at the Tintwistle Cheese Festival who was doing the Brie Blind Taste Challenge. He and Mrs Van Boxtel have been friends for years. He was the one who told me about the meeting.'

'Right,' said Sisely as they turned on to Burnett Road. 'Aldrin, can I say something to you?'

'Er, sure,' Aldrin said, bracing himself.

'I'm sorry,' she said.

'*You're* sorry? I'm the one who took the battery out of the walkie-talkie! I'm the one who took my mum's dream journal from you! I'm the one who refused to help you when you were having that nightmare! Why would *you* be sorry?'

'Because you wasted one of your chances to see your mum.'

'If it stops you having that awful nightmare again, it wasn't wasted. Hey, I wish you could have seen Habeas's face when you **shoved** him in the back!'

'I think I would have liked that!'

'Do you want to do homework together?' Aldrin asked.

'I don't mind.' She shrugged. 'As long you don't try to copy mine.'

Aldrin smiled. Sisely was – and would ALWAYS be – a stickler for the rules.

The shop was packed when they walked through the door. Agatha Rees-Lane was perched at the counter again – and this time she had FOUR friends sitting with her.

'I think we'll try some more of the Laguiole,' she was telling Cerys, who was rushing round the shop like a waitress. 'Oh, and some more of the Caerphilly if it's

not too much trouble. Elizabeth here asked you for it five minutes ago, but you didn't bring it.'

'I'm so sorry.' Cerys continued to smile, even though she must have felt like **screaming**. 'I'll get it for you now.'

'There's a good girl,' said Agatha.

'Aldrin!' Doug exclaimed. 'And Sisely! It's wonderful to see you two together again!'

'Thank you, Mr Adams,' said Sisely.

'Aldrin, *we* are having our busiest day EVER! There's been a constant stream of people since we opened the doors this morning! Who needs Belinda, eh?'

Aldrin looked around him.

'Dad,' he said, 'are these people actually buying any cheese, though?'

He noticed that Mrs Swaby from Conleth Crescent was nibbling on a piece of Jarlsberg and Mr Wiltshire from Beech Road was sampling the Barber's 1833 Vintage Reserve Cheddar.

'Of course!' Doug said. 'Mrs Verner was in this morning. She bought some Emmental.'

Aldrin noticed that Mrs Verner was at that moment standing right behind Doug.

'Dad,' Aldrin said, indicating her with a nod.

Doug turned round.

'I bought this cheese this morning,' she said. 'I was halfway through it when I noticed it's got holes in it.'

'Well, it's *supposed* to have holes in it,' Doug told her. 'It's Emmental.'

'The sign says **no quibbles**,' she reminded him.

'Quite right!' said Doug cheerfully. 'I'll refund you your money in full. You see, Aldrin? Customer care! That's how you run a business! I wouldn't take Belinda back for all the money in the world!'

Out of the corner of his mouth, Aldrin told Sisely, 'I think my dad is having his own moment of hubris.'

They went upstairs to the kitchen. Aldrin saw an envelope leaning against a jar of caramelized red onion chutney in the middle of the table. He picked it up. His name and address were on the front.

'What is it?' she asked.

'I don't know,' he told her.

The writing was different to the writing on the package that had contained his NemeSwiss costume. He turned it over and tore open the flap, then pulled out what was inside. It was a page that had been torn from a newspaper. He opened it out and stared at it for a long moment.

'I don't get it,' he said.

'What is it?' Sisely asked.

It was the front page of the *Higher Dinting Advertiser*. The headline on the lead story read:

FAREWELL, *CHEESE LOUISE*!

And then underneath:

FAMOUS CHEESEMONGER'S TO CLOSE ITS DOORS AFTER THIRTY YEARS!

Aldrin handed it to Sisely, who read the story closely.

'There's no letter or note with it,' Aldrin said, looking inside the envelope again.

Sisely finished reading, then she stared into the distance, like she was performing a sum in her head.

'OK, think about it,' she told him. 'Why is someone so keen to let you know that a cheesemonger's is closing down?'

'I've no idea,' Aldrin shrugged.

'Think, Aldrin! What happened when your dad decided to close his shop that time?'

'Beddy Byes turned up,' he remembered, 'to ask if he could have all the leftover stock. Although I've no idea what he was planning to do with . . .'

Aldrin stopped. He felt his mouth widen in shock.

'Hold on,' he said. 'Do you think someone is trying to tell us where Beddy Byes is going to be?'

'Maybe it's Beddy Byes himself.'

'Why would he do that?'

'You heard what your mum said. She thinks there's still good in him.'

'Sisely,' Aldrin said, his mouth twisting into a smile, 'do you think he's trying to talk to us? Is that why he's telling us where he's going to be?'

'It could be that,' Sisely said. 'Or it could be a trap. If he *is* collecting cheese, then he must be taking it to Habeas's lair. We could stake out the shop. Then, if he does turn up, we could follow him. If we're going to do that, we're going to need to move quickly. According to the article, the shop is closing down today.'

Aldrin felt his heart **sink**.

'I don't even know where Higher Dinting is,' he said. 'Who's going to drive us there?'

'There's only one person in the world we can ask,' said Sisely.

A DIRTY DOUBLE-CROSSER

Mrs Van Boxtel nibbled on a piece of Cheddar as she read the article from the *Higher Dinting Advertiser*.

'Intereshting,' she mused. 'Moooosht innntereshh-hting. And there wash no letter? No way of telling who shent thish newshpaper page to you?'

'No,' Aldrin told her. 'But we think Beddy Byes is trying to lead us to Habeas Grusselvart.'

'Or perhapsh,' Mrs Van Boxtel suggested, 'he ish trying to lure you into a trap.'

'A trap?' asked Aldrin.

'That was *my* first thought,' said Sisely. 'But then I thought, what if Beddy Byes wants us to find Habeas? Aldrin's mum thinks there's still good in him.'

Mrs Van Boxtel nodded slowly.

'She wash very fond of him at one time,' she said. 'They were friendsh – jusht like you two are friendsh. But there ish no good in him any more, jusht anger and bitternessh. Shad to shay, but Beddy Byesh ish now **jusht ash evil** ash hish bossh.'

'We can't just do NOTHING!' Aldrin said impatiently.

'No,' Mrs Van Boxtel agreed, 'but we musht think about our nexsht move very, VERY carefully.'

'We don't have long,' Sisely pointed out. 'The shop is closing today.'

At that precise moment, there was a sharp **BUZZ** on the intercom of Mrs Van Boxtel's flat.

'Ah,' she said, 'thish will be Wilbur. I invited him round to talk about the other little myshtery that we musht sholve.'

She pressed the button to let him into the building, then a minute later she opened the front door to invite him in.

Aldrin and Sisely could hear them talking in the hallway.

'A traitor – in our ranks!' he thundered. 'I still can't believe it, Nel! Do you have any idea who it might be?'

'None whatshoever,' said Mrs Van Boxtel. 'Come in. Aldrin ish here and alsho hish friend Shishely.'

They stepped into the room, first Mrs Van Boxtel, then the tall, moustachioed, sergeant majorly figure of Wilbur Leveson-Gough.

'Hello, Wilbur,' Aldrin said.

'Hello again, chappie,' Wilbur replied. 'And you must be Sisely – is that right?'

'Yes, hello,' said Sisely.

'Well? Is it true?' Wilbur asked Aldrin. 'This Archie chappie who was at the meeting – he's not a Cheese Whizz at all?'

'His real name is Ethan,' Aldrin told him, 'and he works for Habeas Grusselvart.'

'Well, *blow me down*,' Wilbur said. 'You know, I'd never seen him before. I thought someone in the room must have known who he was.'

'There ish only one way that Habeash could have found out about the meeting in Tintwishtle,' said Mrs Van Boxtel.

'We've been betrayed,' Wilbur said, 'by one of our own. So who is it then? Who's the dirty double-crosser?'

'That ish what we musht find out. Who wash he with?'

'I've no idea. I arrived with Aldrin and the chap was

already there. He was sitting on his own, from what I can remember.'

'Did you see him talk to anyone else?' Sisely asked.

'Not that I noticed,' said Wilbur. 'I think everyone was more concerned with Aldrin here and whether or not he was The One.'

Aldrin made a suggestion then. 'Difficult as this might be,' he said, 'we must go through everyone who was at the meeting that night and ask ourselves if they might be a suspect.'

'I still refuse to believe that a Cheese Whizz would sell out another member of the order!' Wilbur insisted.

'What about Maxshine Joli?' Mrs Van Boxtel asked.

'Maxine Joli?' Wilbur repeated, his moustache bristling. 'Have you taken leave of your senses, Nel?'

'Wilbur, EVERYONE musht be conshidered a shushpect.'

'But Maxine Joli? The great-granddaughter of the legendary Didier Durand – the most famous Cheese Whizz of them all? She would never do anything to dishonour the order.'

'Can we say the same about Cormac de Courcy?' Aldrin asked.

Wilbur's eyes bulged at the very suggestion.

'Cormac de Courcy is the greatest living Cheese Whizz and the very finest of men,' he told him forcefully. 'I've stayed with him on his farm in Ireland. I'll not stand by and listen to you defame a great man!'

'What about Estelle Giddens?' Aldrin pushed.

'*Esssteeellle Giddennnsss,*' Wilbur said thoughtfully.

'I think for a long time we have *all* harboured doubtsh about Eshtelle Giddensh,' said Mrs Van Boxtel.

'Look, I'm not overly fond of the woman,' Wilbur admitted, 'but I don't think she would –'

'We have known for a long time that she hash wanted to lead the Cheeshe Whizshesh,' Mrs Van Boxtel reminded him. 'Perhapsh she ish trying to bring down the order from the inshide.'

'But I still find it frankly unfathomable that she would –'

Wilbur cut himself short.

'What is it?' Aldrin asked.

'I've just remembered something,' he said. 'Look, it's probably of no consequence, but after the meeting I saw Estelle and this Ethan chappie talking in the car park. Now that I think about it, there *was* a sort of closeness between them. Like a mother and son.'

'Does she have a son?' asked Aldrin.

'I'm pretty sure she does,' said Wilbur. 'Although I've never met the chap and I've no idea if he's called Ethan.'

'What are we going to do?' Aldrin asked.

'I think perhapsh we should all shleep on it,' said Mrs Van Boxtel, 'and then deshide the besht courshe of action to take.'

'Sensible idea,' said Wilbur.

'NO!' Aldrin suddenly yelled. 'WE CAN'T JUST SLEEP ON IT!'

Sisely cleared her throat to get the attention of the room.

'I just want to point out,' she said, 'that *Cheese Louise* is closing very shortly. If we're going, we're going to have to leave **NOW?**'

'EXACTLY!' said Aldrin.

'*Cheese Louise*?' Wilbur asked. 'What on earth is *Cheese Louise*?'

Mrs Van Boxtel handed the newspaper cutting to him.

'Shomeone shent thish to Aldrin,' she said, 'anonymoushly. He thinksh perhapsh shomeone ish trying to lead him to Habeash Grusshelvart.'

'It was Beddy Byes!' Aldrin insisted.

'What?' Wilbur replied. 'You think he's ready to betray Habeas?'

'It's just a theory,' Sisely said.

'We need to go to Higher Dinting to stake out the shop,' Aldrin said. 'If he shows up, we can follow him and see where he goes.'

Nel raised her eyebrows at Wilbur. 'Sho – what do *you* think?' she asked.

'What do *I* think?' repeated Wilbur. 'I think it's a damn fool idea! What if it's a trap?'

'That ish alsho *my* conshern,' said Mrs Van Boxtel. 'But, on the other hand, thish could be the besht opportunity we have had in a very long time to find Habeash Grusshelvart.'

'EXACTLY!' yelled Aldrin.

'And do what?' Wilbur asked.

'Very shimple,' said Mrs Van Boxtel. **'Deshtroy hish bashe of operashions.'**

'We're running out of time here,' Sisely pointed out.

'I think you're mad to even consider it,' Wilbur insisted.

'Let ush put it to a vote,' Mrs Van Boxtel suggested. 'Aldrin, do you wish to go?'

'Yes!' he answered decisively.

'Shishely?' Mrs Van Boxtel asked.

'Yes?' she said.

'Wilbur?' asked Mrs Van Boxtel.

'You know what I'm going to say,' Wilbur announced. 'I think it's a trick.'

'Sho that jusht leavesh me,' said Mrs Van Boxtel. 'And I am going to shay . . .' She looked up at the ceiling.

'Please, Mrs Van Boxtel,' Aldrin said, 'this could be the best opportunity we ever get to find Habeas Grusselvart!'

'The time for talking is over,' Sisely told her. 'We need to act – now!'

'Then I am going to shay . . .' Mrs Van Boxtel repeated, still staring at a point on the ceiling, 'yesh!'

'So we're going!' Aldrin said, scarcely able to believe it.

'Yesh,' said Mrs Van Boxtel. 'Higher Dinting – here we come!'

Aldrin rubbed his hands together in excitement.

'Well, if you insist on going on this damn-fool crusade,' said Wilbur, 'at least let me come with you. There'll be safety in numbers.'

'We will go in my car,' Mrs Van Boxtel said, picking up her keys. 'How thrilling! To be going on a shtake-out!'

48

THE SHTAKE-OUT

'Unless I'm *very* much mistaken,' said Wilbur, 'I rather think this traffic light coming up is red, Nel.'

'Don't be shilly,' said Mrs Van Boxtel. 'It ish clearly amber,' and her tiny turquoise car putt-putt-putted through it, forcing several cars to brake sharply and drawing angry hoots from their drivers.

Mrs Van Boxtel wound down the window and, from the mouth of this sweet old lady with the dandelion-puffball hair, came an ANGRY roar:

'WHAT ISH YOUR PROBLEM, HUH? THE LIGHT WASH NOT YET RED! OH, *BEEP! BEEP! BEEP!* YOURSHELF!'

Aldrin looked at Sisely, who was sitting next to him in the back, gripping the seat in fear. Not only was

Mrs Van Boxtel the WORST DRIVER IN THE ENTIRE WORLD, she was also the ANGRIEST!

'Honeshtly,' she told her terrified passengers, 'there is sho much road rage in thish country!' and then she shouted out of the window again:

'WHERE DID YOU GET YOUR DRIVING LISHENSHE FROM? A LUCKY BAG?'

It was like her entire personality changed when she got behind the wheel of a car!

Wilbur looked over his shoulder at Aldrin and Sisely.

'You two all right back there?' he asked.

'Er, I think so,' Aldrin answered.

'Just hold on tight, chappie. We should be there in a few minutes.'

Suddenly, they felt a series of **bumps**.

'What ish going on?' asked Mrs Van Boxtel. 'Why ish the car doing that?'

'I think two of your wheels are up on the footpath,' Sisely told her.

'Ah, yesh, you are right, Shishely,' Mrs Van Boxtel confirmed. 'Who is reshponshible for putting a footpath THERE – of all the plashes!!! Ah, here ish the shign for Higher Dinting!'

'You have to take the next left,' said Sisely, who'd

memorized the entire route from Mrs Van Boxtel's map. 'Then it's a right, a left and another right.'

Mrs Van Boxtel took all four turns without using her indicators – or slowing down! She bounced over three speed bumps, clipped the wing mirror of an ice-cream van as she overtook it and narrowly avoided hitting a lollipop lady on a pedestrian crossing, before they finally arrived outside **Cheese Louise** on Brereton Road.

'Now,' said Mrs Van Boxtel, 'the shecret to good shurveillanshe ish to keep a low profile.'

'Er, right,' said Aldrin.

Wilbur indicated the post office on the opposite side of the street.

'Why don't you park the car there?' he asked. 'It's a discreet distance away, but it'll also afford you a rather good view of the shop.'

'Yesh, exshellent idea!' said Mrs Van Boxtel.

After sixteen unsuccessful attempts, she managed to parallel park in a space that was wide enough to accommodate a bus.

'What time ish it?' she asked.

'It's two minutes to five,' Sisely answered.

Aldrin felt a knot of nervousness in his stomach as

he stared at the door of the cheesemonger's. A moment later, it swung open and a woman of approximately his dad's age showed an elderly man out of the shop. She watched him walk up the road, a *Cheese Louise* bag swinging from his fingers.

'A happy customer,' Aldrin said.

Then they watched as the woman pulled a tissue from the sleeve of her cardigan and dabbed at her eyes.

'But shadly her lasht,' said Mrs Van Boxtel.

The woman went back inside the shop and turned the sign on the door from **'OPEN'** to **'CLOSED'**.

'So how long do we intend to sit here for?' asked Wilbur.

'For as long as it takes for Beddy Byes to show up,' said Aldrin.

'We don't even know that he *is* going to show up,' Wilbur pointed out.

At that precise moment, unbeknownst to them, Beddy Byes was reversing his white van into the yard at the rear of *Cheese Louise* – a difficult manoeuvre to pull off with a giant snow-boot cast on his leg. He got out and looked around him. Using his crutches, he picked his way to the back door of the shop and knocked three times.

A woman came to the door. She looked like she'd been crying – which Beddy Byes thought was understandable in the circumstances.

'You must be Louise,' he said.

'Er, yes,' she sniffled. 'And you're Maurice?'

'*Morr-eece*,' he corrected her. 'Are you absolutely sure this is a good time? I *can* come back.'

'No, no,' she insisted. 'I just said goodbye to Mr Christman. He's been coming here for thirty years.'

'I can't imagine how difficult this must be for you,' Beddy Byes sympathized.

'Time catches up with everyone in the end,' she sighed. 'No one seems to want specialist cheesemongers any more.'

'Cheesemaking was once considered an art form,' Beddy Byes said. 'But sadly not any more.'

'You know,' the woman said, 'you're a very nice gentleman, *Morr-eece*.'

'Thank you,' he said, opening the back doors of the van. 'Shall we, erm, start bringing it out? You'll have to do all the lifting – as you can see, I'm a bit incapacitated at the moment.'

While this conversation was happening, Aldrin, Sisely, Wilbur and Mrs Van Boxtel still had their eyes fixed on the *front* of the shop. They stared as the woman inside pulled down the blinds.

'It doesn't look like this Beddy Byes cad is going to show,' said Wilbur.

'What time ish it?' Mrs Van Boxtel wondered.

Sisely looked at her watch. 'Twenty past five,' she said.

'Perhapsh Wilbur ish right,' Mrs Van Boxtel said. 'We have no reashon to believe that Beddy Byesh will come here.'

'Wait!' Aldrin said – because something had occurred to him. 'Does the shop have a rear entrance?'

'Yes,' said Sisely. 'It's accessible from an alley off Grosvenor Parade.'

'What if he's taking the cheese out the back?' Aldrin asked, throwing the car door open.

Aldrin ran across the road, past the shop and turned on to Grosvenor Parade. He found the alley. His heart started beating FASTER and FASTER as he ran along the rear of the row of shops and looked into their backyards. And that was when he heard a voice say:

'Thank you for your help loading the van. How awful for you to have to say goodbye to all this delicious cheese.'

It was Beddy Byes!

Aldrin poked his head into the yard just as the man was about to get into the front of a white van – the same white van he was driving when he cleaned out Aldrin's dad's stock. Aldrin noticed that he was wearing a giant snow-boot cast and was walking with the aid of crutches.

'Goodbye, Louise,' he said cheerfully as he levered himself into the driver's seat.

In that moment, he happened to look up. Aldrin pulled his head back and wondered if Beddy Byes had seen him. Then he heard the engine kick into life and he raced back to the car to tell the others.

'He's round . . . the back!' he told them breathlessly.

He threw open the back door and jumped in.

'He's loaded up . . . the van . . .' he added. 'He's about . . . to go.'

Mrs Van Boxtel turned the key and started the engine.

'No, wait!' said Wilbur. 'Allow *me* to drive, will you?'

'You?' asked Mrs Van Boxtel.

'Nel,' said Wilbur, 'you are, by a considerable distance, the **worst driver** it has ever been my misfortune to share a car with. If this chap is going to lead us all the way to Habeas Grusselvart's headquarters, then we will have to tail him in a way that is inconspicuous. No offence, Nel, but I don't believe you're capable of doing that.'

'He's right,' Aldrin and Sisely said at the exact same time.

'Fine,' said Mrs Van Boxtel, sounding hurt. 'But jusht to let you know, it ish not *me* who ish a bad driver, but everybody elshe on the road.'

They swapped seats. Aldrin spotted the van as it turned right on to Brereton Road.

'THERE HE IS!' he said, pointing.

Wilbur set off in pursuit, through the centre of the town, then the outskirts of town, then out into the countryside.

He stayed a discreet distance back so as not to arouse the suspicion of Beddy Byes. But Aldrin became nervous every time he allowed the white van to disappear round a bend in the road, terrified that, when they took the bend themselves, Beddy Byes would have disappeared.

'Keep up!' Aldrin urged him.

'We want him to lead us to Habeas,' Wilbur reminded him. 'If he begins to suspect that he's being followed, he'll take us on a wild goose chase.'

But Aldrin still believed that Beddy Byes *wanted* them to know where he was headed.

As they pursued the white van through the countryside, it became clear that Mrs Van Boxtel was a worse passenger than she was a driver. She was just as quick to anger when she *wasn't* sitting behind the steering wheel.

'Look at thish joker in the blue car,' she said as they attempted to overtake it on a stretch of winding country road. 'EITHER LEARN TO DRIVE, YOU SHILLY LITTLE MAN, OR PUT AN L-PLATE ON THE BACK OF YOUR SHILLY LITTLE CAR!'

'Nel,' said Wilbur, 'please calm down.'

Aldrin felt his pulse racing as he stared at the back of the white van – like a rabbit's tail in the distance – and he thought about where it was leading them.

'It looks like he's heading into West Yorkshire,' said Sisely.

But then, out of nowhere, Wilbur let out a shout:
'FOX!'

. . . and pulled hard on the wheel.

There was a loud squeal of rubber on asphalt . . .
SQUUUEEEAAALLLL!!!

. . . as Mrs Van Boxtel's tiny turquoise car swerved off the road and into a newly ploughed field. It **BOUNCED UP AND DOWN** for a few seconds before its wheels got caught in the mud and it came to a **juddering** stop.

Aldrin, Sisely, Wilbur and Mrs Van Boxtel felt themselves thrown forward. Luckily, they were all wearing seat belts.

'Everyone OK?' Wilbur asked, looking over his shoulder.

'Yes,' said Sisely.

'Yes,' said Aldrin.

'Yesh,' said Mrs Van Boxtel. 'What happened?'

'A damn-fool fox stepped out in front of us,' Wilbur told her. 'I was trying to avoid hitting the poor blighter.'

'QUICK!' Aldrin shouted. 'We have to get back on the road! We can't let Beddy Byes get away!'

'Yes, of course,' said Wilbur, turning the key in the engine. He pressed his foot on the accelerator. But the car didn't move. The wheels just spun in the mud.

'Oh, no,' said Wilbur. 'It looks like we're bally well stuck!'

And Aldrin felt his heart sink as he realized that Beddy Byes had managed to get away.

49

HIDING IN PLAIN SIGHT

Aldrin popped the lid of his lunch box. Within seconds, he could hear the scraping of chair legs off the floor as first Harry, then Frankie, then Sisely pushed back from the table.

'Oh, come on, it's not that bad,' said Aldrin. 'It's just a bit of Vieux-Boulogne.'

'My eyes are watering!' said Harry. 'Look! There are tears rolling down my face!'

Vieux-Boulogne was a soft cheese with an orange rind that smelled like a pig pen, but tasted divine.

'I've had an idea!' said Frankie, pinching his nose.

'Does it involve Aldrin putting the lid back on his lunch box?' asked Harry, with his hand over his mouth.

'No, it involves the character **NemeSwiss**,' Frankie said.

'I'm, er, not really sure I love the name NemeSwiss any more,' Aldrin told him, embarrassed by the mention of it. 'Maybe Nighty Knight was better.'

'No way,' Harry insisted. 'NemeSwiss is a proper superhero name.'

'Anyway,' Frankie continued, 'I was thinking that NemeSwiss should have to perform some act before he can enter into other people's nightmares. Like, for instance . . . eating cheese.'

'Eating cheese?' Harry asked.

'Exactly,' Frankie told him. 'What if, you know, just before he goes to sleep at night, he eats cheese and he thinks really hard about someone and *that's* how he gets into their dream? What do *you* think, Aldrin?'

'It's, erm, a bit far-fetched, isn't it?' Aldrin suggested.

'Of course it's far-fetched!' said Frankie. 'It's a superhero story!'

'Aldrin,' Sisely said, her hand clamped over her nose and mouth, 'I think you should put the lid on your lunch box before Mr Maskell comes.'

'It's fine,' he told her. 'I'm going to eat it in a second. Harry, can I ask you a question?'

'What?' said Harry, who was still covering his nose and mouth too.

'If you were a supervillain,' Aldrin asked, 'where would you build your base?'

'Probably on an island.' Harry shrugged. 'Middle of the Pacific Ocean – somewhere like that.'

'Right,' said Aldrin.

'I'd build mine into a mountain,' Frankie announced. 'Or a dormant volcano.'

'OK,' said Aldrin, 'but what if you didn't have an island, *or* a mountain, *or* a dormant volcano? What if you were going to build your secret headquarters in – OK, I'm just picking somewhere totally random now – West Yorkshire?'

'West Yorkshire?' Frankie scoffed. 'Why would a supervillain want to build his secret headquarters in West Yorkshire? That makes *no* sense.'

'No, it makes *total* sense,' said Harry. 'It's called **hiding in plain sight.**'

'Hiding in what?' Aldrin asked.

'Hiding in plain sight,' Sisely said. 'It means to go unnoticed, even though you're very noticeable.'

'Exactly,' said Harry. 'If I was a supervillain, I'd set up a base in Uttoxeter. Or Worksop. Or Somersal

Herbert. Then what I'd do is I'd set up a front.'

'A front?' Aldrin asked.

'Yeah, a pretend business,' Harry said, 'like a factory, or a call centre, or a recycling facility – something that doesn't look suspicious. But, at the same time, no one knows what *really* goes on inside.'

'**ALDRIN ADAMS!**' Mr Maskell shouted across the floor of the canteen. '**WHAT IN THE NAME OF GOD ARE YOU EATING?**'

Aldrin quickly stuffed the cheese into his mouth as Mr Maskell made his way over to the table, with his hand covering the lower half of his face to stop himself from gagging.

'Thorry . . . Mithter . . . Mathkell,' Aldrin managed to say through a mouthful of the *stinkiest* of STINKY mush. 'It wath . . . thome Vieux . . . Boulogne.'

'Vieux-Boulogne!' Mr Maskell declared. 'It's going on the **banned list!**'

He turned on his heel and left.

Harry stood up then.

'I'm sorry, Aldrin,' he said, 'I can still smell it. I'm going to be sick if I stay here.'

'Me too,' said Frankie, who followed Harry out of the cafeteria.

Sisely stood up then. She was about to leave too when Aldrin suddenly grabbed her wrist.

She looked him. His face was pale and his eyes bulged.

'Meeea Memummm,' he said.

'Are you choking?' Sisely asked.

Aldrin shook head.

'Meeea Memummm,' he repeated impatiently.

'That's completely unintelligible,' Sisely told him. 'Why don't you finish eating what's in your mouth and then say what's on your mind?'

For three solid minutes, Aldrin chewed and chewed the vile-smelling cheese until it had become a oniony, mushroomy ball of mush, small enough to pass down his throat.

'Theo Redmond,' he blurted out.

'Theo Redmond?' Sisely repeated. 'OK, you're still not making any sense at all, Aldrin. Have you definitely swallowed it?'

'Theo Redmond was the man who Ethan said discovered sequencing.'

'There's no such thing.'

'I know that. I'm just wondering if it was maybe another one of his jokes. What's Theo Redmond spelled backwards. It's Dnomder Oeht! Is there a town in West Yorkshire called Dnomder Oeht?'

'If there is,' said Sisely, 'I've never heard of it.'

'OK, what if his name isn't Theo?' Aldrin suggested. 'What if it was initials – like T.O.'

'T.O. Redmond spelled backwards is Dnomder Ot,' said Sisely. 'There's no such . . .'

She stopped.

'It could be an anagram,' she told him.

'What's an anagram?' Aldrin wondered.

'It's a word formed by rearranging the letters of another word,' she explained. 'Not necessarily backwards – just randomly.'

'OK,' said Aldrin, 'so what word could you make out of Dnomder Ot?'

He knew the answer before he'd even finished asking the question. And Sisely knew too. Because they both said it at exactly the same time:

'TODMORDEN!'

50

A BIT FISHY

But WHERE in Todmorden? That was the question that gnawed away at Aldrin that night. He was still contemplating it the following morning as Cerys unwrapped the cheeses while humming a happy tune and Doug opened the shop for the day.

Aldrin had borrowed a large map of Todmorden from the school library and he opened it on the counter. There was nothing unusual about Todmorden as far as he could see. It looked like just another run-of-the-mill market town. It was surrounded by moorlands and the Pennine Hills, with a river – the Calder – running through it.

Aldrin pored over every inch of the map, looking for something that struck him as being out of place.

'What's that?' asked Cerys as she emptied the cash bags into the till.

'It's a map,' Aldrin told her, 'of Todmorden.'

'Todmorden?' she asked. 'Why are you interested in Todmorden?'

'Oh, it's, erm, a project I'm doing for school,' he fibbed.

Just then, the door pinged and in strode Agatha Rees-Lane. She had an air of urgency about her this morning.

'I'll take some of the Corra Linn and some the Der Scharfe Maxx,' she said brusquely. 'Oh, and some Adelegger, some Coolea and some of that delicious Boerenkaas that I had yesterday.'

'You want to *buy* it?' Doug asked – not unreasonably.

'No, I'll take free samples of each,' she said. 'And I'm in rather a hurry today. The girls and I are going on a picnic. Do you think you could wrap it for me and then bring it out to the car?'

'Now just a minute –' Doug began to say.

'I'll do it,' Cerys said, cutting him off. 'It's no trouble at all.'

So Agatha sat in her open-top convertible while Cerys packed a bag of delicious – but, more importantly,

FREE – cheese for her and her friends. Doug smiled at Cerys as she took it outside, then his expression changed dramatically.

'This can't go on!' he said.

'Agatha can't stay away from the place,' Aldrin agreed.

'It's not just her,' Doug said. 'It's everyone. They're all taking advantage of Cerys's good nature.'

'Belinda would have told them all to sling their hooks,' Aldrin pointed out. 'Why don't you just admit it, Dad. You can't manage without her.'

Doug nodded sadly.

'It's true,' he confessed. 'Cerys is just, well, too nice. At this rate, I'll be bankrupt within a month.'

'This is what's known as your "**All is Lost**" moment, Dad?'

'My what?'

'Harry told me about it. It's the moment – usually three-quarters of the way through the story – where the hero realizes that they're as far away as it's possible to be from what they truly want.'

Doug stared sadly into space and nodded.

'That's *exactly* how I feel!' he said.

'But the other thing I learned,' Aldrin told him, 'is

that the **"All is Lost"** moment is never the end of the story. It's when the hero is forced to look into their soul – and that's when they decide on a course of action.'

'Belinda thinks I was looking for a new version of your mother. But I wasn't. The truth is that there IS no new version of your mother. Cynthia was a one-off. Just like Belinda is a one-off.'

'The shop isn't the same without her, Dad.'

'Nor is my life, Aldrin.'

'Then go and tell her that. Tell her how you feel about her.'

'Maybe I will,' Doug said.

The bell on the door pinged and Cerys stepped back into the shop.

'Agatha forgot that she wants a sample of the Bucheron,' she said, 'and some of the Nocetto di Capra. I'll just get them for her.'

'No,' Doug muttered, 'that's not right.'

At first, Aldrin thought his dad was putting his foot down over the free samples. But then he noticed that he was staring down at the map.

'What's not right?' Aldrin asked.

'*The Codfather Packing Company*,' Doug read. 'Why on earth would anyone build a fish-packaging factory in the middle of West Yorkshire? Todmorden is miles and miles from any sea!'

Aldrin suddenly felt a thrill of excitement shoot through him like a **JOLT OF ELECTRICITY**.

'Yes,' he agreed, 'it's very . . . *fishy*, isn't it?'

Had he found him, he wondered? Had his dad accidentally discovered the secret lair of Habeas Grusselvart?

'Dad, I have to go to Sisely's,' he said.

'Aren't you going to help us in the shop today?' Cerys asked.

'I think you two can manage without me for a few hours,' said Aldrin.

As he walked towards the door, he thought about what he was about to do and the danger he was likely to face. He turned round and said, 'Dad, I love you.'

Doug chuckled.

'You're only going to Sisely's house!' he reminded him. 'It's not like we're never going to see each other again!'

'I KNOW WHERE HE'S HIDING!'

Sisely was standing in the front garden of her house with a brand-new electric scooter.

'WHOA!' Aldrin gasped. 'Where did you get that?'

'From my mum and dad,' Sisely said. 'For my birthday.'

'When was your birthday?' Aldrin asked.

'It's today.'

'Today? Why didn't you tell me?'

'Why would I tell you?'

'Because that's what friends do.' Aldrin smiled. 'They tell each other stuff.'

'Fine,' she shrugged. 'It's my birthday today.'

'Happy birthday!' he told her. 'Sisely, **I KNOW WHERE HE'S HIDING!'**

'Habeas?'

'Do you remember what Harry said? If he was a supervillain and he wanted to build his base in West Yorkshire, he'd set up a pretend business?'

'Yes,' Sisely remembered, 'like a factory, or a call centre, or a recycling facility.'

'There's a warehouse in Todmorden – my dad spotted it on the map – called the Codfather Packing Company.'

'Why would *anyone* build a fish-packaging factory in Todmorden?' Sisely asked. 'It's miles and miles from the sea.'

'Exactly!'

'You think he's there?'

'I do! Sisely, are you thinking what I'm thinking?'

'Probably not.'

'I'm thinking that you and I should go to Todmorden to check this place out – right now!'

'I was thinking we should ring Mrs Van Boxtel and tell her.'

'OK, fine,' said Aldrin, who'd made up his mind to listen to his friend in future.

Sisely invited him into the house. She picked up the cordless phone in the kitchen and she dialled Mrs Van

Boxtel's mobile number, which – like everything else – she had memorized.

'She's not answering,' she said. 'It's going to her voicemail.'

Sisely left a message, telling her about Doug's discovery.

'So, what do we do now?' Aldrin asked after she'd hung up.

'We wait,' she told him.

'Come on, Sisely!' Aldrin said. 'Where's your sense of adventure?'

'I don't *have* one!' she reminded him.

'We'll just go and have a look,' he said. 'That's all.'

'How would we even get there? Todmorden is miles away.'

Aldrin looked out into the hallway where Sisely's brand-new electric scooter was leaning against the wall.

'You *can't* be serious,' Sisely said. 'It would take us about four hours to get there!'

'So?' Aldrin asked. 'What else are you doing today?'

Sisely sighed a long sigh.

'Fine,' she said. 'But we're just going to look at the place from the outside, OK?'

Aldrin's tummy was suddenly turning somersaults at the thought of confronting his enemy – this evil overlord who, for five hundred years, had preyed on people's innermost fears to spread misery and unhappiness throughout –

RRRIBBIT . . . RRRIBBIT . . . RRRIBBIT . . .

'What was that?' Sisely asked.

'I think it was my stomach,' Aldrin said. 'It's just excitement.'

'It wasn't your stomach, Aldrin. It sounded like –'

RRRIBBIT . . . RRRIBBIT . . . RRRIBBIT . . .

Aldrin looked down. And there, sitting snugly in the breast pocket of his jacket, was Silas.

'Oh, no, he must have climbed in there!' Aldrin said.

'Do you need to take him home?' Sisely asked.

'No,' Aldrin told her, 'we'll take him with us. But just promise me, Silas, that you'll stay out of trouble!'

CHEESY RIDER

For once in her life, Sisely was wrong about something. It didn't take them four hours to reach Todmorden. It took almost five!

She had failed to factor into her calculations the additional drag that came from sharing her scooter with her cheese-loving friend.

There was also the fact that she couldn't use the motorway, having promised her mum that she would only ride the thing on the footpath.

'Oh, no!' she exclaimed as they finally entered Todmorden in the early afternoon.

'What's wrong?' asked Aldrin, who was standing behind her, steering.

'The battery light is flashing,' she said.

'So? We're here now.'

'Yes, we're here, Aldrin – but how are we going to get back?'

Aldrin was in such a fever of excitement at the prospect of confronting his enemy that he wasn't even thinking about going home.

And now he had no time to think about it because in the distance he could see the sign for the Codfather Packing Company.

'There it is!' he said.

He could feel his pulse quicken.

'We don't know that it's definitely Habeas Grusselvart's base,' Sisely pointed out. 'And, anyway, they're not going to just let us inside.'

Moments later, they pulled up outside the factory – at the exact moment that the scooter ran out of battery power!

'That's it,' said Sisely. 'We have officially no way of getting home now.'

'Sisely, look,' said Aldrin, pointing at the gate. It was wide open! And the security hut next to it was . . . empty!

'Aldrin, we said we were just going to check it out from the outside,' Sisely reminded him.

'We can still get a bit closer,' Aldrin said.

He walked through the gate and Sisely followed, wheeling her scooter. The factory building looked ENORMOUS.

He sniffed the air like a basset hound trying to pick up a scent.

'I don't smell fish,' he said, 'do you?'

'I'm not sure this is a good idea,' said Sisely as they crossed the car park. 'What if someone asks us what we're doing here?'

'We'll tell them the truth,' Aldrin said breezily. 'We're two out-of-towners whose scooter has run out of battery power, and we're looking for somewhere to plug it in for an hour.'

They reached the factory, then they wandered round the back. Aldrin spotted a loading bay – and, next to it, something that stopped him dead in his tracks!

'Sisely, look!' he said. 'It's the van that Beddy Byes was driving!'

'Let's find a way to tell Mrs Van Boxtel,' said Sisely.

'No, let's go into the building,' Aldrin insisted.

'But what if someone sees us? There's bound be security cameras.'

'Sisely, I think Beddy Byes *wanted* us to find this

place. I think that's why the gate was open and why there's nobody in the security hut.'

'What if it's a trap?'

'I don't think it's a trap,' Aldrin said, stepping through the doors of the loading bay and into the factory. 'Come on, Sisely, we didn't come all this way just to turn round and go back home again – not when we're so close. Habeas Grusselvart is somewhere inside these walls.'

Sisely sighed, leaned her scooter up against the wall of the factory, then followed him inside. Aldrin spotted two hazmat suits with fishbowl helmets hanging from a hook on the wall.

'Here, let's put these on,' he suggested. 'They'll just assume we work here.'

The suits looked enormous on them. They rolled up their trouser legs and sleeves to try to look a bit less like two children wearing adult clothes.

'There's an oxygen mask inside the helmet,' Aldrin said. 'I wonder what that's for?'

'We'd better put them on,' Sisely suggested. 'It's probably part of their health-and-safety policy.'

Yes, even as they were preparing to trespass on the property of the world's most evil supervillain, Sisely remained a stickler for the rules.

They fixed their oxygen masks over their noses and mouths and they put on their helmets.

They wandered around blindly for several minutes – blindly because the glass at the front of their helmets got fogged up. But soon they found themselves standing in front of what looked like a heavy door, with a giant skull and crossbones on it, then underneath was the word '**DANGER!**'.

Aldrin pulled down the handle and pushed open the heavy door. Beyond it was a small antechamber, which turned out to be an airlock, then beyond that was a second door. This one had a large wheel attached to it. Aldrin turned it and the door opened outwards into an enormous room.

Like two astronauts stepping on to a planet where no human being had ever set foot before, they walked slowly and cautiously into it.

The floor beneath their feet felt wet and sticky. But they could still see nothing. It took about a minute for the fog on the inside of their helmets to clear and that was when the full STINKING truth of what went on inside the walls of the Codfather Packing Company was revealed to them.

'It's all . . . CHEESE!' Aldrin said into his oxygen mask.

Which was an understatement.

It was a MOUNTAIN of cheese, big enough to ski down! Millions upon millions of tons of the stuff – and it was all decomposing. Aldrin could see the fumes rising from it like smoke from a volcano, and suddenly he understood the reason for the oxygen masks.

He turned round and he could see the shock on Sisely's face even through her helmet. With a nod, he indicated that they should leave and they headed for the door. They stepped into the antechamber and Aldrin pulled the door closed behind him. He pressed down on the handle of the other door . . .

But it didn't move!

Aldrin turned and looked at Sisely, his

eyes wide with alarm.

He tried the door again – but the handle still wouldn't budge. They were trapped in the tiny antechamber between the two doors.

And then Aldrin and Sisely heard laughter – horrible, mocking laughter.

'MWAH-HA-HA-HA-HA-HA-HA!'

It was coming from a speaker on the wall.

'Nice of you to pop in,' said Habeas. 'So what do you think of my mountain of cheese?'

Aldrin tore off his helmet and his gas mask.

'YOU'RE CRAZY!' he roared.

'Oh, yes,' said Habeas, 'but then *all* villainous masterminds are crazy! I call it . . . Mount Cheddarest.'

Aldrin didn't reply.

'You know – *like* Mount Everest, except it's Mount Cheddarest,' said Habeas. 'I thought you and that father of yours liked a good pun.'

'I'm sorry to disappoint you,' Aldrin told him, 'but I don't think it works on any level.'

Sisely followed Aldrin's example and removed her helmet and mask.

'LET US OUT OF HERE!' she shouted.

'With pleasure,' said Habeas.

At that moment, the outer door opened and Aldrin and Sisely found themselves staring at eight burly security guards.

'I shall see you very shortly,' Habeas said.

Then he laughed again:

'MWAH-HA-HA-HA-HA-HA-HA!'

'THE HILL ON WHICH YOU DIE'

The eight burly security guards escorted Aldrin and Sisely to a lift, where one of them pressed the button for the fourth floor.

'I'm sorry,' Aldrin whispered to Sisely out of the corner of his mouth.

'Why are *you* sorry?' she asked.

'Because I talked you into coming with me,' he reminded her. 'And then I talked you into entering the factory when you wanted to tell Mrs Van Boxtel.'

'You were determined to do it anyway,' she pointed out. 'And I wasn't going to let you do it on your own. You're kind of useless on your own.'

'I kind of am, aren't I?' Aldrin laughed.

The lift pinged. They had arrived at the fourth floor.

They stepped out.

'Keep walking,' said one of the security guards, shoving Aldrin in the back.

As they were escorted along the corridor, Aldrin read the names on the doors:

RITA CHOO

Training Delivery Manager with Special Responsibility for Things that Go Bump in the Night

DON DECADENT

Training Delivery Manager with Special Responsibility for Scary Clowns

HOLT HESSION

Training Delivery Manager with Special Responsibility for Things that Bite and Sting

It was a far bigger operation than Aldrin had even dared to imagine.

He could hear voices – actors apparently practising their lines:

'No, it's not "Boo!". It's "BOOOOOO!!!!!!". Try it again, darling – this time with feeling!'

Moments later, they stopped outside a door. One of the security guards knocked. Inside, a voice called out:

'COME IN!!!'

The door was pushed open. And Aldrin and Sisely stepped into the office . . . of Habeas Grusselvart!

He was sitting with his feet resting on a large desk. Standing at his right hand, with a broad grin on his face, was the young man Aldrin had once thought of as his friend, the young man he knew as Archie, but whose real name was Ethan Marcus.

'Hello, Aldrin,' said Habeas in a mock-cheery voice. 'And hello, Sisely. You remember Ethan, don't you, Aldrin? Or should I say NemeSwiss?'

'I remember that he's a liar,' Aldrin snapped. 'And a cheat and a snake in the grass.'

'Oh, come, come,' said Habeas, 'there's no need for that kind of hostility. Please remember that you are a guest here – an uninvited guest, but a guest nonetheless. Remove those hazmat suits – they're company property, you know.'

'Gladly,' said Aldrin, who was really sweating now.

Sisely and Aldrin stepped out of their protective clothing and threw it to one side.

'Let us go,' Sisely demanded.

'I can't do that.' Habeas smiled. 'You know far too much for me to ever let you leave now.'

'So what are you going to do with us?' Aldrin asked.

'All will be revealed,' Habeas assured him, 'in due course. So tell me, what do you think of the place? Impressed much?'

'You operate a factory that churns out nothing but unhappiness,' Aldrin said.

'I shall take that as a compliment,' said Habeas.

Aldrin felt his attention suddenly drawn to the wall behind the desk. It was filled with TV screens – thousands and thousands of them.

'I call it my **WaLL of Torment**,' Habeas said. 'Each screen is playing a scene from a nightmare that's being experienced by someone somewhere in the world at this moment in time. It was on that wall that I first saw you, sticking your nose in where it wasn't wanted. Well, you should have stayed out of other people's nightmares. And you should have stayed away from Todmorden.'

'I came here to destroy you,' Aldrin told him.

'You're not doing such a good job of it.' Habeas laughed again.

There was another knock on the door.

'ENTER!' yelled Habeas.

A second later, Beddy Byes hobbled in on his crutches.

'They came alone,' he told his boss, 'on the girl's electric scooter.'

He made his way behind the desk and stood at Habeas's left hand. Aldrin and Sisely looked at him searchingly, hoping for some kind of signal from him that he was on their side. This amused Habeas greatly.

'Oh, you thought Beddy Byes led you to me so that you could destroy me?' he laughed. 'Well, I'm sorry to disappoint you, Aldrin, but he brought you here so that *I* could destroy *you!*'

Beddy Byes shot an evil grin at Aldrin.

'You see,' Habeas continued, 'Beddy Byes lives to serve me, his master. We had a little falling-out recently, making it necessary for me to demote him. I think he accepts that he fell down in one or two of his duties. But he is back in my good books now. Beddy Byes, how would you like to *share* the role of my Personal Assistant and Vice President of Global Operations with Ethan here?'

'I would like that very much,' said Beddy Byes, 'Your Highnessfulness!'

'It's good to have you back,' said Habeas. 'And now, Aldrin, in answer to your question, I'm going to tell you what I intend to do with you.'

'If you let us go,' Aldrin said boldly, 'I might spare your life.'

Habeas burst out laughing.

'Can you believe this kid?' he asked Ethan.

'He's a born comedian,' Ethan agreed.

'I could see from the security footage,' Habeas said, removing his feet from the desk and standing up, 'how impressed you were by Mount Cheddarest.'

'I still don't think it works as a pun,' Aldrin told him coolly.

'No matter,' Habeas replied. 'Mount Cheddarest will be **the hill on which you die**. You *and* your little friend here.'

'What do you mean?' asked Aldrin, exchanging a look with Sisely.

'I'm going to put you back in the room,' Habeas told them, 'with all that cheese – but this time *without* your helmets and gas masks. Do you know long you'll last breathing in those fumes?'

Aldrin shrugged.

'I've no idea either,' Habeas quipped, 'but we're about to find out.'

He shouted, 'SECURITY!'

The door opened again and in walked the eight burly security guards. Aldrin fixed Beddy Byes with a look.

'Maurice,' he said. 'Maurice. I know there's good in you. My mum told me.'

'Your mother was a fool,' said Habeas, 'just like you are! Goodbye, Sisely Musa! Goodbye, Aldrin Adams! And good riddance to both of you!'

THE WORST BIRTHDAY EVER

'MWAH-HA-HA-HA-HA-HA-HA!'

With Habeas Grusselvart's evil laugh echoing along the corridor, Aldrin and Sisely were escorted back to the lift, to take them down to the ground floor and the enormous vacuum-sealed warehouse that contained Mount Cheddarest.

'I'm sorry,' Aldrin told Sisely again. 'I'm sure this is turning out to be **THE WORST BIRTHDAY EVER!'**

'I've had better,' she confessed, then she lowered her voice so that the security guards couldn't hear her. 'Aldrin, what are we going to do?'

'Sisely, don't worry,' he whispered.

The lift door opened and large meaty hands shoved them in the direction of the warehouse. One of the

377

security guards opened the first door.

'Aldrin,' Sisely said in a hushed voice, 'if you secretly know kick-boxing and you're about to take on those eight security guards, can I suggest that NOW might be a good time to leap into action?'

'Just be patient,' Aldrin told her out of the side of his mouth.

'It's just that they're shoving us into the airlock,' she pointed out.

The security guards put on their gas masks and fishbowl helmets and closed the first door behind them. Then one of them turned the wheel and pushed open the second door.

The smell hit Aldrin and Sisely INSTANTLY!

Aldrin loved stinky cheeses – the stinkier the better was his philosophy – but this was a pong so overpoweringly vile that it almost knocked him clean off his feet!

Sisely began to retch:

BWUUUHHH!!!
BWUUUHHH!!!
BWUUUHHH!!!'

They were shoved roughly into the warehouse and with a loud . . .

CLAAANNNGGG!

. . . the door was pulled closed behind them.

The air was so thick with noxious gas that Aldrin and Sisely could only take very short breaths. Tears stung their eyes. They COUGHED and SPLUTTERED.

'OK, Aldrin,' Sisely said, 'what's this plan of yours?'

'Plan?' asked Aldrin. 'I don't have a plan.'

'You told me not to worry,' she reminded him.

'I just meant, you know – the prophecy!' Aldrin shrugged.

'The PROPHECY?' Sisely said angrily. 'There IS no prophecy! They made it up!'

'OK, there's no such person as Loofasi Smada,' Aldrin spluttered, 'but my mum still believes that I was born to unite the Cheese Whizzes in destroying Habeas Grusselvart.'

'THAT'S what you meant when you told me not to worry?' Sisely choked in disbelief. 'I wish you'd told me that in the lift. I would have kicked one of the security guards in the shin or something.'

'I think . . . everythiiing's . . . going to beee . . . okaaay,' said Aldrin, slurring his words. He was suddenly feeling very light-headed.

'You're about to faint,' Sisely told him. 'Lie down on

the ground.'

'Whaaat?' said Aldrin. 'Whhhyyy?'

His vision was swimming.

'Because most gases rise,' Sisely pointed out. 'It means the air is cleaner closer to the ground.'

Aldrin and Sisely lay down on their sides and they tried to breathe.

'Maaayyybeee . . . you should haaave . . . kicked theeem . . . in the shiiinnns,' Aldrin slurred.

'Shuuush,' Sisely slurred back. 'You're waaasting . . . valuuuable . . . oxygeennn.'

Slowly, the two friends began to lose consciousness. Their vision became blurred and they started to feel the irresistible urge to sleep.

And that was when a figure suddenly appeared before them.

'I've got you,' he told them in a calm voice. 'You're safe now.'

At first, Aldrin wondered if he was hallucinating due to the effect of the gas. But he watched as a man in a hazmat suit and fishbowl helmet crouched down and placed an oxygen mask over Sisely's nose and mouth, then placed one over Aldrin's nose and mouth too.

And, as he did so, Aldrin could just about make out the face of their kindly saviour through the steamed-up glass of his helmet.

It was Beddy Byes.

'ATTAAAAAACK!!!!!!'

Aldrin and Sisely sat on the floor of the corridor with their backs against the wall and tried to catch their breath.

'You saved . . . our lives,' Aldrin said between gasps.

'I'm sorry it took me so long,' Beddy Byes said.

'Did you send Aldrin . . . the newspaper article . . . about **Cheese Louise** . . . closing down?' Sisely asked.

'Yes, I did,' Beddy Byes said. 'I was hoping you'd follow me here. Which you did. But then Habeas discovered what I'd done. You have a spy somewhere within the Cheese Whizz network.'

Aldrin and Sisely exchanged a look – it was just like Mrs Van Boxtel said.

'Habeas found out about the newspaper clipping I

sent you. But I convinced him that I was luring you into a trap to win my way back into his good books.'

'So my mum *was* right about you,' Aldrin told him, his breathing returning to normal again. 'She told me there was good in you.'

'I'm not sure that the good I've done matters any more,' he said, looking away, 'especially having done so much bad.'

'Of course it matters!' Aldrin assured him. 'It's NEVER too late to do the right thing! And you led us to Habeas Grusselvart!'

Beddy Byes returned a sad smile. 'So when are the others getting here?' he wondered.

'Others?' asked Aldrin.

'Well, I did presume you'd tell all the other Cheese Whizzes,' said Beddy Byes, 'and right now an army of them would be descending on Todmorden to destroy Habeas Grusselvart's base of operations.'

Aldrin was beginning to see the error he'd made in not thinking this plan through.

'They're not coming,' Sisely said. 'We're on our own.'

'On your own?' Beddy Byes repeated, his voice filled with concern. 'Then we'd better get out of here! Right now!'

But Aldrin suddenly remembered something.

'Oh, no!' he said, then he looked down into the breast pocket of his jacket. 'Silas!'

Inside, his pet frog lay motionless, his eyes closed.

'He must have breathed in too much gas,' Aldrin said, tears suddenly spilling from his eyes. 'Oh, Silas. I should never have taken you with me.'

'Aldrin,' Sisely said, 'I'm very sad that your frog is dead, but we REALLY NEED to get out of here.'

'She's right,' said Beddy Byes. 'Let's go.'

Aldrin scrambled to his feet.

'I know every inch of this factory,' Beddy Byes said. 'There's an emergency exit that isn't alarmed. It opens out on to a part of the car park that isn't covered by CCTV. I can help you climb over the wall.'

Beddy Byes opened a door and led them into a large empty room.

'The emergency exit is in here,' he told them over his shoulder. 'It's your only chance to get out of here without Habeas finding –'

And then he suddenly stopped – both talking *and* walking. And Aldrin and Sisely stopped too. Because right in front of them stood . . .

. . . the one and only . . .

. . . and uniquely evil . . .

. . . Habeas Grusselvart!

He was standing in front of the emergency door, next to Ethan.

'I told you he was going to betray you,' Ethan said to his boss.

'I'm just too willing to see the good in people,' Habeas replied.

Beddy Byes, Aldrin and Sisely turned and ran for the door they'd come through. But a very large group of security guards entered through it.

And now they were trapped!

Habeas narrowed his eyes. 'Beddy Byes – you FOOL!' he thundered.

'My name isn't Beddy Byes,' his former Personal Assistant and Vice President of Global Operations informed him. 'It's *Morr-eece* Mackle.'

'After everything I did for you.'

'You did NOTHING for me except exploit my unhappiness to help you spread anxiety and misery throughout the world.'

'And what's wrong with that?' Habeas asked. 'It's a perfectly respectable career. More exciting than being a boring old cheesemonger, I would have thought.'

Ethan chuckled along with him.

'Well,' Maurice announced, 'I don't want to do your evil work any more.'

'I totally understand,' said Habeas. 'I'll make sure you're paid up until the end of the week and I'll talk to Human Resources about getting you a reference.'

'What?' asked Maurice. 'REALLY?'

'Of course not!' Habeas replied – and his laugh NEVER sounded more sinister.

'MWAH-HA-HA-HA-HA-HA-HA! You don't get to just walk away from an operation like this!' Habeas told him in a voice that chilled Maurice to his core. 'Especially with the secrets that *you* know! I can promise you this, Beddy Byes – you will NEVER see the outside of this place again!'

Aldrin took a step forward. 'Habeas,' he announced, 'I'm giving you once last chance to surrender – before I destroy you in line with the ancient prophecy.'

A long moment of silence followed before Habeas burst into helpless convulsions of laughter.

'He really should be on the stage, this kid!' Habeas said, then he turned to one of the security guards. 'Throw them back in the room – all three of them!'

In that moment, Aldrin could hear a noise outside,

like a distant lawnmower engine.

No, he thought. *It* couldn't *be. Could it?*

'What *is* that CONFOUNDED noise?' Habeas asked as it rose in volume.

Before anyone could investigate, there was a loud **BANG** – and an enormous hole was blown in the wall, forcing Habeas, Ethan and some of the security guards to dive out of the way in fright.

Poking through the hole, Aldrin noticed, was the nose of Mrs Van Boxtel's tiny turquoise car!

'She must have listened to my message,' Sisely whispered.

Outside, they could hear the slamming of a car door and then what sounded like an elderly woman, with a strange European accent, muttering to herself. 'The parking shpashesh in thish country are far too shmall. It ish shomething I have alwaysh shaid.'

Every pair of eyes in the room stayed glued to the enormous hole, waiting for something to happen. Then, a few seconds later, a sweet-looking old lady with a giant dandelion-puffball hairdo, wearing a surgical collar, walked in, brushing the dust from her cardigan.

'Hello, Aldrin!' she said. 'Hello, Shishely! Shorry I am late!'

'Nel . . . Van . . . Boxtel!' Habeas said, spacing out her name. 'We meet at last!'

'Habeash Grusshelvart,' she replied, 'I can't shay that it givesh me any great pleashure to lay eyesh on you for the firsht time. But shtill I'm sure I will feel better when I watch you being deshtroyed today.'

Habeas gave a sort of half-laugh, like he couldn't believe what he was hearing.

'This one's even funnier than the Adams boy!' he declared. 'Well, at least they'll have each other for amusement when they're breathing their last – on the slopes of Mount Cheddarest!'

'Mount Cheddaresht?' Mrs Van Boxtel asked.

'It's what he calls his giant mountain of rotting cheese,' Aldrin told his teacher. 'He's been collecting the stuff.'

'Mount Cheddaresht?' Mrs Van Boxtel repeated.

'Yes!' said Habeas impatiently. 'It's *like* Mount Everest, except obviously made of cheese.'

'I am not sho shure that it worksh ash a pun,' Mrs Van Boxtel said.

This was the trigger for Habeas to lose his temper.

'Put them in the room!' he growled. 'ALL OF THEM!'

Several security guards started to walk towards

Mrs Van Boxtel. Suddenly, and VERY unexpectedly, she bent her knee and lifted one foot off the floor. At the same time, she hung her two arms in the air, with her wrists all limp.

'I think it only fair to warn you,' she said, 'that ash a little girl growing up in the Netherlandsh, I learned the Japaneshe form of unarmed combat known ash judo.'

The security guards stopped walking towards her. They all took a step or two backwards.

'What are you doing?' Habeas asked them.

'She said she knows judo,' one of them replied.

'When she was a little girl,' Habeas reminded them, 'which was a long time ago – probably when dinosaurs walked the earth. Nel, put your leg down – you'll dislocate your hip.'

'I might shurprishe you,' she told Habeas. 'Or perhapsh shome othersh might shurprishe you inshtead. Habeash, I would like to introdushe you to shome of my friendsh.'

Suddenly, another figure appeared through the hole in the wall, then another, then another, until they were streaming in. Aldrin recognized Maxine Joli and Cormac de Courcy and Wilbur Leveson-Gough and most of the other forty Cheese Whizzes who had been at the meeting in Tintwistle.

Mrs Van Boxtel had summoned an army to storm the place!

Aldrin watched as, one by one, they all assumed fighting poses.

'Well,' said Habeas, 'what are we all waiting for?'

'We are waiting for Aldrin to give ush the order,' said Mrs Van Boxtel.

Aldrin looked around him.

'Order?' he asked.

'According to the propheshy,' she said, smiling at him, 'a boy would bring together all of the Cheeshe Whizshesh and lead them to the evil Habeash Grusshelvart. Sho perhapsh it wash true after all. If it wash, Aldrin, we are humbly awaiting your inshtructionsh.'

Aldrin smiled at his English teacher, whom he'd grown to love like a second mother. And then he shouted:

'ATTAAAAAACK!!!!!!'

THE BATTLE OF TODMORDEN

All HELL broke loose then!

The security guards rushed at the Cheese Whizzes. But, whatever skill set they possessed in keeping nosy strangers off the factory premises, they were no match for the Cheese Whizzes in the art of hand-to-hand combat.

As if by magic, Maxine Joli started conjuring up red-wax-covered balls of Edam from nowhere, then rolling them across the floor – one after another – like an expert boules player. The security guards who were charging at her stepped on them and fell – one, two, three, four, FIVE of them – landing in a tangle of arms and legs. Aldrin rushed straight into the middle of the fray with his head lowered like a rampaging bull.

A security guard, who bore an uncanny resemblance to the bulldog who lived on Burgess Road, came running towards him, snarling. Aldrin caught him FULL in the stomach . . .

WOOOMMMPPPFFF!!!

. . . and the man fell on his back, winded and yelping like a chihuahua.

All around him the battle raged.

Arthur Ladd, the former coal miner from Northumbria – a man who, to Aldrin, looked at least eighty years old – moved with the grace and agility

of an Olympic gymnast. From the pockets of his well-worn tweed jacket, he started pulling out giant strings of cheese. In a blur of movement, he used them to trip up the security guards, in much the same way that Aldrin had taken down the Tyrannosaurus rex, winding the strings round their knees to bring them down, then tying them up in yet more cheese strings – of which he seemed to have an endless supply.

Maxine was now armed with what looked a giant Super Soaker. From it, she shot huge globules of Mont d'Or – a melty cheese that Aldrin especially loved – right into the faces of Habeas Grusselvart's henchmen.

'I *have* to get one of those for Christmas!' Aldrin noted to himself.

Temporarily blinded, they stumbled about uselessly, trying to wipe the melty cheese from their eyes, while Arthur tied them up with cheese strings.

Meanwhile, Cormac de Courcy, the Irish farmer with the eyepatch, was wielding a giant cheesy breadstick like a sabre, forcing three security guards to back away with their hands raised in submission. One security guard who made a grab for Sisely found himself the recipient of a painful kick in the shin. He hopped around on one leg, howling in pain and using the foulest of language:

'You LITTLE –'

. . . until Sisely decided she couldn't listen to any more and just pushed him over.

Aldrin was admiring this move when suddenly he felt his legs kicked from underneath him. He hit the floor and looked up. The security guard he'd knocked on to his back had recovered and was now bearing down on him angrily.

But then, out of nowhere, a hand appeared from behind, placed a cloth over the man's mouth, and . . .

WOOOMMMPPPFFF!!!

. . . the man's eyes rolled backwards and he fell to the floor, unconscious.

In the chaos unfolding around him, Aldrin couldn't immediately tell the identity of his saviour. But then he saw that it was Estelle Giddens – the traitor! – who was still pretending to be on the side of the Cheese Whizzes.

'He'll be asleep for a minute of two,' she said. 'It was just some concentrated essence of Limburger.' Which Aldrin knew was one of the **STINKIEST** of **ALL** stinky cheeses.

Estelle offered him her hand.

'No thank you,' Aldrin told her. 'I'm more than capable of standing up by myself.'

'Please yourself,' she said and shrugged before returning to the battle.

As Aldrin climbed to his feet, he noticed three more security guards hopping around on one leg and Sisely standing with a giant circle of space around her and a face that seemed to say, 'OK, who's next?'

Then, out of the corner of his eye, he spotted Habeas running at Mrs Van Boxtel with a fist raised and a look of sheer rage on his face. She had her back to him and didn't appear to see him coming.

'MRS VAN BOXTEL!,' Aldrin roared. **'LOOK OUT!'**

But then something EXTRAORDINARY happened.

In one fluid movement, she lifted one leg, spun round in a semicircle and caught Habeas with a roundhouse kick – flush on the chin! The evil overlord collapsed like a detonated building!

Aldrin shook his head. His English teacher really WAS a judo master.

He felt a tap on his shoulder then. It was Maurice.

'Look!' he said, pointing his finger.

Aldrin followed his line of vision and saw Ethan heading for the door.

'Where's he going?' Aldrin asked.

'They're probably going to abandon the building,' said Maurice.

Aldrin cracked a smile.

'So we won!' he declared. 'SISELY, WE WON!'

Maurice shook his head.

'Not yet,' he said, then he started to pick his way towards the door after Ethan. 'I have to stop him!'

Aldrin looked around him. He saw Maxine Joli rolling balls of Edam across the floor with one hand and firing her Super Soaker with the other. He saw

Cormac using his breadstick like a skilled swords-man, forcing Habeas Grusselvart's guards to back away and then turn and run.

And he saw Mrs Van Boxtel judo-throwing one of the security guards over her shoulder like he weighed nothing.

'I didn't know she did judo,' Aldrin said to Sisely, shaking his head.

'I have a feeling,' Sisely replied, 'that there are LOTS of things about Mrs Van Boxtel that we don't know yet.'

'Sisely, I think they've got this,' Aldrin told her. 'Let's go and help Maurice.'

They followed him in the direction of the door.

'What's going on?' Aldrin asked as they caught up with him, now picking his way on his crutches down a corridor towards the heart of the factory.

'This building is just bricks and mortar,' Maurice reminded them. 'The only part of the operation that's of any real importance is contained in the computer system.'

'The nightmares,' Sisely said.

'You're a very smart girl,' Maurice replied. 'Almost four million of them. They're like short movies – many of them were filmed here using actors standing in front of a green screen, then digitally enhanced using the latest graphics software. The computer has been programmed to play them on a two- or three-times-weekly loop in the dreams of seventy million people across the world.'

'Seventy MILLION?' Aldrin asked. This thing was bigger than even he had imagined. 'So *that's* what Ethan has gone to get?'

'We can set Habeas back to Year Zero,' Maurice declared, 'if we can just prevent Ethan from uploading all that information to the cloud.'

'And how are we going to do that?' Aldrin asked.

Maurice suddenly turned into a small room that contained a series of large grey electrical boxes that had hundreds of switches, red levers, clocks, buttons, knobs, wires of all colours, and flashing green and yellow lights all over them.

'Simple,' said Maurice. 'By shutting off the power to the building.'

He walked over to a computer and tapped on the keys.

'Just as I thought,' he said. 'He's uploading everything.'

'Oh, no!' Aldrin said.

'It's only sixty per cent complete,' Maurice said. 'There's still time.'

He ran over to one of the electrical boxes and started flicking some switches up and other switches down, then pressing buttons and turning knobs left and right.

'Sixty-five per cent,' he said, stealing a quick look at the screen. 'Almost there. Aldrin, that giant red lever next to your left elbow – if you pull that down, it should cut off the power.'

Aldrin reached for the lever. Then he heard a voice behind him say, 'I wouldn't do that if I were you.'

Aldrin and Maurice spun round. Standing in the doorway was the tall, moustachioed figure of Wilbur Leveson-Gough. And what they couldn't fail to notice was that he was holding Sisely prisoner.

'Step away from that lever,' he said, 'or the girl will get hurt. There's a good chappie!'

57

NINETY SECONDS TO SAVE THE WORLD

'It was YOU!' Aldrin spat. 'YOU were the one who betrayed the Cheese Whizzes – not Estelle Giddens!'

'Classic diversionary tactic,' Wilbur said proudly, the two ends of his moustache dancing like happy caterpillars. 'And you fell for it. All of you.'

Maurice stared at the man. 'I presume it was you who told Habeas that I sent Aldrin the newspaper cutting about **Cheese Louise**,' he said.

'Guilty!' Wilbur chuckled.

'And *that's* why you insisted on driving,' Aldrin said, 'when we followed Maurice from Higher Dinting. And why you drove into that field!'

'I *knew* there was no fox on the road!' Sisely said.

'Quit wriggling!' Wilbur ordered, tightening his grip on her.

'Why?' Aldrin asked. 'Why did you betray the order?'

'I would say there were many reasons,' Wilbur explained. 'Chief among them being family. Specifically, my grandson.'

The penny suddenly dropped for Aldrin.

'Ethan?' he said. 'Ethan is your grandson?'

'Ethan should have been a Cheese Whizz,' Wilbur said bitterly. 'As you know, the power is passed down the family line from father to daughter, then from mother to son. His mother was a Cheese Whizz. But then, for reasons I never understood, we lost our powers. I lost mine. My daughter lost hers. And Ethan – that's Ethan Marcus Leveson-Gough to you – didn't inherit. We were clearly considered . . . unworthy.'

'You *are* unworthy!' Aldrin snapped. 'All of you!'

'Careful, chappie,' Wilbur said, raising a warning eyebrow at him, 'that's my family you're talking about.'

Maurice turned his head to the right to see the computer screen.

'Upload eighty per cent complete,' he said with an urgency in his voice.

'**ALDRIN**,' Sisely shouted, '**JUST PULL THE LEVER!**'

'I wouldn't advise it,' Wilbur reminded him. 'I *will* hurt the girl.'

'**I DON'T CARE!**' said Sisely. '**JUST DO IT, ALDRIN!**'

But Aldrin didn't. He wanted more answers.

'So how did Habeas get to you?' he wondered.

'He didn't,' Wilbur told him. 'It was my daughter. After she was stripped of her powers, she dedicated years of her life to tracking him down. She pored over maps and eventually found out about this place. I mean, a fish-packaging factory – in Todmorden! It's miles and miles from any sea. She wanted to reach out to Habeas. Figured if she wasn't good enough to be a Cheese Whizz, she might as well work for the opposition. So she told Ethan to look for a job here. And he made a career for himself creating computer-animated nightmares for Habeas.'

'Until he displeased him,' Maurice said, filling in the blanks, 'and found himself sacked.'

'Absolutely correct,' Wilbur confirmed. 'That's when he asked me if I could get him into the meeting at Tintwistle – and get you there as well.'

Aldrin experienced a sudden flashback of him whispering in his ear after the Brie Blind Taste Challenge.

'For twelve generations,' Wilbur said, his eyes narrowing into spiteful almond shapes, 'the Leveson-Goughs have been proud to be part of the Order of the Cheese Whizzes. And we were stripped of our powers without any explanation!'

'Wilbur,' Aldrin reminded him, 'it's not all about *you*, you know?'

'I beg your pardon?' Wilbur growled.

'We're on the point of ending this. Five centuries of Habeas Grusselvart using nightmares to spread fear and misery throughout the world. All I have to do is pull this lever – and it all stops!'

'I suspect there's a reason he doesn't want it to stop,' said Maurice. 'How much is Habeas paying you?'

Wilbur laughed scornfully. 'The small matter of ten million was mentioned,' he said. 'It will allow me, my daughter and Ethan to live out the rest of our days in comfort – and, who knows, maybe even luxury.'

'Upload ninety per cent complete,' Maurice announced.

'Wilbur,' Aldrin said, his hand snaking slowly up

from his side, 'I'm going to pull the lever now.'

'Don't *touch* that lever,' Wilbur warned him again.

'**PULL THE LEVER!**' Sisely shouted.

'You lay one hand on that lever,' Wilbur repeated, 'and I'll take your friend up to the roof and throw her –'

Wilbur's flow of speech was suddenly interrupted by a dull . . . **THWACK!**

Aldrin watched the man's eyes roll upwards, then he flopped to the floor like an empty sock puppet. Standing behind him, holding a giant wheel of Double Gloucester over her head, was Mrs Van Boxtel.

'Shtill got it!' she congratulated herself.

'Mrs Van Boxtel!' said Aldrin. 'It was Wilbur who betrayed the Cheese Whizzes!'

'Oh, I knew that from the very shtart,' she said. 'I wash jusht playing dumb until I could get all the other Cheeshe Whizshesh to come here. Aldrin, perhapsh now might be a good time to pull that lever.'

'Upload ninety-five per cent complete,' Maurice said.

Aldrin turned, gripped the lever in both hands and pulled it down . . .

But NOTHING happened.

'Oh, no,' said Maurice, his voice collapsing in on

itself. 'He must have switched the power to the back-up generator.'

'Where's the back-up generator?' Aldrin asked in an urgent voice.

'There's no time to reach it,' Maurice said gravely. 'It's in another factory on the far side of town.'

'Then I'll have to stop Ethan from uploading it myself!' Aldrin said.

'Ninety seconds until the upload is complete,' said Maurice.

Aldrin made his way to the door.

'Aldrin, no.' Mrs Van Boxtel told him, 'It ish too dangeroush for you!'

He stood in the doorway with his hands on his hips.

'Whether I like it or not,' he said, 'I've been given this superpower –'

'It's not a superpower,' Sisely reminded him.

'I've been given this superpower,' Aldrin persisted, 'and right now I have ninety seconds to save the world from Habeas Grusselvart.'

'It's, er, more like eighty seconds now,' Maurice pointed out.

Aldrin turned and ran in the direction of the stairwell.

58

'IT'S GOING TO BLOW!'

Heehhh . . .

Aldrin could hear the wheeze in his chest as he held on to the banister and pulled himself up the final flight of stairs to the fourth floor.

Heehhh . . .

He could possibly do with going to gym class a bit more often, he thought, especially when he remembered how fit the rest of the Cheese Whizzes looked in dispatching all those burly security guards.

Heehhh . . .

He'd finally reached the fourth floor, the nerve centre of Habeas Grusselvart's evil empire. He made his way along the expensively carpeted corridor, back to the evil one's office.

Heehhh . . .

He walked in – only to discover it empty.

There was no sign of Habeas and no sign of Ethan. All the TV screens on the **Wall of Torment** were switched off. He ran over to Habeas's desk. The drawers had been pulled open in an apparent hurry and emptied of their contents.

'You're too late,' he heard a voice say.

He turned round. Habeas stepped into the room, grinning at him.

'It's all up there,' he said, throwing his eyes skyward, 'in the cloud. Like I will be too – very soon.'

Aldrin could hear the distant sound of a helicopter.

'So you're running away?' asked Aldrin.

'It's not running away,' Habeas insisted. 'It's what's known in military circles as a **tactical retreat**.'

'That certainly *sounds* like running away.'

'This wasn't a victory for you – and deep down you know it. Yes, you discovered my secret lair. And you and your weirdo friends broke in and caught my security staff unawares.'

'How's your head?' Aldrin asked. 'I saw Mrs Van Boxtel knock you out cold with a roundhouse kick.'

'She didn't knock me out cold,' Habeas insisted. 'I . . . *slipped*.'

'Sure you did,' said Aldrin.

'You might have driven me out of Todmorden,' Habeas said bitterly, 'but I'll be up and running again within a matter of months. Isn't that right, Ethan?'

Ethan suddenly appeared next to him.

'Possibly even weeks.' Ethan smiled. 'Yeah, everyone can enjoy a little break from their nightmares and then they'll suddenly return – even more terrifying than before!'

Aldrin noticed something under Ethan's arm. It was his mum's dream journal. And, even though he didn't strictly need it any more, seeing Ethan holding the diary that Cynthia had kept as a gift for her son made Aldrin furious.

'So,' he said, 'you're the new Beddy Byes, are you?'

'No,' Ethan replied, 'we haven't settled on a name yet. Although, yes, Beddy Byes *is* one of the names under consideration.'

'Habeas is using you,' Aldrin told him, 'just like he used Maurice. He's taking advantage of your anger and bitterness.'

'What bitterness?' Ethan asked.

'Your bitterness at not inheriting the power. Your anger at your mum and your granddad being considered unworthy.'

'Don't you DARE talk about my mother!'

'I'm telling the truth.'

'Yes,' Ethan said, looking Aldrin up and down, 'she said you were a snivelling little toad.'

'What?' Aldrin asked, confused.

'Oh, yes, you've met her – hasn't he, Mum?'

Outside in the corridor, Aldrin could hear footsteps approaching. Seconds later, Ethan's mother appeared in the doorway. And Aldrin couldn't believe his eyes.

'Cerys!' he said.

She smiled at him.

'It's actually Nerys,' she revealed. 'Nerys Leveson-Gough.'

All at once, Aldrin understood how Habeas knew they were coming to Todmorden that day.

'You only came to work in *C'est Cheese* so you could spy on me!' he said.

'Well, it wasn't because I enjoyed watching that awful Agatha woman stuff her face with cheese,' she said. 'Or because I enjoyed your father looking at me all gooey-eyed. Or because I liked sharing a workspace with that ignorant girlfriend of his.'

'Don't speak about Belinda like that,' Aldrin told her. 'She's worth twenty of you.'

'Is that right?' Nerys said, stepping into the room.

'That's no way to speak to a lady,' Habeas said, egging her on. 'I think you'd be well within your rights to slap him across the face.'

'She's no lady,' Aldrin told him.

Nerys walked right up to Aldrin and stood in front of him. She pulled back her hand. And then:

RRRIBBIT ... RRRIBBIT ... RRRIBBIT ...

Silas suddenly sprang from Aldrin's breast pocket! He was alive! And, not only was he alive, he was hell-bent on protecting Aldrin!

SPLAT!!!

He landed on Nerys's face – and he stuck to it, while she screamed:

'GET IT OFF ME! GET IT OFF ME!'

She stumbled backwards, waving her arms frantically. Habeas and Ethan were forced to step out of the way as she staggered past them with Aldrin's slimy pal still attached to her face.

Behind her was the window that looked down on the giant mountain of rotting cheese. Nerys smashed against the glass, cracking her head loudly. Silas leaped from her face on to the ground and hopped back to Aldrin, who picked him up.

'Well done, Silas!' he told his little friend, before returning him to his pocket.

But, whatever pleasure it gave him to see Nerys get her comeuppance, it didn't last long. Suddenly, there was a splintering sound as the window cracked in a spiderweb pattern.

Aldrin stared at Ethan, who stared at Habeas, who stared at Nerys, who stared at Aldrin, no one daring to say a word, or even move a muscle.

Then, suddenly, the window exploded into tens of thousands of pieces.

Ethan dropped Cynthia's dream journal with the fright of the window breaking. Immediately, Aldrin covered his nose and mouth with his hand as the noxious air flooded from the warehouse into the room.

An alarm resembling a foghorn started to sound throughout the building.

Aldrin could hear the helicopter overhead now.

WOOO-ZOOO!!!
    WOOO-ZOOO!!!
        WOOO-ZOOO!!!

'Run along,' said Habeas teasingly. 'You have about five minutes before this building explodes!'

'But there's still people inside!' Aldrin reminded him.

'Oh, well,' Habeas said, 'perhaps NemeSwiss could save them!' and then he laughed his evil laugh.

'**MWAH-HA-HA-HA-HA-HA-HA!**'

Wilbur rushed into the room then, rubbing his neck where Mrs Van Boxtel had dealt him the knockout blow.

'Let's go,' he told the others.

'It looks like this is goodbye,' Habeas told Aldrin drily. 'Until we meet again, Aldrin Adams.'

Habeas, Ethan, Wilbur and Nerys ran out of the room, and headed for the roof. Aldrin made a desperate run for it, stopping to pick up his mum's dream journal. With the book tucked under his arm, and Silas safe in his pocket, he hurried to the stairwell.

It was full of factory staff who had heard the alarm and smelled the gas and were making their slow way out of the building.

'**HURRY!**' Aldrin roared down at the them. '**IT'S GOING TO BLOW!**'

There were gasps and even screams from the

hundreds of members of staff descending the stairs.

For Aldrin, it was like being caught in a human flood. He was carried down four flights of stairs and outside into the car park by the heavy flow of people desperate to escape the vile stench that was spreading rapidly throughout the building.

Outside, the car park was filled with people. Aldrin could see men and women dressed up as scary clowns and monsters and vampires and zombies and all the other characters who haunt people's nightmares. Some were being sick. Others were fanning their faces, discussing what they all presumed was an accidental gas leak.

Here, out in the open air, he could see them for what they were – not the scary characters who struck terror into people while they slept, but a bunch of cowards hiding behind make-up and masks.

As the helicopter landed on the roof, Aldrin roared:

'EVERYBODY, MOVE AWAY FROM THE BUILDING!!'

'What?' the people asked him as they started to scatter.

'ANY MINUTE NOW, IT'S GOING TO TURN INTO A CHEESE FIREBALL!'

he shouted. **'STAND BACK AS FAR AS YOU CAN!'**

Aldrin heard his name being called. He spotted Mrs Van Boxtel and Sisely standing a short distance away.

'You got out!' Sisely said, sounding highly relieved. 'And you got your dream journal back!'

'What about Habeash?' Mrs Van Boxtel asked.

'He got away,' Aldrin told her sadly. 'And Ethan managed to upload everything to the cloud.'

Mrs Van Boxtel nodded, taking the news in her stride.

'We all live to fight another day,' she said.

Aldrin looked around him. He saw Maxine Joli and Estelle Giddens and Cormac de Courcy and all the other Cheese Whizzes standing around, reliving their memories of the battle. He saw the teams of burly security guards nursing their various injuries.

Wait a minute, Aldrin thought.

'WHERE'S MAURICE?' he shouted.

'He said he was going back into the building,' said Cormac de Courcy, 'to look for you!'

Aldrin took Silas from his pocket and handed him to Sisely.

'Look after him, will you?' he said.

Then he did what real superheroes do. He ran

towards the danger.

'**ALDRIN, NO!**' Sisely screamed as he headed back into the building.

The poisonous smell hit him immediately, searing his nostrils and making his eyes water. He covered his nose and mouth. He had no idea where he was going. The tears were pouring from his eyes, reducing his visibility to almost zero.

But he walked straight ahead. And then he took a left turn. And then he took a right turn. And then he took another left. It was as if someone – or some supernatural sense – was directing him. Because that's when he suddenly spotted a figure in front of him, stretched out, face down, on the floor.

It was Maurice.

Aldrin rushed to him and turned him over. He was barely conscious. Aldrin took off his jacket and pressed it to Maurice's face.

'Here,' he said, 'breathe into this.'

'Am I dead?' Maurice mumbled.

'No, you're not dead,' Aldrin promised him. 'Come on, I'm going to get you out of here.'

Overhead, Aldrin could hear the helicopter taking off from the roof.

He put his hands under Maurice's arms and he started to pull him backwards along the corridor and towards the door. Thirty seconds later, he was dragging him outside into the car park.

The helicopter circled the building.

Cormac and Estelle came running towards them. They picked Maurice up and ran with him, determined to get him clear of the building, with Aldrin following closely behind.

Aldrin dived for cover just as the air was ripped apart by a series of seven devastatingly loud explosions. The windows of the factory shattered and the roof blew off the building like a hat being lost in the wind.

Flames engulfed the entire factory. There were gasps of surprise from the hundreds of people standing around in small groups, watching the Codfather Packing Company burn to the ground.

The last explosion was almost deafening. A dark cloud of smoke, shaped like a mushroom, stretched up into the sky and the air over Todmorden was suddenly filled with the smell of toasted cheese.

Sisely and Mrs Van Boxtel came and found Aldrin. Sisely had managed to retrieve her scooter from where she left it.

'We'd better get you two home to your familiesh,' said Mrs Van Boxtel, 'before they realishe you are misshing.'

'Who's going to drive us?' Sisely asked.

'I will, of courshe,' Mrs Van Boxtel said – but then she suddenly realized something. 'My beautiful car! It wash deshtroyed in the exploshion!'

Perhaps that wasn't such a bad thing, Aldrin thought. The roads of the country would certainly be a lot safer without Mrs Van Boxtel on them.

Sisely and Aldrin exchanged a look. He could tell that she was thinking exactly the same thing.

'I don't mind sho much,' Mrs Van Boxtel sighed. 'The car wash inshured. And anyway it hash been a long day. While I am obvioushly an exshellent driver, shometimesh when I'm tired I make mishtakesh. Let ush shee if shomeone can give ush a lift home!'

59

ALDRIN ADAMS . . . AND THE CHEESE NIGHTMARES!

'I can't BELIEVE you're eating cheese!' Sisely said.

'What do you mean?' Aldrin asked, nibbling on a piece of deliciously herbaceous Pecorino Romano. 'I'm ALWAYS eating cheese.'

'After being locked in that warehouse today,' Sisely said, 'I'll *never* eat cheese again!'

'I actually had a toasted Gruyère sandwich as soon as I got home.'

'You're so odd.'

'I know!' he said proudly. 'Shall we get on with it?'

It was late on Saturday afternoon, just hours after the fire that had reduced the Codfather Packing Company to a pile of stinking rubble. And the two friends had a job to do.

They were in the little yard at the back of **C'est Cheese**. Aldrin lifted the lid of the wheelie bin, then he looked down at the pile of clothes at his feet.

'Oh, well,' he said, 'here goes.'

He bent down and gathered them up in his arms. Then, one by one, he dropped the pieces of his superhero suit into the bin:

The onesie.

The mask.

The gloves.

The belt.

The cape.

Then the boots.

He took one last look at his old superhero costume. The eyeholes of the mask seemed to be staring up at him.

'Goodbye, NemeSwiss,' he said.

Then he put the lid on the bin.

'Goodbye and good riddance,' said Sisely.

'I'm kicking myself,' Aldrin told her, 'for letting him get away.'

'What could you have done differently?' she asked.

'Maybe if I'd got up the stairs a bit quicker,' he said, 'and stopped Ethan uploading all the information to the cloud. In a few weeks, they'll be back in business.'

'And we'll be ready,' Sisely vowed, 'to fight them – nightmare by nightmare.'

'I'm sorry again,' Aldrin told his friend, 'for treating you so badly.'

'Well, I kept secrets from you,' Sisely said, 'so I'm sorry too.'

'Let's agree to never fall out again,' Aldrin suggested. 'After all, the universe needs us too much.'

Sisely looked him up and down.

'The universe?' she said sceptically. 'Seriously, Aldrin, you have to stop talking like you're some kind of superhero. And take your hands off your hips.'

'Sorry,' Aldrin said, 'I didn't even realize I was doing that.'

There was a short silence between them then.

'Although I am prepared to admit,' Sisely said, 'the way you ran back into the building to rescue Maurice – that *was* like something a superhero would do.'

'So maybe I *do* need some kind of suit?' Aldrin suggested.

'No,' said Sisely, 'your ego is already out of control.'

'Well . . .' Aldrin smiled, 'maybe just a cape then?'

'I *hope* the lesson you've learned,' Sisely said, 'is to keep your feet firmly on the ground in future.'

They heard voices behind them then.

'All right, Aldrin? All right, Sisely?'

It was Frankie and Harry.

'Your dad told us you were out here,' Frankie said. 'You are not going to BELIEVE what's happened!'

'Er, what?' wondered Aldrin.

'We got a letter – from Life on Mars Comics,' Harry said, between blasts on his asthma inhaler. 'They saw a copy of *The Oddballs*. And they want to publish it every month – not as a bunch of photocopied pages stapled together, but as a proper glossy comic. And it's going to be sold in comic-book stores!'

'**WOW!**' said Aldrin. 'Everyone is going to know about *The Oddballs*.'

'Well, one thing's for sure,' said Frankie, 'everyone is going to know about you, Aldrin! Show him, Harry!'

Harry had a folder in his hand. He opened it and pulled out a drawing.

'This is the new version of the boy who can access other people's nightmares,' Harry said.

Aldrin cast his eyes over the comic strip. The hero

was certainly different from the one he'd seen before – the tall, handsome boy with blond hair, a square jaw and biceps like bowling balls. The new version was a short and slightly chubby boy, with a friendly face, two front teeth that stuck out prominently and a head of wavy russet hair. And he was dressed in blue pyjamas with little yellow wedges of cheeses on them.

'It's actually . . . ME!' said Aldrin.

'That's right,' said Frankie. 'We decided *that's* how we want NemeSwiss to look. Except we're not going to call him NemeSwiss any more.'

'No?' asked Aldrin.

'We're going to call him . . . Aldrin Adams!'

'Oh, no,' Sisely muttered under her breath. '*How* are we going to keep your ego under control now?'

'I mean, who says that superheroes can't look like you?' said Harry. 'No offence, Aldrin.'

'Er, none taken,' Aldrin told him.

'*Aldrin Adams*,' Frankie said dramatically, '*and the Cheese Nightmares!*'

'It, er, definitely has a ring to it,' Aldrin said, failing to suppress a smile. 'As a matter of fact, I kind of like it.'

Sisely put her head in her hands.

Aldrin couldn't believe he was about to be immortalized as a real comic-book hero! Could this day get any better, he wondered?

The answer, it turned out, was yes.

Suddenly, the four friends heard a woman's squeals, then a moment later, Belinda – in her white work overalls – ran out into the backyard, followed by Doug, whose face was flushed red.

Belinda was holding her left hand like she'd injured her wrist. And on her ring finger Aldrin saw the almost blinding glint . . . of a diamond!

'Oh, Aldrin,' Belinda said tearfully, 'your dad's only gone and asked me to marry him, the daft beggar!'

Aldrin looked at his dad. He couldn't remember the last time he'd looked happier, and he didn't need to ask what Belinda's response had been.

'That's brilliant news!' said Frankie and Harry.

'Congratulations,' said Sisely.

'I thought he were in love with that Cerys,' Belinda said. 'I were being daft.'

'Well,' Doug said, 'you shan't be seeing her around here again. Did I tell you what happened, Aldrin? She left – just after you did this morning. I was about to pop round to Belinda's to ask her to come back and

Cerys just rushed out the door without saying a word.'

'Forget about Cerys.' Aldrin smiled. 'You're getting married!'

'We're going to be a family,' Doug told him. 'Are you pleased, son?'

'Pleased?' Aldrin said, throwing his arms round Doug and Belinda. 'I couldn't be happier.'

And he meant every word.

EPILOGUE: PART ONE

It was a beautiful, sun-drenched day in paradise. So beautiful, in fact, that Habeas Grusselvart – stretched out to his full length on a sunlounger – was actually toying with the idea of opening the top button of his long black coat!

He sipped his spinach-and-broccoli detox smoothie and listened to the sound of the waves licking the shore.

'You know, in a way,' he said, 'the boy has done me a favour. I think I needed a break – just to recharge my batteries. Five hundred years is a long time to go without a holiday.'

'How long have you had this place?' Ethan asked, referring to the luxury seafront villa with the helicopter landing pad on the roof.

'For more years than I can remember,' said Habeas. 'It's the first time I've ever seen it, though. My life for the last five centuries has just been work, work, work! What's *in* this again?'

'Spinach,' said Ethan, 'and broccoli.'

'Spinach and broccoli,' Habeas repeated. 'And what's it supposed to do?'

'It cleanses your, erm, insides,' Ethan told him.

'I see,' said Habeas. 'Healthy body, healthy mind, eh? Yes, I should have done this years ago, Beddy Byes.'

'Beddy Byes?'

'I beg your pardon?'

'Er, you just called me Beddy Byes.'

'Yes, I've settled on that as my new name for you!'

'Oh, er, right.'

'You don't mind, do you?'

'I suppose not.'

'I just think it's a good, solid name for a Personal Assistant and Vice President of Global Operations. And, by the way, I've been letting it go up until now, what with you being new and everything, but I'd like you to address me as Your Wonderfulness.'

'Your Wonderfulness?'

'Yes. Or Your Highnessness. Or Oh Great and

Handsome One. Or Oh Powerful and Fragrant One. The last Beddy Byes had a whole list of pet names for me that he used to use. He made me feel quite nauseous sometimes with all the sucking up he did – although, looking back now, I did rather enjoy it.'

'So what are your plans,' Ethan asked, 'Your, erm, Highnessness?'

'To build a brand-new secret lair,' Habeas answered. 'The last one served my needs for thirty years. But it was time to move on. They always say the trick is to get out of Todmorden before it changes you.'

'What kind of secret lair do you have in mind this time,' Ethan asked, 'Oh Handsome and Robust One!'

'Perhaps an island in the middle of the ocean!' Habeas mused. 'Or maybe somewhere a few hundred feet underground! Or maybe inside a dormant volcano! The world is our oyster, Beddy Byes!'

'That's, erm, very exciting,' said Ethan.

'But for now,' Habeas continued, 'it's going to be all rest and recuperation.'

He closed his eyes and felt the heat of the sun on his face. He breathed in the sea air and listened to the sound of the waves as they fizzed on the sand.

'And yet,' he said, suddenly opening one eye, 'when

I think about those seventy million people around the world who **SHOULD** be having nightmares tonight, but aren't . . . it makes me **HATE** that boy even more!'

'Aldrin Adams, Your Excellentness?' Ethan asked.

Habeas opened his other eye and sat up on the sunlounger.

'Right,' he said, 'that's quite enough rest and recuperation for me, thank you.'

'Really?' asked Ethan.

'The boy is laughing at us,' Habeas growled, 'no doubt pleased with himself for bringing together the Cheese Whizzes to disrupt our vital work. And here I am, lying on a sunlounger, sipping this **DISGUSTING** concoction and considering opening the top button **ON MY COAT!** Where's that mother and grandfather of yours?'

'*He's* asleep in a hammock over there,' said Ethan, 'and *she's* having a mani-pedi done, Your Lordshipfulness.'

'Well, wake him up! And tell *her* to **STOP** having a mani-pedi – whatever that even is! We have work to do! Bring me my laptop! We're going to check the property websites and see if we can't find ourselves an **ISLAND** or a **DORMANT VOLCANO** somewhere whose owner requires A QUICK SALE!'

'Right away, Your Worshipfulness,' said Ethan.

Habeas pounded the sunlounger's pink mattress with a furious fist.

'HOW DARE HE COME TO MY SECRET LAIR AND TRY TO DESTROY FIVE CENTURIES OF WORK!' he shouted – then he roared into the cloudless, sun-kissed sky: '**Watch out, Aldrin Adams! Habeas Grusselvart is coming back!**'

EPILOGUE: PART TWO

'I know he's out there somewhere,' Aldrin said, 'plotting his return.'

'There ish nothing you can do about thish,' said Mrs Van Boxtel. 'Jusht be ready when that day comesh.'

'I still feel like I failed,' Aldrin said. 'I had a chance to destroy all those nightmares – and I didn't!'

'But you succeeded in doing something else,' Sisely pointed out.

'She ish right,' said Mrs Van Boxtel. 'You helped bring the Cheeshe Whizshesh together in a common caushe.'

'They've seen Habeas Grusselvart now,' Sisely added. 'They know how close they came to defeating him.'

They were sitting in Mrs Van Boxtel's brand-new tiny turquoise car, about to pay someone a special visit.

'What you did,' said Mrs Van Boxtel, 'in tracking him down and leading everyone to him, hash filled everyone with sho much hope and happy feelingsh.'

Mrs Van Boxtel's 'happy feelingsh' lasted only as long as it took for a giant eighteen-wheeler truck to overtake them on the road. Then she wound down the window.

'WHERE DID YOU LEARN TO DRIVE?' she shouted, at the same time leaning on the horn. 'IN A SHCHOOL FOR CLOWNSH?'

BEEP!
BEEEEEEP!!!
BEEEEEEEEEP!!!!!!

'Mrs Van Boxtel,' Aldrin said, touching her shoulder gently, 'we're not in any hurry, are we?'

'It ish jusht the shtandard of driving in thish country ish SHO, sho bad!' the teacher said.

Aldrin and Sisely looked straight ahead and said nothing. A moment later, they passed the sign for Higher Dinting, then shortly after that Mrs Van Boxtel took four turns without using her indicators or slowing down, bounced over three speed bumps, clipped a moped with her wing mirror and swerved to avoid hitting the local vicar on a pedestrian crossing, before she brought the car to a merciful halt outside the shop on Brereton Road.

Aldrin smiled when he read the sign over the door. It said:

Yes, Louise had changed her mind about retiring from the cheese business following a visit from the nice man who'd taken away her leftover stock. He showed her a business plan and suggested several ways in which she could make her cheesemonger's more appealing to customers so that it could compete with the cheaper supermarkets.

So confident was he that he could help make a success of **Cheese Louise** that he'd offered to work as her assistant.

Aldrin pushed the door of the shop. Maurice looked up. He smiled when he saw Cynthia's boy in the doorway – and, with him, his friend Sisely and his teacher, Mrs Van Boxtel.

'Hello,' he said. 'Welcome to **Cheese Louise**.'

'Hello, Maurice,' Aldrin said. 'We heard a rumour that you were back in the business.'

'Back doing what I loved . . .' Maurice nodded. 'Before I got distracted.'

'How ish bushinessh?' Mrs Van Boxtel asked.

'Improving,' he said. 'Next year, we're considering taking a stall at the Tintwistle Cheese Festival.'

'How exciting!' said Aldrin.

Just then, Louise walked in from the refrigerated stockroom behind the counter.

'Maurice,' she said, 'can we order another wheel of that Red Leicester?' and then she noticed that he had company. 'Oh, hello.'

'Louise,' Maurice said, introducing them, 'this is Aldrin. His late mum, Cynthia, was a dear, dear friend of mine a long, long time ago – as a matter of fact, we learned to be cheesemongers together. And these are his friends, Sisely and Mrs Van Boxtel.'

'It's lovely to meet you all,' said Louise, before returning to the stockroom.

Maurice used a cheese wire to cut three slices from a block of Gouda, then he handed them round.

'You'll love this,' he said. 'It's so caramelly.'

He wasn't wrong, Aldrin discovered. It was sweet and delicious.

'Gouda is one of my all-time favourite cheeses,' Aldrin told him.

'Thank you again,' Maurice said, 'for saving my life.'

'Thank you for saving mine,' Aldrin responded.

'Mine too,' added Sisely.

Maurice smiled.

'You three,' he told them, 'you really are a formidable team. Don't underestimate what you achieved that day in Todmorden. You put Habeas Grusselvart out of business – for the first time in five hundred years.'

'He'll be back, though,' Aldrin said sadly. 'He's probably rebuilding his empire somewhere as we speak.'

'It's likely,' Maurice agreed. 'But he fears you, Aldrin. And now I understand why.'

'But why would he fear me?' Aldrin asked. 'He's invincible, isn't he?'

'No,' Maurice said, shaking his head. 'It's true that he's not fully human. He's a supernatural being. But there is a way that he can be destroyed – and I can show you how to do it.'